THE WELL OF EXILE

An Autobiographical Novel

Khalil Hamad

'building bridges of cultural understanding'

Credits

Author
Khalil Hamad

Introduction and Critical Analysis
Ibrahim Joher

Translator
Dr. Fayeq Oweis

Editor
Raneen Saadah

Cover Design
Dr. Fayeq Oweis

General Information

THE WELL OF EXILE
An Autobiographical Novel
Khalil Hamad
1st Edition: 2025

Publisher Information:
Inner Child Press
intouch@innerchildpress.com
www.innerchildpress.com

$ 21.95

Introduction, Critical Reading, and Analysis

By the esteemed writer and critic,
Ibrahim Joher

Khalil Hamad, in The Well of Exile, portrays the struggles of an ambitious young man yearning for a better life, striving to break free from the cycles of poverty, occupation, and discrimination. This is the story of a writer who refused to succumb to the obstacles of orphanhood, poverty, and deprivation. Instead, he persevered with determination, armed with a culture of self-reliance. He had no doting mother to comfort him, nor a father who could spare time as he toiled to feed the mouths of his children, who found themselves in an environment of scarcity.

Khalil Hamad completes his university education with a bachelor's degree, believing that the doors of opportunity will swing open for him in the dreamlike desert lands of Kuwait. Yet, he soon realizes that he must rely on his patience as he steps into the grinding world of work. What unfolds is a tale of trials and tribulations, meticulously recounted by the experienced writer in the pages of his autobiography here.

Khalil writes his life story in a style that blends narrative storytelling, characterization, dialogue, and detailed depictions of situations. At times, the hurried reader might find these details excessive, but I believe that the events or moments he describes with such precision—sometimes resembling the meticulous details of a screenplay—reveal the depth of his emotional impact and the strength of his memory, which still retains those moments from over 45 years ago.

In this memoir, readers will find shocking revelations about the lands of youthful dreams—Kuwait and the United States, places rife with crime, gang wars, and murder. The author has done well to expose the hidden, grim realities of life in these countries, as if warning young people captivated by glossy, deceptive propaganda.

The author employs various artistic techniques while maintaining a direct, conversational tone with his reader, as though speaking to them face-to-face. He also engages in intertextuality, drawing from the Quran, world literature, the fantastical and imaginative tales of *One Thousand and One Nights*, and historical references.

Khalil Hamad, known to his Facebook followers as an adventurer who traverses mountains and plains, climbs peaks, and explores mountain caves, is the same person who began these adventures in the lands of exile. He is the same individual who armed himself with popular, religious, and social fortifications, ensuring he did not fall into the well of exile or succumb to the clutches of the social monster born from the cultural shock experienced by those who migrate from Eastern to Western culture, particularly in the United States.

Readers of this memoir live alongside its author, urged forward by his compelling narrative, carving more of this valuable information, especially for those aspiring to live abroad in pursuit of knowledge or wealth. Khalil cites real-life examples from his own experiences, offering warnings and advice.

The experience of "Arif," a fellow townsman who traveled to those distant lands, remained ever-present in Khalil's actions and conscience. He internalized Arif's story from a young age, and it became a tale of the innocent village. This is why we find Khalil deeply loyal to that incident where Arif left and never returned. Khalil made a solemn vow to himself never to repeat Arif's sorrowful experience.

At the age of sixteen, the idea of orphans as projects of excellence and distinction took root in his mind. He lived with this idea until it materialized, leading him to write his master's thesis on the subject. He passionately debated with his professors, eager to prove the validity of his concept.

This artistic, realistic autobiographical novel shines in all its manifestations. There is no fantasy, exaggeration, or muscle-flexing—neither in language nor in the claim of false heroics without real-world experiences. Khalil openly shares where he failed, when he was afraid, how he moved from one dwelling to another in search of safety, how he feared stepping out into the street, how he endured hunger, and how he the last ten days of each month barely scraping by, waiting for the monthly allowance sent by his brother from Kuwait. He also recounts working as a porter in a university bookstore.

This autobiographical novel carries the culture of its author, his personal experiences, and the Eastern culture in confrontation with Western culture. Notably, what stands out is the author's extensive knowledge of the English language and his ability to use it to distinguish between situations and concepts emphasized in Western frameworks. Meanwhile, he deals with these concepts as if they hold no difference in our Eastern culture. Observe how he describes university students in their first, second, third, and fourth years with different titles, each carrying a meaning and description of what the student achieves in each academic year.

Khalil Hamad writes here with a torrential flow. He narrates events and conveys his emotions during transitions or decision-making moments, capturing feelings of anxiety, anticipation, and waiting. He never forgets to draw comparisons, constantly reminding himself and the reader that he came with a goal and must achieve it successfully. In this context, he directly advises those who wish to settle abroad, urging them to fortify themselves and not deceive their families. Through this, he shares the experiences of young men who were lost, others who suffered severe psychological illnesses, or those who wandered aimlessly through the streets of the United States.

The author, in this autobiography, frequently invokes popular proverbs that have become part of the nations and generations' cultural fabric. He also references Quranic verses and historical figures, both from Islamic conquests and contemporary events.

I was struck by one of the chapter titles he uses here: "As if you, Khalil, never ventured..." This is a variation of the well-known saying etched in popular memory: "As if you, Abu Zayd, never ventured." To this, I say: Thank God Abu Zayd did venture, and so did Khalil, allowing us to live through this rich experience that he pens with his words and emotions. He takes us with him, making us grieve when he grieves, wait in suspense when he waits, and hold our hearts when he faces hostile situations in one of the states of the well—the well of exile that he constantly reminds us of.

Thanks to Abu Zayd, to Khalil, and to Arif, whose sword remained unsheathed over Khalil during his exile, reminding him to return to his homeland. For the well of exile in one's homeland is better than the well of exile in exile.

Prologue

My life is a tale brimming with tempestuous events and shocking drama, much of it steeped in pain and loss. This description holds true for my entire journey, from my birth on April 17, 1954, to this very moment in early 2024, when I sit down to chronicle the memories etched deep into my memory. Yet, I must clarify that my life has not been devoid of happiness. But, as is often the case, joy has a fleeting nature, slipping quietly from memory, leaving only the shadows of its passing.

I could easily divide my life story into three distinct chapters, each marked by its own unique trials and tribulations. Each of these phases, on its own, could fill a volume of a lengthy autobiographical novel, deserving of its own title due to the coherence of the experiences it holds.

The first chapter of my life, the most harrowing and agonizing, spans my early childhood and youth, from the day I was born until my graduation from Bethlehem University in mid-1978. Writing about this chapter is an arduous task. The pain of those years, tied to their time and place, is overwhelming—like opening a black box containing terrifying events that shaped every stage of my life thereafter, leaving their indelible mark on my soul.

I was born in the Palestinian village of Kifl Haris, a small rural community 22 kilometers southwest of Nablus. The Palestinian countryside of the early 1950s was a place of extreme poverty and isolation, still reeling from the aftermath of the Nakba of 1948. At that time, the village was nearly cut off from the rest of the world due to a lack of roads and vehicles, deprived of basic infrastructure such as electricity and running water. The nights in the countryside were cloaked in pitch darkness, steeped in fear and uncertainty.

Life was a relentless grind, shaped by the crushing weight of poverty, the sting of meager earnings, and the backbreaking labor of tilling the land. But hardship was only part of the story. Fear was a constant companion, lurking in the shadows of every day and night. The pitch-black darkness, the howls of hyenas, the whispers of jinn, the tales of ghouls, the slither of snakes, the sting of scorpions—these were just a few of the many dangers that haunted our lives. Together, they wove a tapestry of terror, turning existence into an unending nightmare.

During that chapter of my life, I endured two profound and shattering events—each leaving behind echoes that refuse to fade and wounds that defy healing. It was as if the sky itself had crumbled and fallen to the earth. And so, I have chosen to name the first chapter of my story *'When the Sky Fell to Earth.'*

The first of these tragedies was my early orphanhood. My mother passed away when I was just two years old, leaving me to be raised by my maternal aunt, who married my father shortly after. Yet, the true weight of my upbringing fell on the fragile shoulders of my eldest sister, Aisha. She was only ten years old when our mother died.

The second seismic event was the Naksa of 1967—a disaster that left in its wake a bitter taste of defeat, a wrenching sense of loss, and the grim realities of life under a harsh and unrelenting occupation. Like a shadow, the occupation's arrogance and brutality settled over the people, pressing down on their hearts and stifling their spirits.

In those early years of my childhood, I lived in a world steeped in fear, much like every other child in the countryside. Palestinian rural life was a tapestry of dangers, both real and imagined. Even the bedtime stories my older sister told us—tales of ghouls, jinn, and the oppressive darkness—only added to the terror, weaving nightmares into the fabric of our nights.

Yet, among the many fears that haunted my childhood was the wells that scarred the rural landscape. Some were simple, their depths plumbed by buckets to draw water for daily life. Others were hidden in gardens, like The garden where bees are kept or Jinanat Al-Taboon. Wells such as Birka and Badi seemed to hold secrets in their shadows. They were everywhere—beneath your feet, at the edge of your vision— a constant reminder of the relentless need for water that drove people to carve these pits into the earth, collecting precious rainwater. But to me, they were more than just sources of life; they were portals to a world of darkness, their gaping mouths whispering of dangers I could not name.

The wells scattered far from the village were even more terrifying. One such well was Omar Ibrahim Bouzia, standing near our land in the Marajem area. Its gaping mouth, often uncovered by an iron lid, seemed to beckon with a silent threat. We would draw water from it during the olive harvest or on days spent tilling the earth, each time staring into its shadowy depths, torn between necessity and an unshakable fear.

The legendary well of Nakhrur was a place shrouded in dread and mystery—a yawning abyss whose depths defied comprehension. Whispers and legends clung to it like shadows, each tale of its origin more haunting than the last. Some claimed it was born from a meteorite's fiery descent from the heavens, while others insisted it had been carved by jinn, those elusive spirits of the unseen world. We would often circle its crimson-tinged mouth, wide and gaping amidst the jagged rocks, daring one another to peer into its darkness. Our curiosity, both thrilling and perilous, drew us to its edge as we passed by on our way to the well of Haris for a swim. Nakhrur Well lay along the route to the spring, about five kilometers from the town, nestled in the rugged mountains between Kifl Haris and Salfit.

The Haris Well, shrouded in its own legends, was no less fearsome than the others. It was here, in its shadowy depths, that we learned to swim. The spring's source, which surged with crystal-clear waters in the winter, lay hidden 42 steep steps below the earth, carved into ancient stone. Beneath a massive overhanging rock was a dark, yawning cave—a place where adventurous divers sometimes vanished, their lives nearly claimed by the well's secrets. What made this well truly terrifying, however, was the myth of the Rasad, a creature said to lurk within its depths. Shaped like a lamb, the Rasad was believed to steal a child each year from those who dared to swim in the well after the rains filled it and the springs overflowed.

Even the bedtime stories we heard were often woven around a terrifying well—this time, it was the well of Khanifsa. In the tale, a mouse tumbled into the well and cried out for help, but no one could save her except her mouse husband. My sister would often link this story to a real well near our land in the Musmad area, belonging to the Samara family of the Kayed clan. Its roof was half-collapsed throughout my childhood, and I would often stand on the crumbling edge, staring into its shadowy depths, half-hoping to catch a glimpse of the mouse from the story of Khanifsa's Well— the same tale my sister would recount to us before sleep claimed our weary eyes.

It is here, in the echoes of Prophet Yusuf's story—cast into a well by his brothers in an attempt to rid themselves of him, only to emerge as the guardian of Egypt's treasures under the Pharaohs—and in the shadow of other sorrows, that I find the roots of my own tale. From this time and place, with its haunting wells and dramatic turns of fate, the title of the second chapter of my life was born: *The Well of Exile*. It is a story that begins with my graduation from university and my swift departure to Kuwait, and ends with our forced expulsion years later—a journey so rich with upheaval and wonder, it feels as though it were spun from the threads of *One Thousand and One Nights*.

THE WELL OF EXILE

An Autobiographical Novel

Khalil Hamad

THE WELL OF EXILE

Khalil Hamad

Journey to Kuwait and My First Job in Exile

Despite the harshness and difficulty of the circumstances that shaped my life from birth and throughout my youth, despite the poverty and occupation that nearly robbed me of a university education, and despite all the trials and tribulations I endured during my studies, I managed to graduate in mid-1978 from Bethlehem University with a Bachelor's degree in English Literature and a diploma in Education and Psychology.

In May of that year, clutching my hard-earned certificates, I traveled to Jordan and waited for a visit visa to Kuwait, arranged by my eldest brother, Mustafa. He had been the first to follow our brother Hamad to Kuwait in the early 1970s. Mustafa had abandoned his studies after failing the high school final exams 'Tawjihi' by a single mark in Chemistry. He went on to work in the printing industry, quickly climbing the career ladder to become a printing press manager within a few years, a feat attributed to his charismatic personality and exceptional leadership skills.

After receiving the visa, I traveled to Kuwait by land with my cousin, Taysir Salem, who was visiting Jordan at the time, along with his nephew, Ahmed. I remember that journey vividly, the tires of Taysir's car bursting repeatedly, but thankfully, we didn't get stranded in the desert, as he would rush to fix the damage at the first repair shop we came across.

I also recall that throughout the journey, my cousin kept us entertained by playing songs by Saadoun Jaber to help him stay awake.

Finally, I crossed into Kuwait with ease through the Saudi border, and the next day, I set out to search for a job. So, this marked the beginning of my exile, stretching over many years. A life that felt like dwelling at the bottom of a well, brimming with events, travel, and suffering. It was a dramatic, stormy existence, woven with both profound pain and enduring hope.

I had been under the illusion that companies would welcome me with open arms, eager to hire me because I held a degree in English Literature—a rare specialization at the time.

But that didn't happen. I achieved nothing, and I suspect my brother Mustafa knew this all along, that I would hit a dead end, and he would intervene only, when necessary, after I had lost hope and learned a harsh lesson.

When my visa was about to expire, my brother Mustafa, the manager of the printing press, finally asked me: "Do you really want to work?"

I replied: "Yes, of course."

He told me to buy a navy-blue pair of trousers, a white shirt, and a maroon tie. He instructed me to cut my shaggy hair to a number two or maybe a four, and to polish my shoes with 'boya' until they gleamed, and to let him know when I was ready. It seemed I had arrived in Kuwait and started looking for a job while still maintaining the appearance of a student—more akin to a 'hippie' or a 'young person'.

I followed his instructions meticulously, determined not to return home empty-handed. I didn't want to end up working in the construction of settlements or be consumed by the poverty that had already claimed my brother, Hamad.

Mustafa then sent me to see a man named Mahmoud Al-Ghazawi, who worked at a printing press in the Hawalli area. I went to the address he gave me and found Mahmoud seated among stacks of books. He asked about my specialization, and I told him it was English Literature. Then he asked me the meaning of the word 'promotion.' I stumbled over my words and couldn't answer. He simply said: "Never mind, never mind".

He handed me the address of a manager at Burgan Bank, a Palestinian man named Mohammed Al-Naji. He was a large man with a protruding belly, often drenched in sweat. I later learned he was a leading authority in his field and a pivotal figure at the bank, nicknamed "The Bulldozer"—a man who got things done, no matter the obstacle.

The bank's main headquarter was located by the sea, near Seif Palace. I went straight to the manager and found him on the second floor. When he noticed my presence, he gestured for me to sit at an empty desk directly in front of him. As I waited, boredom set in, and I began fiddling with the calculator on the desk. Suddenly, I felt the manager's hand on mine as he said: "'You've broken the machine. Be careful with it."

His words embarrassed me, and I thought the job I had hoped for had slipped through my fingers, but the opposite happened. After returning to his office for a few minutes, he told me to start work the next day—no questions asked. He approached me, shook my shoulders, and said: "Don't think your degree matters! My dear, forget your degree at home and come get a certificate from me."

I nodded my head, not uttering a word, still in shock from everything that had happened that day.

And just like that, in the blink of an eye, I became an employee in the Letters of Credit department at Burgan Bank, earning 150 Kuwaiti dinars—a paltry salary, barely enough to cover the rent of a small apartment. I estimated it would take me at least 150 years to save enough money to get married. So, I made a decision—and oh, how I wish I hadn't.

THE WELL OF EXILE

Me, Kuwait, the Financial Boom, and Departure to the United States

During the period when I left my homeland as an expatriate and set out for Kuwait in the latter half of 1978, in search of financial stability and peace of mind. At that time, Kuwait was experiencing an unprecedented economic and financial boom. International economic reports hailed it as the richest nation in the world, with the Kuwaiti dinar trading for at least three dollars. The stock market, Souk Al-Manakh, was witnessing extraordinary activity.

Truthfully, after I began working at the Burgan Bank, I noticed that Kuwait in those days was a land floating on two seas: one of oil and the other of money. This abundance was mirrored in the banking sector, where deposits soared to astronomical figures. When I started my first job abroad at Burgan Bank, handling the bills of the exchange department, the value of those bills alone were worth 16 million Kuwaiti dinars. I also handled several checks, one of which was worth a mere four million dinars.

I imagine that this overwhelming financial abundance led to a relaxation of the regulations governing financial transactions. Banks operated with freedom and ease, following lenient lending policies and offering facilities that seemed almost too comfortable. This, in turn, contributed to the Manakh Crisis—a stock market crash with massive financial, social, and psychological repercussions. It led to the bankruptcy of many individuals, companies, and institutions, plunging countless people into the depths of mental anguish and financial ruin, with its effects that rippled across the globe.

Though my role at the bank was confined to handling bills of exchange and checks in that department, I couldn't shake the feeling of being like the character from Shakespeare's literature who found himself in the ocean and uttered the famous line: "Water, water everywhere, nor any drop to drink."

I began murmuring my own version of that old saying: "Money is everywhere and nothing in my pocket." Picture it—someone like me, who hadn't even owned a single penny before stepping foot in Kuwait, suddenly found himself surrounded by conversations about millions.

When I started working at the bank, I was no longer the wild, free-spirited young man I once was—the hippie with ripped jeans, a striped shirt, and messy long hair. I had to adhere to the bank's strict dress code, which required me to wear a suit or, at the very least, a tie. One day, I forgot to wear the tie, and they sent me back home to fetch it.

Of course, despite my joy at becoming a bank employee with a monthly salary and a bank account, a deep sense of frustration simmered. My tasks were largely archival, involving the tracking bills of exchange scrawled in Arabic, which required no knowledge of English or any real banking expertise.

I often found myself wishing I had been assigned to the documentary credits department next door, where stacks of papers were prepared and executed with foreign banks in English. This work often involved commercial correspondence, which would have sharpened my language skills and offered me real banking experience. Such a role would have allowed me to grow in the banking field, giving me a sense of fulfillment as I worked in a domain that aligned with my academic efforts and personal aspirations. And, of course, it would have meant a better income

This feeling of frustration with the nature of my job and the tasks assigned to me became the catalyst for my decision to travel to pursue a master's degree in the United States. I hoped to return with a higher qualification that would open new opportunities and improve my financial situation.

However, as the future unfolded after a long journey through the estrangement of exile and my eventual return to Kuwait from the United States, I realized that I had been "chasing a thread of smoke," as Nizar Qabbani once wrote. In time, I will share how, upon my return, I felt "defeated and heartbroken, and undoubtedly mistaken," much like the protagonist in Qabbani's timeless poem, *"The Fortune Teller."* My decision had not been a fortunate one, nor did it yield the financial returns I had hoped for, for several reasons.

And you will see how mistaken I was in my decision to travel to complete my studies when I tell you about a man who was hired at the same bank, on the same day as I was, and the state I found him in upon my return compared to my own newfound circumstances—even though I had always thought of him as a simple man, even shambolic.

What prompted me to say this about him was an incident one day after work, when he couldn't start his Volkswagen. A group of employees rushed around, eager to assist, and I stood by, watching. After several attempts, one of them asked him when he had last put oil in the car. He replied, baffled: "Does a car even need oil?!"

The other reason that compelled me to make the decision to leave my job and travel was the suffocating loneliness that bachelors endure in that country. Unmarried men are treated as outcasts, exacerbating their profound sense of isolation.

Although I lived with my brothers and a handful of other bachelors like myself, a suffocating loneliness often crept into my days. To cope, I would wander to the Arabian Gulf to fish or lose myself in reading and writing. In 1979, I published my first complete short story in the literary section of *Al-Watan* newspaper, under the guidance of the esteemed Mahmoud Al-Rimawi. The story, titled *"Layla and the Sea,"* was a milestone for me, as was a journalistic piece I wrote about education in the occupied territories.

The final push that compelled me to make up my mind and leave that miserable, low-paying job and travel to pursue my master's degree was my encounter with Dr. Ishaq Al-Qutb. He was the director of the local branch of the International Foundation for Assisting Arab Students, headed by Prince Turki bin Abdulaziz. The foundation helped students secure university admissions and offered scholarships to many. Gratefully, they assisted me in obtaining admission to the University of Riverside for a program in English for Foreign Students—a bridge that eventually led me there and later enabled me to enroll at the San Diego State University, where I pursued my master's degree in Comparative Literature.

Honestly, if it had been only for the reasons I mentioned earlier, I might have hesitated to leave, clinging to my comfort zone. But I followed that roaring inner voice that was urging me to continue my research on the relationship between orphanhood and literary creativity—a theory born in my mind when I was just sixteen, one that had never received proper recognition or attention during my undergraduate studies.

I was determined to delve deeper into this topic, to gather the evidence needed to support such an academic study. I was ready to sacrifice everything to prove that the relationship between orphanhood and literary creativity was one of profound cause and effect.

In the end, I made my decision. On January 1, 1980, I boarded a plane, leaving Kuwait after a year and a few months, heading to the United States much to the bewilderment of many acquaintances. What followed was a rich, transformative experience that lasted four years. God willing, I will share its most significant moments with you in due time, for they are truly worth following.

The Great Adventure: Traveling to the United States – The Earth receives what the heavens bestow

Traveling to the United States was no simple matter, and for a peculiar reason. A man from our village named Arif had sailed for America at the dawn of the twentieth century, leaving behind his infant son, Saleh, who was barely forty days old—or so the village tales went. Not long after, Arif vanished without a trace, his absence becoming the stuff of proverbs and folk poetry. I grew up hearing my father recite the refrain: "I could never understand how Arif could leave and abandon his children."

For the people of our village, traveling to the United States meant a good riddance. The myth of Arif is deeply rooted in our collective memory, casting a long shadow over any dream of America. To embark on such a journey meant breaking free from that folkloric legacy, shattering the myth, and confronting the fears and anxieties it had sown.

Had I waited for my family's approval, especially my father's. I would never have set foot in the land of the Native Americans. The myth was too powerful, too entrenched. And so, I became the first person from our village to travel to America since the ill-fated Arif.

When I received my university acceptance letter and secured the necessary visa from the American embassy, I began preparing for the journey. My brother, Mustafa, arranged the trip, booking a flight that would take me from Kuwait to Queen Alia International Airport, then onward to Amsterdam, and finally to New York on a long, direct flight. From there, I would travel to Los Angeles and make my way to Riverside, the city near Los Angeles where my university was located.

I packed my belongings into a single suitcase, clutching all my savings—no more than a thousand Kuwaiti dinars, roughly three thousand dollars. I also carried the phone number of a man I had never met: Adel Hermas, a friend of a friend from Bethlehem who then lived in Los Angeles. My colleague at the bank had arranged for him to meet me at the airport and help me get to my university. Beyond Adel, I knew no one, and I had no idea what I would do if that person didn't show up to meet me at the airport.

We were on our way to Kuwait International Airport when we received joyous news that my eldest brother, Hamad, had been blessed with a daughter named Hiba. We made a detour to the hospital to visit her and check on her mother before my departure. It was the night of January 1, 1980.

And then, the plane took off, marking my first experience of flight. Before long, we arrived at the transit point, where we waited for the plane that would carry us to the United States. After a few hours of waiting, we took off at the scheduled time, heading toward the Netherlands. Our first stop was Amsterdam Airport, where the plane refueled, or so I understood, and soon we were soaring over the countries of Western Europe. The massive aircraft, a Boeing 747 operated by Royal Jordanian Airlines, carried us across the Atlantic Ocean in a journey that lasted about twelve hours.

On the same flight was a group of students traveling to study abroad through an international organization dedicated to supporting Arab students. It was undoubtedly their first time on a plane, and their faces betrayed their fear and unease. I'm certain they recited every Quranic verse and prayer they could summon. The look of terror on one young man's face, in particular, remains vividly etched in my memory.

I won't deny the anxiety about flying, especially over the Atlantic. But I found myself repeating a phrase that had puzzled me: "The Earth receives what the heavens bestow." My mind was preoccupied with a morbid question: Which fate would be more terrible—a catastrophic crash on land, or to plunge into the ocean, leaving the passengers as prey for sharks?

During the flight to New York, I struck up a conversation with the man seated next to me, a fellow traveler from Salt, Jordan. He, too, was traveling to Los Angeles on the same TWA flight. He mentioned that his relatives would meet him at the airport and, upon learning that I was alone and knew no one on the other side, reassured me. All I had was a phone number for a man named Adel Hermas, and I wasn't even sure if he would answer my call.

My new companion promised not to leave me alone and insisted on ensuring I reached my destination safely. He even offered me a place to stay with his relatives until I figured out how to get to the university.

I thanked him for his generosity and kindness, and by the end of the journey, we became friends. When the plane touched down at the vast, intimidating New York airport, he stayed by my side without hesitation. Together, we searched for the TWA airline offices, and at one point, I think we even stepped outside the airport. My Jordanian friend helped me use a payphone on the street corner to call Adel Hermas, who had promised to meet me at Los Angeles Airport and guide me to the University of Riverside.

To my immense joy, Mr. Adel Hermas answered my call, as if he had been eagerly awaiting. He assured me he would be there at the appointed time and even mentioned he would be wearing a red shirt so I could spot him easily.

As soon as the call ended and I hung up, we resumed our search for the offices of the airline that would take us to Los Angeles. Standing at the corner of the street, we spotted a taxi driver and asked him for directions to the TWA offices. He told us it would take at least half an hour by car to reach them. Just as he finished speaking, my Jordanian companion turned his head —and there they were, the very offices we were asking about, right in front of us. It took us no more than a few steps and less than ten seconds to reach them. We exchanged glances, suspecting the taxi driver had planned to take us on a needless half-hour ride, only to bring us back to where we started—if he even intended to bring us back at all. This experience marked our first encounter with what felt like an attempted scam in the United States.

We completed the necessary procedures and boarded the flight to Los Angeles, a five-hour journey that carried us over the vast expanse of the United States. Night had fallen by the time we landed, and it was nearly ten in the evening when we reached the exit gate. To my delight, I spotted him—Adel Hermas, the man in the red shirt—waiting for me.

Once Al-Salti's companion saw that I was in safe hands, he left with his relatives. I never saw or heard from him again. Yet, he left an indelible mark on my memory and heart, one that neither time nor years could ever erase.

Exhaustion had consumed us after the long flight, which had lasted 35 grueling hours, carried us across deserts and seas. Adel, my friend's friend, explained that Los Angeles transformed into a war zone at night, and it was too dangerous for him to reach his own home. Instead, he would take me to his brother Imad Hermas's house in Pomona, a less violent area and closer to my university.

Khalil Hamad

My First Days in the Land of Exile—In the Belly of the Whale: Uncle Sam's Country

The science of public relations is a formidable discipline, one that wields the mass media to craft desired images, conceal flaws, and beautify the unsightly. Over time, it creates mental pictures that become alternative reality.

The Americans have masterfully invested their intellectual advancements in psychology and communication sciences (mass media), harnessing their unparalleled resources in the field of media since the early 20th century to paint an idealized portrait of the United States for the outside world. They have succeeded in masking the immense flaws that rarely cross the mind of a foreigner yearning to reach this paradise on earth—the land of dollar, a land paved with the resonant metal, 'gold.'

This is what countless people believed, many of whom perished chasing the American Dream. Even residents of wealthy Western Europe migrated under the illusion that the streets of New York were paved with gold—a sentiment echoed by a German immigrant, who, like millions of others, fell victim to the overwhelming power of American media dominance.

I imagine that every immigrant to the United States carried a mental image of America as God's paradise on earth, only to be struck by a devastating cultural shock upon arrival. They discovered the staggering chasm between the mental image etched in their minds and the stark reality of certain aspects of life there.

I had already sensed the danger lurking in America's streets after an incident with a taxi driver at New York Airport. My fears were confirmed by Mr. Adel Hermas. the man who volunteered to pick me up at Los Angeles Airport. As he drove me from the airport—I had assumed he was taking me to his home—he informed me that just before leaving his house in a suburb of sprawling Los Angeles, armed clashes had erupted in the neighborhood's streets. He assured me such skirmishes were common among rival gangs with flashy names like 'The Black Hand' and 'The Red Hand.' He added that the number of gangs often matched the number of ethnic groups in the area—and there were many: whites, browns, yellows, and reds. The most violent clashes, he said, were often between gangs of the same ethnicity, battling for dominance. The danger was so imminent that police officers often refrained from intervening—after all, it wasn't their circus, nor their monkeys.

To be honest, I doubted his words at first, suspecting that he simply wanted to rid himself of the burden of hosting me, content with merely picking me up from the airport. He informed me that, due to safety concerns, he would send me to stay with his younger brother, Imad Hermas, who lived in a less dangerous area closer to Riverside, where my university was located. Imad would take responsibility for getting me to my destination.

As the days passed, however, I began to realize the truth in what he had said. It became clear to me after I settled in San Diego, a city that, while not as perilous as cities like Los Angeles, Chicago, or New York, still carried its own undercurrent of dangers. The threat was most severe in the city center, where it was not uncommon for people to be killed every night—or even during the day. The farther one moved from the heart of the city, the safer it became.

Riverside, by contrast, was the first city I lived in after arriving in the United States. It was a relatively rural area near Los Angeles, quiet and peaceful— or so it seemed. The tranquility was deceptive, though, as a serial killer was on the loose during those years, dumping the bodies of his victims not far from the city. By the time I arrived, the death toll had reportedly reached sixteen.

When I eventually moved to the 72nd Circular area in San Diego—the "Circular" referring to a ring road that looped around the city center, numbered sequentially from 1 onward—I was told it was a relatively safe neighborhood. It was home to affluent residents and close to San Diego University, where I was pursuing my master's degree. But "safe" was a relative term. I witnessed police chases that felt like scenes ripped straight from a Hollywood movie. Once, I saw a group of young men in a car open fire on someone standing at a traffic light near my home, killing him—just for amusement.

During my time in San Diego, I became acquainted with a Libyan student who was working on his PhD in sociology. He lived in the 58th Circular area and once complained to me about burglars had broken into his home and stolen his television through the window. The next day, he bought another one, despite my warnings that they would return if he didn't install an alarm system. Sure enough, the second TV was stolen the moment he left his house unattended.

After the drive from Los Angeles Airport to Pomona, where Imad—Adel Hermas's brother—lived, we finally arrived at his home. During the drive, we spoke of our mutual friend in Kuwait and of Adnan Hermas, who, as it turned out, was the eldest brother of Adel and Imad. Adnan had been my classmate at Bethlehem University. When we reached Imad's housing, he welcomed me warmly and treated me with great hospitality that left no doubt he had fulfilled his duty as a host in the best way possible. Even though I was most likely exhausted from jet lag, from the flight, the lack of sleep, the stress of travel, and the overwhelming unfamiliarity of the place.

Sleep was my primary need, but it was elusive. As I waited for the god of slumber, I sat in front of the television, which was broadcasting a local news bulletin. The first news I saw was a live report of a fire raging through a Saudi prince's mansion in Hollywood, allegedly set by an arsonist. The news that followed was a relentless stream of murders, assaults, robberies, and clashes. It reached a point where I began to believe that America was nothing but a land of murders, thefts, accidents, and assaults. I was stunned. Such scenes, I had never imagined, existed outside of Hollywood movies—ironically, not far from where I sat at that very moment.

Eventually, sleep took hold of me, like the slumber of the Seven Sleepers. When I awoke, Adnan Hermas suggested that he take me to stay with some Jordanian friends of his who lived near Riverside University, where I would be enrolling in a few days. True to his word, he drove me to their place. The young men welcomed me warmly, almost as if I were one of their family, and even handed me a copy of their house key. But my stay with them was short-lived—and for a very serious reason.

I soon noticed that they slept during the day and stayed awake at night. I couldn't discover if they worked or were students, while I attended university during the day and slept at night. This went on for a few days, during which I spent little time with them due to our conflicting sleep schedules. Then, on the third or fourth night, around three in the morning, one of them suddenly sat on top of me on the bed, a gun in his hand, its barrel pointed at my head. "Get up and stay awake with us, man," he said. "You're always sleeping."

Truthfully, I was terrified that the sight of the gun was unnerving, and I feared that a stray bullet might cause an unintended tragedy. I couldn't tell if the gun was real or just a water pistol, or if this was a serious breach of control or just part of their nightly antics.

Though I opened my eyes and saw the barrel pointed at my head, I pretended to be too groggy to wake up. The others eventually pushed him away, and the incident ended there. I went back to sleep—or at least pretended to, waiting for the morning.

As soon as the darkness lifted and the morning sun rose, I gathered my belongings, slung them over my shoulder, and left the house while the young men were still lost in the depths of sleep. I never returned to that place again.

THE WELL OF EXILE

Internal Imprisonment – and the Red Gold

Despite my profound gratitude for the kindness of Mr. Adnan Hermas—his gracious hospitality, his effort to arrange my stay at his friends' home, and despite my appreciation for the young men who welcomed me into their house, the incident with the gun left me deeply shaken. It casted a shadow over my life, disrupting the fragile peace I had clung to.

I couldn't help but wonder if these young men were truly sound of mind, given their reckless behavior. Later, I heard about students who deceived their families into believing they were enrolled in universities while, in reality, they had dropped out. They spent their days lost in sleep, only to emerge at sunset like nocturnal creatures, plunging into a world of goatling. It was said that they would ask their families to send tuition fees, but instead they spent it on car installments and fleeting pleasures.

Later, I discovered that more than 50% of the young men who travel to the United States for their studies eventually dropping out of university. Many of them fell into the labyrinths of indulgence and forbidden pleasures, and the rate of losing one's way is even higher among younger students—those pursuing their first university degree—especially those who lack the support system and social oversight typically provided by family and relatives. Only those who manage to overcome the shock of cultural difference succeed.

Now, let me recount what happened to me regarding my first accommodation situation after I left the youth housing for good. That morning, I went to the language institute's administration office and explained what had happened. I asked for their help in finding new accommodation, preferably on-campus housing if possible.

The institute's director reassured me that she would take me to her own home if she couldn't find a place for me. Meanwhile, a delicate blonde woman, the secretary of the English Language Institute for Foreign Students, made a few calls while I waited in the office. After a short while, she asked me to grab my luggage and follow her. I obeyed, and to my surprise, she managed to secure a spot for me in the on-campus dormitory adjacent to the institute's building. This, of course, felt like a miracle, given the overcrowding in these dormitories and the high demand for them. Often, rooms were booked long in advance.

And so, I willingly entered this "internal prison," for a mere eighty dollars a month, which covered both lodging and meals. I call it a prison because life in these dormitories was closer to incarceration than living—even if the door remained unlocked.

On the third floor of the dormitory, I became roommates with a man named Michael. He was a white American, strikingly pale, from the northern states, specifically Georgia. He had come to Riverside University to study physics, as it was reputed to be one of the top universities in that field, or so I was told.

Despite the fact that our beds were barely a meter apart, we rarely spoke. For several days, I assumed he harbored some dislike for Arabs. He was a man of few words, and we never sat together or shared anything, not even when a 5.4-magnitude earthquake struck, shaking us so violently and nearly fell to the floor. When it happened, he went his own way, and I went mine.

Though sharing a room as roommates for nearly eight months, only one incident remains etched in my memory.

One day, he received a small package in the mail from his family. He opened it in front of me, almost boastfully, as if he already knew what was inside. To my astonishment, it contained a single apple—a large, gleaming red American apple. I had never seen an apple so big, so perfect. Had it been mine, I might have split it in half without a second thought, sharing it with him, or perhaps even distributing it among the other residents on our floor. But he devoured it alone, right in front of me. As I watched him, I couldn't help but mutter to myself, "Wherever the stream flows, it runs."

As for the food at the dormitory, it was nothing short of astonishing. I wouldn't call it five-star—it was more like six or seven stars. The dormitory cafeteria served three meals a day: breakfast, lunch, and dinner. Breakfast was a lavish spread of scrambled eggs, sunny-side-up eggs, omelets, boiled eggs, mashed potatoes, and other delights. There were slices of mortadella, toast with jam and butter, an assortment of cheeses and yogurts, fresh herbs, strawberry and banana sandwiches, and an array of juices and milk. Everything was laid out in open buffet-style containers, and students could eat and drink to their heart's content—or until they were stuffed, if they so desired.

Lunch was also served as an open buffet, featuring main dishes including every kind of meat imaginable—chicken, fish, beef steaks—alongside vegetables and other delicacy one could imagine. My personal favorite was the barbecued-seasoned beef ribs, roasted in massive ovens, and served with baked potatoes and sour cream. If you were to ask me now whether I ever ate pork at those open buffets, I couldn't rule it out, though I can't say for certain it happened.

Dinner followed the same pattern, though bread—both white and brown—was conspicuously absent, replaced by what they called pita bread. Remarkably, my chronic stomach pains that had plagued me since my days at Bethlehem University, where I often ate falafel, hummus, and fava beans from a local eatery called Fateem, were beginning to ease.

The residents were bound by this dietary system and its strict timings. If someone missed a meal, they had to wait for the next one or buy food from the market at their own expense. For me, I never missed a single meal to avoid paying extra for food, especially since it was abundantly available. With my limited budget, I couldn't afford such luxuries. As a result, I didn't need any financial assistance during this period and avoided buying anything from the market to keep my expenses in check. The thousand Kuwaiti dinars I had brought with me were stretched just enough to cover all my costs and obligations throughout the nine-month language course, which lasted until the beginning of September 1980. I remember this was during the era of Democratic rule, with President Carter still in office. However, that same year, he lost the election to President Reagan, and the Republican victory had a noticeable impact on the economy. Prices soared across the country.

Over time, I became acquainted with an American young man in the cafeteria. His name was David, and he had curly red hair and a face sprinkled with brown freckles. One day, I noticed he had brought an enormous amount of food. After devouring everything on his plates, he returned with another mountain of food, as much as he had taken the first time. Astonished, I approached him and asked, "David, what are you doing? For heaven's sake, what's with all this food? Have you gone mad?"

David sighed deeply and confessed that he had just sold units of his blood to pay for his dormitory fees. Every time he did so, he would binge on food to replenish what he had lost and to keep himself strong enough to continue selling his blood to cover his living expenses.

I was utterly stunned by this revelation. I realized David wasn't the only one selling his blood for a handful of dollars. It turned out that blood trading was a thriving business there, referred to as "red gold"—a nod to the color of blood, drawing a parallel to "Black gold." I kept this information to myself, quietly storing it away as a potential solution should I ever find myself in desperate need of money.

Despite the life of comfort I now enjoyed, a stark contrast to my bachelor days in Kuwait, I began to feel an overwhelming sense of loneliness seeping into the corners of my heart. This emptiness was especially acute on weekends, when the world around me erupted into a whirlwind of appointments, dances, and parties. These were moments when lovers would meet, while I, with an empty heart, retreated into my solitude, left to simmer in my isolation.

For a stranger like me, who did not belong to the openness of this environment and still bound by the moral restraints I carried within, such feelings were magnified. While the world around me buzzed with life, I spent much of my time painting a mural—an olive tree—on the wall of the dormitory hallway.

I had met a young Lebanese man from the Al-Khatib family at the university cafeteria. I believe he was pursuing a doctorate in agriculture as was his Iraqi friend, Zuhair. The Lebanese man was friendly, always smiling, and brimming with humor and joy. He always wore a suit and tie as though he were the sultan of his time. I had asked him to help me buy a printer, and he gladly took me to a store where I purchased one for a hundred and fifty dollars.

Perhaps he noticed the shadow of melancholy etched on my face, a trace of my isolation in the dormitory and my near-complete disconnection from others. Wanting to cheer me up, he invited me to join him one evening. To my surprise, he took me to a nightclub where women danced half-naked. I didn't stay long and asked him to take me somewhere more modest, which he did.

It was with this man and his Iraqi friend, the engineer Zuhair, I experienced an incredibly awkward situation—one that time has stubbornly refused to erase from my memory, no matter how much time has passed. The incident didn't happen to me directly, but I was there, alongside another companion from Gaza, from the Al-Ayesh family. I was a witness to it, and perhaps even a participant, as I found myself inclined to support my Gazan friend's words. I remember being deeply affected by what transpired.

The Great Leap and the Awkward Situation

Once I settled into the university dormitory, I threw myself into studying English at the university's language institute. Language, I soon realized, is a realm entirely separate from literature. No matter how much literature you devour, you cannot master a language unless you study it diligently, grasp its rules, and unravel its secrets. This is why universities treat the two as distinct disciplines. Truthfully, I hadn't grasped this before enrolling in my major. I had assumed that mastering the language would come naturally through studying literature. But I soon discovered that literature professors often turn a blind eye to linguistic errors, focusing instead on the literary content.

My journey with learning English was anything but easy. I came from government schools where foreign language education was inadequate. Were it not for a teacher named Mohammed Al-Qadah, from Tulkarm, who had taught in Kuwait before being appointed at Deir Istiya Secondary School—the school I graduated from—I might have failed the English subject of my high school exams 'Tawjihi'. Al-Qadah was an exceptional teacher, clearly well-educated in the field of language, and his teaching skills were nothing short of brilliant. Thanks to him, I scored a relatively high mark of 73% in my English tawjihi exam, one of the best in my class that year (1972).

When I was accepted to Bethlehem University, I discovered that half the students in the Faculty of Arts came from Frère schools and other institutions where English was the primary language of instruction, with Arabic as a secondary language. One student, Jean Lama, boasted of scoring a perfect 300 out of 300 in English on her high school exams.

When I expressed skepticism, she brought her transcript the next day, proving her claim true.

Because of this stark disparity, the university divided first-year students into two groups: Group A, which included graduates of private schools who were more fluent in English than Arabic, and Group B, which consisted of graduates of government schools whose English proficiency paled in comparison.

The gap between the two groups felt insurmountable. I began to doubt whether I could ever specialize in English literature, no matter how hard I tried. Yet, I was deeply passionate about this field, not only because of the scarcity of specialists but also because it was the arena where I hoped to prove my theory about the source of creative energy. But that, of course, is another story.

But I managed to navigate my predicament with resourcefulness and cunning. I struck an agreement with Sister Pia, the Irish-born instructor of the English language courses. I attended all her lectures for Section A—comprising students from private schools and the Frère school—as a listener. For Section B, which included graduates of public schools, I enrolled as a regular student. I also spent countless hours in the library, earning myself the nickname "Abu Al-Maktaba" (Father of the Library). To further immerse myself in the language, I took up a job at the Senturiat of the Al-Aziza family, where I practiced English with foreign tourists, though my time there was short-lived.

I remember how, every time I looked up a word in the Al-Mawrid dictionary, I would draw a faint pencil line beneath the word whose meaning I had just learned. Once, I counted the lines under a single word and found there were twenty-one of them. This meticulous method became my hellish strategy that helped me embed words and their meanings deep into my memory—as deep as the roots of a eucalyptus tree, which plunge into the earth's depths, uncovering mines of gold and reflecting their brilliance in its leaves.

I also approached the university's monk-professors, asking them to spare me some time for personalized language lessons. Brother Brendan, the university's vice president, graciously agreed. Every Wednesday, from three to four in the afternoon, he dedicated an hour to teaching me—a commitment that lasted for a long time. I believe I learned from him an amount of English equivalent to half of what I had gained from my entire university education.

However, I suspect my performance in the novel course taught by Brother Brendan during my third year was far from stellar. The exam coincided with the fire that broke out at the Abu Aita plastic factory in Beit Sahour. In our naivety, we went to watch what we thought was a fireworks festival. Personally, suffered a severe allergic reaction and took the exam in a state of disorientation. To my surprise, I received a "Very Good" grade in that course.

Despite all the effort I had poured into earning my first university degree in English Literature, the TOEFL exam— a prerequisite for admission to American universities— exposed my weaknesses in the language. I couldn't surpass the 500-point mark, and so I chose to enroll in a language course offered by American universities for international students before embarking on my master's program. Time would prove that this decision was not only wise but indispensable.

After completing the course at that institute, and thanks to my immersion in American society and daily practice of the language in its native environment, I made a tremendous leap in my proficiency. I achieved a near-perfect score on the

TOEFL exam and came to a firm conviction: the right place to study a language is at its source. Learning a language outside its native land always feels incomplete—unless, of course, one attends foreign schools where English replaces the mother tongue. In such cases, the dance begins early, as the saying goes: "Early start, grow smart."

I am utterly certain that this tremendous leap in my language skills came not just from the numerous skills I acquired from the specialized language institute, but from the confidence I gained from being surrounded by native speakers. I felt as though I had become one of them.

Now, before I close this chapter of my memories, my life story, and my experience of learning English in the land of exile and estrangement—which is the heart of my story—I must return to a promise I made earlier. I would recount the story of what happened in that awkward situation I mentioned earlier, and I intend to do so before I pause.

What happened was that Eng. Zuhair Al-Iraqi and his Lebanese colleague, a fellow from the PhD program, from the Al-Khatib family, hosted us. They invited me and the young man from Gaza, from the Al-Ayesh family, to dinner. They were gracious hosts, and the evening took place at Eng. Zuhair's home, where his gracious wife prepared a delicious Arabic meal, and we spent a wonderful time together.

Wherever you find a Palestinian, you find politics, and endless conversations about it. We were discussing a myriad of topics, though I can't recall how we stumbled onto the subject of Shiites and Shiism. At that point, my Gazan friend began to unleash a torrent of cursing and criticizing against adherents of that sect, leaving no insult unuttered. Deep down, I think I agreed with much of what he said, but I left the talking to Ayesh, who was fervent in his speech, his passion reaching its peak. Meanwhile, our Lebanese friend sat quietly, smiling faintly and nodding his head, saying little. Our gracious host, Eng. Zuhair swallowed his words and remained completely silent.

Suddenly, our Lebanese friend broke into a smile, looked Ayesh straight in the eye, and said, "Are you done with the insults? Don't you know that Eng. Zuhair is a Shiite and that you've been cursing him for the past hour?!"

What a shock. What an awkward, mortifying moment. Here was a man who had hosted us into his home, and we had repaid his hospitality with insults. He had shown us respect, and we had cursed his roots and lineage. What kind of apology could possibly suffice in such a humiliating situation? I was overcome with shame, my face burning with embarrassment, while Ayesh looked as though someone had poured a bucket of cold water over his head. He was drenched in sweat, utterly speechless.

After this unfortunate and deeply awkward incident, we hurriedly left the home of our kind and generous host. From that day on, we avoided him in the cafeteria and the university hallways, ashamed of what we had done, despite Ayesh's feeble attempts to justify his words.

But life goes on, no matter how many stumbles and pitfalls one encounters.

What follows is a discussion about the themes of exile and estrangement, before I return to recounting some of the experiences I faced during my life abroad.

Khalil Hamad

Have You Heard the Tale of Exile and Alienation?

The deepest form of exile is to feel like a stranger in one's own homeland. A person's humanity is ultimately measured by their ability to secure even the simplest of rights in the place they once called home. Yet, exile endures, a relentless and bitter truth. And when exile merges with alienation, life itself becomes an intolerable hell.

I believe that from the very moment the umbilical cord is cut, an invisible thread forms between the soul and the land of its birth. This delicate, unseen tether nourishes the soul with an irreplaceable sense of comfort, reassurance, and peace. And it is for this reason that no place, no matter how distant or vast, can ever truly replace the sanctuary of one's homeland. And the moment a person departs from their homeland, forsaking both the land and those they hold dear, their soul withers, turning barren like an empty desert. They sink into a profound abyss of loneliness, exile, and longing, as though a child has been cruelly ripped from the comfort of their mother's embrace. How desolate it feels to be so far from the earth's nurturing embrace, their true mother, with the life-giving cord that once bound them to peace and serenity severed by the cruel forces of distance, abandonment, and ceaseless wandering.

Abdul al-Latif Aql unveils a deeper truth about exile—it's not merely the act of physical displacement, but a profound betrayal of the very roots that bind us to our homeland. In his words, he laments:

'I am the pulse of the earth, my blood flows with it.

31

How could I betray the rhythm of my own blood and wander?'

In the end, the essence of exile is not found in mere physical distance, but in the profound violation of one's humanity. Even within the familiar confines of one's homeland, the denial of fundamental rights can transform the very soil beneath one's feet into an alien place.

America, with its sprawling lands and the allure of Western capitalism, may at times appear a more favorable choice—a place abundant in opportunity, freedoms, and human rights. Yet, it remains a foreign soil, a land that cannot erase its inherent strangeness. The divide between Arab and Western cultures is immense, a gulf so profound that its depth often goes unnoticed until one is plunged into its labyrinthine realities.

I have observed that many young Arabs grapple deeply with the weight of these cultural differences. For some, the clash is so profound that it leaves them teetering on the edge of psychological collapse—especially those who arrive unmoored, with no support network to steady them, armed only with shallow cultural awareness and the naivety of limited life experience. Their fragile illusions about the place, spun from distant dreams, only magnify the shock of an unfamiliar reality.

As I seen young souls crumble, their tears falling like silent confessions just days after their arrival, consumed by the weight of exile and an aching nostalgia for the familiar rhythms of home and the embrace of family. Some, lost in the haze of their misplaced expectations, found themselves behind bars within days—victims of impulsive, ill-fated decisions born of naïve illusions.

I have seen up close the tragic fates of young men, wandering helplessly through the labyrinth of psychological turmoil, ensnared by the weight of these cultural disparities. As I previously mentioned, my ties to the university's office for international students—where I was often called upon to assist with Arab students, given my role as a graduate student and my age, which set me apart from the younger undergraduates—offered me a front-row seat to a deeply unsettling reality. I witnessed, time and again, how a significant number of young men floundered in the face of overwhelming cultural and societal disparities. For many, the cost of this struggle was steep, and withdrawing from their studies was often just the beginning. What followed was a gradual descent into confusion, psychological distress, and in some cases, something far worse, as they buckled under the weight of cultural shock.

I remember a day when I was sitting with a group of Arab students in the cafeteria at San Diego University, shortly after my arrival to begin my master's program. Among them was a young Palestinian man who had come from Kuwait. Back home, he had excelled academically, ranking among the top ten in his high school exams—perhaps even first in all of Kuwait. Without warning, he rose from his seat and bolted toward the door, his movements frantic, his face a mask of distress. We watched, bewildered, as he vanished from sight, leaving us to wonder at the suddenness of his departure. Time seemed to stretch on endlessly as we speculated, unable to grasp the cause of his apparent panic. When he finally returned, I asked him what had so unsettled him. With a sheepish look, he admitted he had feared he'd left his keys in the dorm door. In reality, the keys had been resting innocently on the table before him all along, untouched, waiting patiently for his return.

When I spoke with him and his roommate, hoping to grasp the depth of his condition and offer some help, I came to understand that he often displayed signs of mental instability. At times, his actions betrayed a subtle chaos—he would absentmindedly place a towel and soap in the refrigerator, or tuck cucumbers and tomatoes into the cupboard or even the bathroom.

There was another Palestinian young man who lived on the streets. He would come to the Arab students in the cafeteria, asking for money to buy food and drink. I often found him sitting or sleeping under the bus shelter. Some of the students—those who hadn't lost their minds to the alienation of exile—would try to contact his family to bring him back and save him from those tragic circumstances.

Stories like this are numerous, and perhaps I will return to share some of them with you, as they highlight the dangers of ignoring the profound cultural and civilizational shock that comes with such displacement.

The problem in technologically advanced capitalist societies doesn't stop at feelings of exile alone. There is something far more difficult to bear—something ten times worse than exile—and that is the feeling of alienation. This is something every human being suffers under the ruthless capitalist system, whether you are a local citizen or a foreigner living within its grip.

To illustrate the difference between American capitalist society and Eastern society, let me share a conversation I had with a professor of mathematics. He was a dark-skinned man of Indian origin, teaching at the University of San Diego State. One day, as we sat together in the university cafeteria, he wanted to explain to me the difference between Western and Eastern civilizations, so he offered this analogy:

"Listen, my friend," he said, "when someone in India thinks about having children, their family takes on the responsibility of finding a bride. Once they find her, rituals, celebrations, and joyous nights are held in homes, halls, and temples. They perform numerous ceremonies, slaughter sacrifices, and distribute sweets to seek God's blessing for the marriage and future children. Then, weddings and festivities go on for several days. But here, in contrast—in Western society, specifically in America—when people think about having children, they call a sperm bank."

This might sound like a joke coming from the Indian professor, but it's no joke at all. It's serious and real. A wealthy individual once established a sperm bank for this very purpose in the United States, and since then, the phenomenon of single mothers has become widespread and is now deeply entrenched there.

Even the renowned psychologist Carl Jung, in the later years of his life, turned to Eastern culture as a solution to his psychological struggles, having lost faith in Western psychotherapy.

The byproducts of technological and civilizational progress, along with the philosophy underpinning the capitalist system—its love of possession, selfishness, and individualism—coupled with the breakneck speed of society and the rapid pace of development, have given rise to numerous social problems. These include racism, unemployment, homelessness, the proliferation of weapons, and consequently, organized and unorganized crime perpetrated by individuals and gangs. These issues stem from the absence of social justice and, taken together, create an enormous labyrinth that makes life closer to hell—even for Americans born into the heart of this inhumane system. So, imagine the impact of these conditions on an expatriate burdened by their Eastern culture, living through the full spectrum of exile and alienation in all its meanings and dimensions... It is nothing short of hell itself.

For an individual who cannot find a way to harmonize, coexist, or integrate into such conditions, life becomes an unrelenting torment. We can only begin to fathom the magnitude of suffering endured by Arab students in such a society and the profound pain they experience if their relationship with Western society and culture remains confrontational and discordant. The psychological and social repercussions of such a clash are immense.

It was necessary to delve into the topic of exile and alienation in detail, to shed light on the circumstances one finds themselves in due to cultural and civilizational differences. But now, it's time to return to the other amusing anecdotes I personally experienced... Many more moments await their telling, so stay tuned.

Oh, Khalil… The Mountain… The Mountain

It is well known that universities organize preparatory orientation workshops for new students before they begin their academic journey, and aim to bridge the gap between the life of school and the life of university. But what about when the leap from a conservative Eastern society to an overwhelmingly open Western one, with vast cultural and societal differences?

Naturally, we can expect that a significant number of young Arabs experience cultural shock when they travel to the United States, whether for education, work, or permanent migration. These individuals are in dire need of specialized preparatory workshops—ones capable of dismantling the mirage-like dreams and illusions planted by powerful media narratives and mental programming. They need to be shown the harsh reality that awaits them and the vast civilizational divide they will encounter.

Yet, because such crucial preparation is often unavailable, the student or individual traveling there becomes vulnerable to cultural shock. Even if they have friends or relatives there, the overwhelming societal current is far stronger than any preparation they might have received. Especially, if they fall victims to the allure of media portrayals, carrying in their minds bright, idealized images that starkly contrast with reality.

I have known more than one person whose reaction went beyond academic failure or psychological crises. Some plunged into alcoholism and drug addiction, while others lost their sanity.

There is also a large segment of people who reacted as though they had dodged a bullet, immediately upon arriving in the embrace of capitalism. They rushed back to the monotony of their previous family and societal lives, seeking the safety of their comfort zones.

Even this group, which escaped the clutches of capitalism, pays a heavy price in the days to come. They are tormented by guilt, feeling the weight of their mistake every time they realize the enormity of their decision to withdraw too soon, to choose avoidance over confrontation and adventure. The feeling of having squandered an opportunity remains a bitter lump in their hearts, lingering until the end of their days. In the future, they often face relentless ridicule from their unforgiving surroundings, as they are blamed for wasting the chance that once came their way, compounding their suffering.

Often, what those who flee lack—those escaping what they perceive as a living hell and a source of unrelenting terror—is psychological flexibility and the patience when making decisions. For them, escaping the 'boogeyman' becomes an emotional reaction, the only choice available to them as an insurmountable monster, magnified by their fears.

There is another group who mistakenly believe they are immune by their upbringing, thinking that their moral, religious, and social grounding provides them with enough strength to confront, adapt to, and overcome the behavioral and social differences imposed by Western society. Yet, they fail to grasp the true power of the dominant culture they suddenly find themselves immersed in.

They are also unaware that the maximum duration a person can resist the roaring tide of a new societal current is forty days. This popular saying did not emerge from nowhere: "Dwell among people for forty days. You will either become one of them or flee them." It was undoubtedly born from the painful experience of someone who had been scorched by the fires of exile throughout history.

I recall a young Palestinian man named Fuad, who arrived from the United Arab Emirates to study at the University of San Diego. I was among the first to meet and welcome him when he stayed with his friend, who happened to be my neighbor. We sat together, and I tried to guide him, warning him of the cultural shock that awaited him. But he assured me that he had come to this country armed with faith and awareness, vowing not to assimilate into society and to preserve his values, prayers, and convictions.

Forty days passed, and unlike many others, he did not leave. More days followed, and eventually, he came to me, complaining and suffering from a severe psychological crisis. He was searching for a way out and a compassionate hand to pull him out of his predicament.

From what I gathered, he was in an extremely precarious situation. I feared he might do something reckless—to himself or to others—without immediate intervention. So, I felt compelled to put all my effort into helping him.

From him, I learned that he had fallen in love with a strikingly beautiful young woman, and he was no less handsome or charismatic in his demeanor and presence. The problem arose when he saw her speaking with someone else by the swimming pool. His Eastern Arab pride flared up, and the dormant codes of honor buried deep within his soul and mind were provoked. His world turned upside down, and the relationship crumbled, leaving him in the throes of a painful breakup. No one truly grasp the devastating impact of a shattered relationship unless they have lived through it themselves or possess the knowledge and insight into the effects of trauma and its aftermath.

Psychologists say it takes half the duration of a relationship to fully rid of the negative emotions and heal from its collapse, especially if the bond was sacred.

Imagine, then, the anguish of a young Arab man, raised all his life on the principles of honor, dignity, and noble morals, suddenly become a victim of betrayal by someone he believed to be his soulmate—someone for whom he had raised the white flag of surrender and moved heaven and earth for her.

I tried with all my persuasive power to pull him away from her, to untangle the emotional and psychological ties that bound him to her. I reminded him of our first meeting and the promises he had made to himself back then. Instead of blaming him, I showed him empathy and understanding, and even wagered that if he walked across the university campus, he would find more than one girl eager to be with him. I played on the strings of his self-worth, encouraging him to rebuild the shattered pieces of his confidence. I urged him to take up sports, to avoid isolation, and to step out of the shadows of loneliness.

But his crisis had rendered him deaf and blind in his love for her. He didn't want to hear or see anything that contradicted his feelings for her. Every time I thought I convinced him to cut ties, he would return the next day, telling me he had to see her to retrieve this or that. Over time, though, I finally managed to pull him out of the well of shock, depression, and negative emotions that had engulfed him after the ordeal. The days passed, and when I decided to return to my homeland before the six-year permit expired, he came to bid me farewell. I confided in him, struggling to express how difficult it was to leave the space station we had been living in and return to Earth. He responded, incredulous:

"You'll be fine. If you can't handle a situation like this, what does that say about the rest of us?"

His eyes welled up with tears. I think he learned a harsh lesson, overcame his ordeal, and will be alright.

As for me, my life was far from easy in the early days of my time in the belly of the whale. A crushing sense of loneliness and isolation, even though I lived in a dormitory that housed more people than a large village. Yet, I kept my distance from the students around me, especially the younger ones, to avoid their pranks and terrible bullying, which were frequent and unbearable. I was selective about whom I interacted with, preferring graduate students.

One of the pranks I witnessed, which filled me with pity for its victim, involved "Sami," a Palestinian student I believe was from the town of Anabta or one of its surrounding villages. Sami was short, stocky, and blond, with a protruding belly and a long, reddish beard. He lived on the same third floor of the dormitory at the University of Riverside as I did. Since the bathrooms and showers were shared, whenever Sami hung his clothes to bathe, some of the so-called friends he trusted would steal his clothes while he was in the shower. He would then be left with two choices: wait for divine mercy or emerge naked, "as God created me."

To distract myself from the gloomy atmosphere of the dormitory, the difficulty of navigating around without a car, the scarcity of money, and the lack of accessible places, I turned to sports and swimming for release and entertainment. But what I loved most was climbing the mountains surrounding the university, despite the fear of a serial killer who had been dumping his victims near the highway that ran through the area at the time.

I favored a spot close by, with a spring, high rocks, and trees. It's worth noting that Riverside was a beautiful city, with towering trees, and the university buildings were scattered amidst a eucalyptus forest, reminiscent of the lovely forests of the University of Jordan.

Sometimes, I would go climbing in the surrounding mountains with an American friend named Dirk. He was a strong, athletic man who wore thick glasses and had an American girlfriend of average beauty. She had a hooked nose that bent slightly to the right, which somewhat marred her appearance. Once, I expressed my surprise to Dirk about his choice of her, especially when we were surrounded by a paradise full of stunning, captivating women, many of whom dreamed of making it to the magical world of nearby Hollywood. He replied:

"I know my limits, and she's enough for me," as if to say, "Allah bless those who know their capabilities."

Khalil Hamad

A Confession

I must confess—yes, I must confess. The tale of my fellow villager, Aref al-Aref, who ventured to the distant lands of Waq Waq at the beginning of the 20th century, leaving behind his young children and never returning, became a folk ballad. I often heard my father sing it: "I could never understand how Arif could leave and abandon his children." This tragedy from the history of my village, Kifl Haris, became a dark nightmare that clung me. I was determined not to share Aref al-Aref's fate. Throughout my time in the United States, I was consumed by the fear of meeting his destiny, a fear that shackled me and caused me to withdraw into myself. It paralyzed me, preventing me from taking any action or engaging in any activity that might threaten my future.

It was not in my nature or upbringing to fear adventure or risk itself. On the contrary, I was the son of a harsh rural environment, where we grew up surrounded by snakes, scorpions, and hyenas. We surrendered to long, dark nights, their gloom pierced only by the faint light of an oil lamp or the flicker of a lantern, while tales of ghouls and jinn filled the air.

As a young boy, I roamed the mountains herding cows, and over time, our hearts turned to iron. When the opportunity arose, I did not hesitate to defy the folkloric legacy and travel where no one from my village had gone before.

Yet, what terrified me most was disappointing my father, who must have lived in a parallel terror for the same reason. I was also afraid of returning empty-handed, without a university degree to hold my head up with pride, as they say. I cannot imagine anything more difficult than failing in my studies and returning in defeat, a failure that would inevitably cast its shadow over the rest of my family.

My fears only grew stronger after what I witnessed and experienced in the early days of my arrival in the United States in the early 1980. On my very first night of my arrival, I remember watching the pervasive crime in American society on the television of my host, Adnan Hermas. Then there was the gun incident, from which I believe I miraculously survived, followed by news of a serial killer near the University of Riverside, where I had enrolled. The ongoing violence, murder, and crime made it seem as though society there was engulfed in an unending civil war.

For all these reasons, I poured all my efforts and focused into my studies and succeeded in them, obtaining my advanced degree, and surviving the deadly perils of capitalist society.

This, however, placed me in another dilemma: my hesitation to take on the kinds of jobs that Arab students typically worked, jobs that were among the most dangerous in the country. Every month seemed to bring news of one of them falling victim to armed robberies—specifically, those working at gas stations, grocery stores, and liquor shops.

Yet, I had no choice but to work. The money I had brought with me was nearly exhausted, and I did not expect anyone to fund my studies. I had to find a job as soon as possible.

Compounding my crisis was the need to move from one city to another in search of university admission for my master's degree, which multiplied my challenges and left all possibilities wide open.

Amidst all these circumstances, I found myself in a wretched, desperate state. I had no idea what would become of me if my money ran out before I could secure a job that would meet my needs. Yet, I was adamant about avoiding menial, high-risk jobs, despite the temptations of the market and the allure of high wages, a conscious decision.

Naturally, as a result of these circumstances and fears, my movements became confined to the university campus and its immediate surroundings. My social relations shrank to a small circle of mature individuals, keeping my world tightly controlled.

Then, the arrival of a young postgraduate student from Gaza brought me a glimmer of relief. We began meeting frequently, sharing stories and comforting each other. He had rented a small studio near the university, one of those modest spaces designed for student.

As I frequented his place, I became acquainted with a Brazilian student living in the adjacent studio. Over time, as our acquaintance deepened, I visited the Brazilian student's studio one day and found him busy installing a new landline telephone he had just acquired. As he recounted his story about a letter he had mailed without a postage stamp, I saw an opportunity to play a trick on him. I discreetly memorized his new phone number, which was written on the device's packaging, without him noticing.

Returning to my Gazan friend's studio. picked up the phone and dialed the Brazilian student's number. Adopting a stern tone, I introduced myself as the post office manager and scolded him, "How could you send a letter without a stamp?" At first, he thought it was a joke, but I maintained a serious and authoritative demeanor. I scolded him for his carelessness, and he began apologizing profusely, saying: "I'm sorry, my English is weak," and offering excuses in broken language.

After a while, I hung up and returned to his studio. As soon as I walked in, I noticed he looked so disturbed and pale. "Is something wrong?" I asked.

He replied hesitantly, "No, it's just... the post office."

The moment he mentioned the post office, I slapped my chest dramatically and said, "Don't worry, I'll take care of it.

When I saw him weighed down by worry, I confessed that it had been me who called him. I explained that I had memorized his number from the box and that the post office had no way of knowing it. I tried to calm him down, assuring him that it must have been some devilish prank.

As for my Japanese friend, he visited me at my new place. By then, I had moved out of the university dormitory and into an off-campus apartment.

As a gesture of hospitality, I got up to make him tea, and decided to add a touch of dried mint to it. He asked me curiously:

"What's that?"

I replied spontaneously: "It's high-quality Middle Eastern contraband."

He raised an eyebrow: "Does it make you feel good?"

"Of course," I said. "Would you like to try it?"

He said: "Yes."

I said: "Give me a cigarette." He was a smoker. So he handed me one, and I carefully emptied some of the tobacco from it, replacing it with the dried mint leaves mixed with tobacco to hold it together. I sealed the cigarette with a bit of tobacco, lit it, and handed it back to him. He took a few puffs, and within moments, he began to show signs of being high. He was under the influence.

But the scene didn't end there. When he decided to leave, I walked him to the elevator—an old, creaky, and painfully slow contraption. After he stepped inside and pressed the button to descend, I rushed down the stairs. I stopped the elevator on the second floor and stood there, pretending I was still on the third floor. When the doors opened, he looked utterly confused to see me standing there. He pressed the button again, and as the elevator descended, I hurried down the stairs once more, this time stopping at the first floor. I stood in front of the elevator doors, maintaining the same posture as before, as if I hadn't moved from the third floor. When he saw me again, he spun around like a frantic chicken. I finally embraced him and said, "Forgive me, I was just joking with you." I don't think he will ever forgive me. And with that, the scene came to an end.

Soon, it was time to move on to San Diego to seek admission into a master's program after completing my language course. I had to go there in person to submit my application, as some friends had suggested. But first, I had to solve the puzzle of how to get to San Diego, which was no small feat. The city was a considerable distance away—at least a two-hour drive, if not more.

Eagles Soar Alone

As I approached the end of my English language course at the specialized institute in teaching foreigners, affiliated with the University of Riverside, and after achieving an outstanding score on the TOEFL exam, a remarkable improvement compared to my best results before joining the institute and arriving in the United States, I felt a surge of confidence. This confidence was born from my studies at the institute, coupled with living among native English speakers and improving my ability to communicate with them fluently and effectively. Yet, all of this only deepened my awareness of the immense loss I had suffered while trying to learn the language in the wrong environment.

The loss lay in the sheer effort I had expended, the time I had wasted, and the pain I had endured while struggling to grasp the basics of the language—efforts that could have been drastically shortened. After all these years of toiling to understand the intricacies, elements, and applications of this foreign language, with the goal of mastering it and speaking it fluently, I realized that learning a language far from its native soil, away from qualified teachers, experts, and specialized institutions, is like watching an ant laboriously drag a seed many times its weight. In contrast, a learner at a specialized institute, guided by qualified instructors and immersed in the language among its native speakers, leaps forward like a hare escaping a predator. Soon enough, they soar into the skies of language like an eagle, gliding with ease, joy, and pride in its vast expanse.

Based on my own hard experience and the tremendous loss of time and effort, I strongly advise anyone considering learning a foreign language to go straight to the heart of where it is spoken. Enroll in specialized institutions there, and practice the language directly with native speakers. This approach not only helps overcome the fear of speaking a foreign language but also builds confidence in mastering it, saving immense time and effort that would otherwise be wasted learning it in the wrong environment. If you were to calculate the cost in both scenarios, you would find that drawing the language from the source is far less costly and yields far better results.

This is what I felt as I approached the end of my language course, and it intensified my sense of the tremendous loss— the time and effort that had brought me to where I was.

Now, with a firm grasp of the language and confidence in my level of proficiency, I thought I had left that burden behind me. But suddenly, I remembered that I did not yet have acceptance into a master's program. I had assumed I would automatically enroll at the University of Riverside for this purpose, but it turned out that the requirements for federally funded universities like Riverside were exceedingly high. The alternative was state-funded universities, so I began consulting my language institute professors and friends. The consensus was clear: head to San Diego University and avoid Los Angeles to steer clear of the risks of living there.

During my search for the best opportunities, I had a conversation with one of my language institute professors. I asked him for his opinion on whether it was better to take a comprehensive exam at the end of a master's program or to write a thesis. His response was that it depended on my future plans and what I intended to do after graduation.

If I planned to continue my academic journey toward a PhD, he advised that writing a master's thesis would be the better option. It would serve as training for the doctoral dissertation, and while I was still young, it would make the process easier once I had acquired the research and writing tools I would learn while preparing my master's thesis.

But if you intend to stop at the master's level and move on to work or teaching, there's no need to waste time preparing a thesis. You can simply take the comprehensive exam instead.

The professor's words settled the matter for me, though I had already been inclined to write a master's thesis. I was eager to explore my theory about the source of creative energy, particularly the presumed connection between orphanhood and creativity, an idea that had taken root in my mind at the age of sixteen. This lofty goal had been one of the primary reasons I had traveled abroad to pursue my master's degree. Now, my mind was consumed with finding a way to get to San Diego. The urgency grew after the semester ended, and I had to vacate the dormitory and leave the University of Riverside behind for good. Amid the uncertainty, a young acquaintance named Victor offered to drive me there in his car. Victor, a student of Spanish descent at Riverside was heading home to his family, who lived in San Diego.

And so it happened. I packed my belongings and set off for San Diego with Victor, unsure whether I would succeed in my quest to gain admission to the university there. Still, I was banking on the personal interview, hoping to leverage my persuasive skills and pitch my pioneering idea about the source of creative energy. The truth was, I had no clear plan for what I would do if I failed, especially since the money I had brought with me to the United States was nearly exhausted.

As we drove south on the highway, Victor maintained a steady pace, never exceeding 80 miles per hour. He had set a speed lock on the odometer to ensure he never went over the speed limit, aiming to save fuel and avoid traffic tickets We journeyed through mountains and breathtaking landscapes teeming with wild grasses and trees—nature at its most stunning. We encountered towering bridges stacked in layers, sometimes reaching over ten levels, each one branching off into a different direction. These architectural wonders were a sight to behold, with every road marked by its own number. I now believe we were traveling on Route 505, the highway connecting Los Angeles to San Diego, passing through the city of Riverside. It was the same route we had seen in adventure films.

Victor explained to me that these bridges and tunnels cutting through mountains were born out of economic crises that had swept through the United States. In response, the federal government had invested heavily in infrastructure to stimulate the economy and resolve the crises. The first of these plans was implemented after the 1928 crisis, and the solution lay in pouring funds into infrastructure. As a result, the United States ended up with the most beautiful and extensive network of roads and public facilities in the world. We made several stops along the way, driving as if we were part of a river of cars flowing in both directions. The highways were a marvel in themselves, with multiple lanes—some for fast-moving traffic, others for slower vehicles—sometimes totaling up to ten lanes.

What struck me about these roads was how cars would slow down and follow behind motorcycle gangs if they happened to pass by, a scene that hinted at the dominance of these groups.

Finally, we arrived in San Diego, the last major city on the map in the southwestern corner of the United States. Nestled along the Pacific Ocean, this city boasted some of the greatest tourist attractions in the world, including the largest zoo, SeaWorld, and countless other landmarks that drew tourists from every corner of the globe.

Victor dropped me off at San Diego State University and went on his way. I don't quite remember how, but I ended up that day at the home of a Kurdish man named Saif Al-Din, a graduate student working on his master's thesis about the communist revolution in South Yemen. I spent the rest of that day and the following night at his place, intending to stay with him until I could figure out my housing situation. But a miracle happened the next day, my housing crisis was solved, and I felt an overwhelming sense of relief, as though I were back among my family and tribe.

Khalil Hamad

O fire of Exile, be thou cool and safe for Khalil!

They say in psychology that change produces tension, and when that tension mounts, it may transform and manifest in pathological forms, dominated by feelings of anxiety and stress.

And here I am, in the eye of the storm, swept up by the waves of forced change. I am leaving my comfortable zone, which I had grown accustomed to during the months I spent in the town of Riverside. Behind me, I leave the tranquility of the place, the monotony of life, the warmth of friendships, the simplicity of living, the peace of mind, the affordable prices, the most delicious food, and the breathtaking scenery. Now, the tempest of change hurls me into a new, undefined space—a place of uncertain directions and open destiny that awaits the restoration of routine and the replacement of one safe zone with another.

Change ignites a fire in the chest, especially when it occurs in a land of exile. It becomes like a deep, dark well when it is aimless, with no clear destination or timeline.

And here I am, swept up by change, hurled into a new city and a different mode of life—one that is more bustling and open to all possibilities. Once again, I find myself searching for my safe zone, starting over from scratch.

Thus, I have fully immersed myself in the city of San Diego. This marks the end of a chapter defined by calm, rural atmospheres, dormitory living, open buffets, limited expenses. It heralds the beginning of an urban phase of noise, commotion, the hunt for housing, soaring prices, mounting expenses, and the drudgery of the necessary details for living as a student in a land of exile, far from family.

It also means the end of playful times and enjoyable language study, and the start of a serious phase, diligence, pursuing a master's degree, and diving into the labyrinths of research and studies, conducting research, taking exams, and awaiting results.

San Diego is a vast, sprawling city, home to millions, with administrative boundaries stretching to astonishing extents. A beautiful city with sandy beaches extending for kilometers, reaching the borders of Mexico to the south. It houses the largest park they call Balboa Park, near which lies the greatest zoo in the world. Not far from there is SeaWorld, with its playful whales.

A city home to several public, private, and community universities, as well as bustling commercial centers and markets. Among its landmarks, San Diego University, a public institution managed by the state, stands out as one of the city's most beautiful features. Perched atop a hill, it draws students from across the United States and around the globe, with an enrollment of around 50,000 students across its various colleges. Half of these students are strikingly beautiful women, and among them, those who are captivating dreamers aspiring to reach Hollywood through the media and arts colleges, which have gained a reputation over time as a backdoor to reach stardom.

The day after my arrival in the city, I left early from the home of my Kurdish host, Saif Al-Din. I can't quite recall now how I found my way to the university, but once I arrived, I went straight to the student affairs office and submitted my application, following the required procedures. After completing the application, I made my way to the English Literature department and inquired about the dean. Dr.

George, as I came to know him, was a humble, smiling man. A white American who, hailed from the bustling city of New York, he had moved to teach at San Diego University to escape the noise, fast pace, and harshness of New York life, as he told me, seeking a quieter, less chaotic, and more peaceful existence.

Dr. George welcomed me into his office, and we got acquainted. I expressed my desire to study at the college and shared with him my theory linking orphanhood to literary creativity, explaining that I intended to pursue a master's thesis on this topic.

After listening to my detailed explanation, Dr. George welcomed the idea but offered his perspective. He pointed out that the theory couldn't be generalized to all literary creators, as while some writers were orphans, others like Hemingway were not. I conceded the point but insisted on the importance of orphanhood in fostering creativity, drawing from my own experience and drawing parallels between my story and Tolstoy's orphanhood. The discussion stretched on, and I passionately defended my perspective. At the end of our conversation, we agreed to expand the scope of the thesis under Dr. George's guidance. Instead of assuming that orphanhood (parental loss) was the sole cause of creativity, Dr. George suggested broadening the idea to include the concept of a general loss (object loss) in the life of a creative writer.

I stepped out of the office of the Dean of the English Literature Faculty, leaving behind a strong impression that I would be a diligent student. The professor had expressed his admiration for my enthusiasm and my defense of my theory, which was still an idea in its infancy at the time.

I remember hearing him say that day, with a sense of awe: "So you're coming from Palestine, carrying an idea that none of the American students have even considered?!"

I felt that the professor was inclined to accept me into the Master's program, but I still had to wait. After all, who knows how the standards would be applied?!

Leaving the faculty building, I felt a fleeting sense of relief after my meeting with the Dean of the English Literature Faculty. This was especially true when he gave me the opportunity to present my idea and accepted it with an open mind, even praising and commending it, unlike how it was usually received by the majority.

As my work at the university ended that day, I headed out through the main gate to return to the home of my Kurdish host, Saif Al-Din. But I walked heavily, burdened by the worries of housing, finding a job that would provide me with a decent income, the concern of acceptance, the city's hustle and bustle, and the open possibilities, in addition to the tension resulting from leaving my safe zone and being in a new place.

I walked as if I were through a dark tunnel, a deep, obscure well. Alienation consumed me like a blazing fire, at its peak. My greatest fear, despite the promising signs, was not being accepted into the faculty. I couldn't bear to think of that possibility and its consequences, and the complications it would bring upon me.

Amidst that turmoil and the overwhelming feelings of loneliness and exile, my eyes fell on the face of a familiar person, smiling and walking in the opposite direction. I never expected to see him in this place, and at first, I couldn't believe, but soon I exclaimed:

"Oh my God, it's Nabil... Nabil... Nabil??!"

That smiling face belonged to Nabil Kokaly, a son of the city of Beit Sahour. He was my colleague at Bethlehem University, graduating in the same cohort as me. He was more than a friend, our bond has deepened into something far stronger, as had my relationship with his brother, Munir Kokaly, and their entire family. This closeness began after I rented and lived in a small room attached to their house during my first year at Bethlehem University. That year, I lived with them as if I were one of the family. Their mother, kind-hearted, treated me like one of her own sons, often feeding me, quenching my thirst, and doting on me.

Suddenly, in the blink of an eye, the fire of my exile turned into coolness and peace, as if it had never existed. I was as though I had glimpsed light at the end of the tunnel or been thrown a lifeline in the dark well of alienation.

Nabil asked how I was doing, and I explained my situation to him. Without hesitation, he suggested I stay with a group of Palestinian youths living near the university until I could find permanent housing. True to his word, he helped me gather my belongings from my gracious host, Saif Al-Din Al-Kurdi, and accompanied me to meet the young men. He introduced me to them, and I stayed with them for a short while. They were led by a spirited young man named Amer. Though I eventually found independent housing close to the university. I maintained a good relationship with those young men, whose own situation was far from ideal, to say the least.

Meeting my friend Nabil Kokaly, who, as it turned out, had preceded me in earning his doctorate—which he indeed obtained later—and returned to work as a professor in Palestinian universities, where he remains to this day, solved all my logistical problems entirely. All that remained was for me to secure admission to the university, find a job, and ensure an income sufficient to cover my study expenses. What happened in this regard was astonishing, miraculous, and almost unbelievable.

Khalil Hamad

O people! Hear and understand!

If Tariq bin Ziyad had not burned his ships, he would never have triumphed in his battles, nor would he have conquered Andalusia. If you are among those who strive for success and seek to achieve their goals, you must burn your ships, charge boldly toward your aim, and never look back—only then will you see.

Scholars and experts in human development labor to present theories on the tools for achieving success. There is near-universal agreement that thoughts and mental images are the blueprints for a future reality waiting to be realized. The speed at which these ideas transform into reality depends on the clarity of the mental image and the effort exerted in striving to achieve and materialize them.

In 1948, the English novelist George Orwell wrote a novel titled *1984*, a novel in which he wove ideas and imagined scenes depicting what the world might look like in the year 1984—thirty-six years after the novel's creation. Astonishingly, much of what Orwell envisioned came to pass, transforming into actual reality.

Analysts have worked tirelessly to interpret this phenomenon. Some believe that Orwell was able to accurately read the reality of the trajectory as it existed when he wrote his novel. His predictions, they argue, were based on that reality and the natural progression of events, which inevitably led to the outcomes outlined in his book. Others contend that he was a visionary, a heightened sensitivity that allowed him to glimpse what lay ahead.

Today, neuroscientists and human development experts lean toward the belief that thoughts shape future reality. Orwell's novel may have served as a blueprint—a set of mental schematics that the collective mind unconsciously sought to realize. Much of what he envisioned came to pass because that is what always happens.

Rhonda Byrne, the Australian author behind the widely celebrated and admired theories of the modern era—*The Law of Attraction*—she claims that all historical geniuses like Aristotle, Plato, and many others had intuitively harnessed this law to achieve their goals and, in turn, attain great accomplishments.

Yet, Rhonda Byrne offers no concrete evidence for the existence of the Law of Attraction. She overlooks the fact that her own success came only after the seismic shock of her father's death, which upended her life at the age of thirty-six. Before that, she had lived a comfortable, stable life as a bank employee. The shock of her father's passing shattered her world, plunging her into depression and grief. As she recounts, she was brought to the brink of despair, teetering on the edge with one foot in the grave, before she clawed her way back to life. It was then that her mind began to operate in a way it never had before, leading her to formulate the *Law of Attraction*. Through this concept, she achieved fame, unprecedented success, and immense wealth.

She attributes her achievements to her accidental discovery of the *Law of Attraction* after that life-altering trauma, claiming it was the key to her monumental success.

As for what happened to me—my chance encounter with my friend Nabil Kokaly—someone I hadn't even known he was in the United States—was nothing short of miraculous. His presence alone resolved a third of my problems, making his mere presence feel like a guardian angel to me. This meeting was not the result of any preconceived thoughts I had visualized or the workings of the *Law of Attraction*.

Had I known of his presence there, I would have reached out to him before my journey, perhaps even visited him while I was in the neighboring city, and arranged for my enrollment at San Diego University.

But I believe that our meeting, which occurred at the most critical moment of my life, was orchestrated by a divine, miraculous hand. I doubt that Nabil was even a regular student at San Diego University at the time. Rather, he happened to be passing through the university building at that precise moment. What transpired was purely celestial intervention—a lifeline, a companion, and my salvation from those dire circumstances.

The same can be said for what happened next, which also smoothed the path ahead for me. After my meeting with my friend Nabil and my brief stay with the group of Palestinian young men he introduced me to, I headed to the university. I made my way to the Faculty of English Literature, where I met with Dr. George, the dean of the faculty. It became clear that I had been accepted into the master's program—but with a conditional basis. This meant I had to work hard and achieve grades higher than 80% in the first semester; otherwise, my acceptance would be revoked, and I would have to leave without completing my studies.

While this conditional acceptance meant, in practical terms, that a sword would remain hanging over my neck throughout the first semester—it was still the better of two difficult options. It was less costly, and it kept the door of hope open. Imagine, dear readers, the repercussions if my application to join the faculty had been rejected. What would it have meant for me financially, psychologically, emotionally, and practically? What a crushing disappointment it would have been! Where would I have gone next, with my financial situation already so strained? Where would I have found stability?

Yet, I never doubted for a moment that I would overcome this unexpected challenge. I was confident I could achieve the required grades to remove the conditional status. In fact, the decision served as a motivation rather than a discouragement, and I resolved to earn the highest marks possible.

Instead of faltering or losing my direction, I rushed to register for the required courses. I remember standing in line for the English Literature program, one of only nine students. In stark contrast, the line for Business Administration stretched for over three kilometers, with some students having camped out overnight just to secure a spot in their desired courses.

Once I completed the registration process, I went to the bookstore near the main cafeteria building to purchase my textbooks. And there, as if orchestrated by fate itself, another miracle occurred, as everything unfolded with such ease and smoothness that felt nothing short of astonishing.

At the entrance of the bookstore, named Aztec Book Store after the indigenous Aztec people of the Americas—stood a tall, slender woman whom I guessed to be in her sixties. I later learned her name was Madame Pat. Something about her demeanor suggested she was in charge, perhaps because she stood near the door of a small office to the left of the entrance. Her authoritative presence was unmistakable, etched in her expression.

I approached her and asked:

"Madam, do you have a job for me?"

What followed was a thunderous surprise. Without hesitation, without questions, she replied:

"Can you start now?"

I didn't miss a beat. I slang my bag of books off my shoulder, dropped it by the office door, bypassing all formalities: "Show me," I said, ready to work.

She led me to the basement and explained the job. It was simple, mostly manual labor: unloading boxes of books from trucks, unpacking them, stamping prices on the first page, then wheeling stacks of books on a handcart to their designated shelves, where they awaited sale.

Just like that, I had a job—a porter at the bookstore nestled within the university walls. It happened almost miraculously, right after I had registered for my courses. It's worth noting that half the students at the university, if not more, dreamed of landing such a position. Yet, once again, it seemed to be God's will for me.

Securing this job resolved a significant crisis for me. I no longer had to work in the market, where the work was dangerous. That had been a pressing concern for me, especially after what had happened to Arif, who had left and never returned.

During the academic term, I worked four hours daily, and eight hours on holidays and weekends. I stayed in that job for over three years, until I completed all the required coursework for my master's degree and began the arduous task of writing my thesis. At that point, I had to stop working to focus entirely on my research—a grueling endeavor that demanded countless hours, relentless effort, and meticulous attention.

Now, years later, when I look back on those moments and how everything I wished for fell into place with such miraculous timing and precision, I am certain it was all orchestrated by divine will. I've come to believe that a person always attains what they strive for:

"And that man shall have nothing but what he strives for, and that his striving shall soon be seen". (Surah Al-Najm 53:39-40)

Especially when the goal one pursues is noble—and what could be nobler than the pursuit of knowledge and serving orphans?

Khalil Hamad

A Wife: Either a Source of Tranquility or a Double-Edged Sword

Life is built on struggle—this is how the world has always been, and this is how it shall remain for as long as God wills it. In ancient times, the primary struggle was against nature and its perils. Divine laws, however, frame the central struggle as one against Satan and the soul that is a persistent enjoiner of evil. Later, Darwin posited that the struggle was between species for survival, while Freud argued that it was between the individual's desires—especially sexual ones—and society's refusal to accommodate them. Marx, on the other hand, saw the primary struggle as a class conflict.

In truth, all these forms of struggle—and more—coexist in capitalist society. But for new immigrants to the United States, particularly Arab students, the fundamental struggle is for citizenship and a passport that unlocks the doors of the world, elevates one's status, and opens the path to a better income. In this sense, it is a document worth risking everything for, even going out on a limp.

You will not find an immigrant to the United States, regardless of their nationality, who does not hunger to obtain American citizenship, lured by the promise of its privileges. Arabs are no exception in this regard. Yet, every Arab student who arrives in America carries with them a long and painful story about obtaining citizenship—stories that often resemble those found in *One Thousand and One Nights*.

In the early 1980s, there were two paths to American citizenship. Either you were wealthy and established a business with a six-figure capital, which would secure citizenship through investment, or you resorted to the more common route: marriage.

Marriage for citizenship, however, comes in several forms. One was marrying a suitable life partner from a respectable family, a wife who would be a source of tranquility, becoming the apple of his eye, and support.

However, in all my years in the United States, I never encountered anyone who managed to marry a girl from a respectable family and obtain citizenship as a natural outcome—except for one young Christian man from Jordan. He was blessed with striking blue eyes, a magnetic personality, and a handsome, well-built frame. At first glance, you'd think he was Scandinavian or Anglo-Saxon.

The second type of marriage was finding a wife to serve as a permanent life partner, but with the hidden goal of obtaining citizenship that promises residency, privileges, and work permits. Securing a wife of this kind was no easy feat. Such marriages were often hastily arranged, with the wife—who was supposed to be a life partner—and husband inhabiting entirely different worlds. It was inevitably a marriage of convenience, even if it appeared to be a genuine union aimed at tranquility and a peaceful life. More often than not, it failed to achieve even the barest minimum of that ideal, and instead became a source of discord.

More often than not, those who enter into such marriages of convenience—cloaked in the guise of genuine matrimony—become entangled in discord and disharmony, frequently ending in divorce. This, in turn, gives rise to endless problems, including issues involving their children.

The third category of marriage is one of mutual agreement, where both parties understand that the arrangement serves a singular purpose: the husband gains citizenship, in exchange, he pays the other party a sum of money. Once the transaction is complete, both parties go their separate ways.

This type of union feels more like a business contract than a lifelong commitment. Of course, it requires certain formalities, such as creating the illusion that the wife lives with the husband in their marital home. The husband might scatter the wife's clothes and her belongings to create the appearance of cohabitation, all in preparation for unexpected visits from immigration officials. Eventually, the wife must accompany him to the immigration office to finalize the citizenship application.

The consequences of such marriages are countless, seemingly without end, and often culminate in disaster. The vast majority of women who agree to participate in these arrangements are, more often than not, drawn from the fringes of society—individuals with questionable pasts, so to speak. Rarely does one find a respectable woman from a well-established family willing to enter into such a contract, no matter the financial incentive.

The issue is, despite the risks, this type of marriage remains a common path for those who seeking citizenship resort. It is not only exorbitantly expensive and riddled with conditions but also fraught with peril. The husband may find himself caught in the crosshairs, and at any moment, the "wife" may withdraw from the agreement—especially if a more lucrative opportunity arises. The risks with immigration authorities are immense; the husband could be accused of fraud, often paying a heavy price, including deportation.

To make matters worse, in many cases, the fraudulent wife exploits the arrangement to blackmail the husband, demanding endless sums of money under the threat of reporting him to immigration authorities. This forces the husband into a nightmarish cycle of extortion, turning his life into a living hell.

The tragedies born from such marriages are countless, and I witnessed some of them firsthand.

Take Amer, for example. He married Linda, a young man in the prime of his life—vibrant, energetic, with a striking physique and a personality straight out of a movie. Linda, the woman he married, was his polar opposite in every way. To avoid the risks of exposing their sham marriage, she lived with him and a group of his friends.

When the legal period passed, and he completed the necessary interviews with immigration authorities, Amer finally secured his citizenship and promptly divorced her. She then married one of his friends who had been living with them, biding his time for his turn. However, when the second man married her, she refused to accompany him to apply for citizenship. Instead, she lived with him as a genuine wife, and he continued to appease her and trying to win her affection to avoid trouble with immigration. As far as I know, he is still waiting, though he now has the option to obtain citizenship through their children. Ironically, this second husband was no less handsome or charismatic than Amer—in fact, he was even more striking.

Then there's my close friend Maher. He waited patiently for years until his friend Youssef obtained his citizenship. The moment Youssef divorced his fake wife, Maher married her. To make their marriage appear legitimate, Maher even went so far as to keep women's clothing in his apartment. No one knows how much this charade cost him, but I do know that he lived in constant anxiety, always anticipating problems to arise at any moment. Yet, like his friend, he managed to survive the scrutiny and testing period, eventually securing his citizenship.

I also recall a man from Beit Sahour whom I once met at a tennis court. As I got to know him, he revealed that he had fled from New York to San Diego—from the northernmost point to the southernmost point—to escape the blackmail he was subjected to by his fake wife. I never found out what became of him later, but he was most likely deported if she had reported him.

As for me, none of these types of marriages were suitable, especially the costly and high-risk ones that could lead to deportation. This was something I could neither endure nor allow before obtaining my degree. So, despite the many opportunities that came my way through friends, I made a deliberate decision to avoid gambling in this matter. I imagined that these opportunities did not carry the same risks.

Of course, even if someone managed to navigate all these dangers unscathed, they would still have to raise their hand and swear an oath of allegiance to the American flag upon receiving their green card. Then, they would have to wait five years to obtain a passport. If they decided to work abroad or return to their homeland, they would have to prove their presence in the U.S. every year—a process that is both financially draining and exhausting. This has led many to abandon their green cards and, consequently, their citizenship, after suffering all kinds of troubles to obtain it.

And, of course, anyone who enters into such an arrangement remains perpetually threatened with deportation if it is discovered that they obtained their citizenship through fraud and a sham marriage.

69

All Men to the Square of Prophet Yusha

The military orders came on the second or third day of the occupation in 1967, directed at the men of our village, Kifl Haris. They were issued by the appointed military governor, who had emerged victorious in the war. Such orders were typical for imposing curfews—you needed soldiers, a governor, force, and military commands to enforce the rules, though people did not always comply.

However, in America's large, bustling cities, the situation was entirely different. There, the streets empty themselves as the sun dips below the horizon, especially in areas near downtown, where gangs and the homeless roamed freely. By nightfall, the streets appear deserted, as if a curfew had been forcibly imposed by a military governor. This was not due to orders but out of fear—fear of the crimes that often claimed three or four victims daily in major American cities, even in less violent ones like San Diego.

The contrast between rural environments and small towns on one hand, and America's big cities on the other, was stark and palpable. Geographically, Riverside might be the closest city to San Diego, but when I arrived in San Diego after completing my English language program in Riverside, it felt like stepping into an entirely different planet.

It reminded me of my migration from my village, Kifl Haris, to Bethlehem in the early 1970s, where I had gone to study at the university. That same sense of displacement resurfaced when I moved from Riverside to San Diego in the early 1980s. The differences were overwhelming, touching almost every aspect of life. Walking through San Diego's streets, I was gripped by a deep sense of alienation, like someone stepping out of prison. Life in the big city was loud, crowded, and intimidating. I often hesitated to enter certain stores, unnerved by them.

Although I lived far from the intimidating chaos of downtown—on El Cajon Boulevard in the 72nd District, a relatively quiet area inhabited by the wealthy. However, during my time there, I encountered two dangerous incidents.

The first occurred when a group of young men fired shots from a passing car at a man standing at a traffic light—one I often crossed on my way to the nearby 7/11 store. They killed him in cold blood, and it later turned out they were drunk, betting on hitting their target.

The second incident took place as I was entering a restaurant near my home, a place I frequented to avoid cooking. Suddenly, an armed robber burst in, brandishing a gun. He stormed out just as quickly after robbing the restaurant of its cash.

The danger lay in the fact that things could have taken a turn for the worse, spiraling out of control. A single bullet could have been fired from that gun, but by God's grace, it never came to that.

On one occasion, I witnessed a group of bikers—men with an intimidating presence, their bodies covered in tattoos, dressed in strange attire, and their hairstyles wild. They were brutally assaulting a man in front of a supermarket called VONS, where I often shopped for groceries. The store was about two kilometers from where I lived. They beat him mercilessly, without a hint of compassion, until the blaring sirens of approaching police cars forced them to scatter. They fled on their roaring motorcycles, leaving the man battered and broken. I never learned the reason for the attack, but I wouldn't be surprised if it was over something trivial— perhaps the victim's face had simply displeased the bikers.

The phenomenon of biker gangs in the United States is truly unique. What Hollywood portrays about these outlaws—is not far from reality. Yet, there is a darker, grittier side to these groups of thugs. They live by the code of gangs, asserting their authority. For instance, when they take over a highway, the road becomes theirs. No driver dares to overtake them; everyone is forced to trail behind at their pace. I witnessed this firsthand on the freeway, and I couldn't help but wonder what they might do to anyone bold enough to challenge their dominance.

And you certainly wouldn't want to be near nightclubs when their patrons spill out onto the streets in the dead of night, drunk and rowdy.

Despite its beauty and status as a tourist destination, San Diego has its share of shadows. Tens of thousands of homeless people sprawl across its streets, they make the earth their bed and the sky their ceiling. This is especially true in public parks, most notably Balboa Park—the city's largest and most famous green space. It's not far from popular tourist attractions such as the zoo and SeaWorld, which draw millions of visitors each year.

On another occasion, from the balcony of my apartment, I witnessed a Hollywood-style police chase in my neighborhood.

Truth be told, the streets of San Diego were remarkably clean, lined with fig and olive trees that evoke a sense of familiarity, almost as if I were walking and strolling through the streets of Palestine, with their familial Mediterranean climate and the same trees. Throughout my time in the city, I don't recall ever seeing or ever sensing the presence of a single mosquito or flying around me.

Over time, I even forgot the blaring of car horns, for you rarely hear them there. Yet, strangely enough, after I returned to Jordan upon completing my master's degree, I was walking down the street near the City Hall, heading toward Hashemite Square, when a massive sixteen-wheel truck rumbled past in the same direction—let loose a horn so deafening it shook the ground beneath me. Instinctively, I leapt into the air, nearly a meter high, convinced it was the blowing of the trumpet blast heralding the Day of Judgment. The sound, so foreign to my ears, had become a forgotten memory from the streets of San Diego.

Among the countless memories that have faded over time, there is one that remains etched in my mind, which is the image of an old man I encountered several times. He would wander along El Cajon Boulevard, meticulously inspecting public payphones, hoping to find a dime left behind by a caller to take it.

All this while I remained bound by the invisible chains of my cultural upbringing, with the sword of Arif hanging over my head. I was determined to avoid the hotter, more dangerous zones, always seeking safety. I can only recall venturing into downtown San Diego once, and even then, I moved as though treading through a minefield. Had I dared to step outside the boundaries I had drawn for myself, perhaps this narrative would have been far more dramatic than it is now.

The Way to Man's Heart Is Through His Stomach

There's no denying that university students face many challenges during their studies. One of the most significant is the cultural shock they experience at the beginning of their university journey, followed closely by the bullying freshmen often endure at the hands of upperclassmen.

I remember one of my sessions with Brother Branden, the vice president of Bethlehem University, which were held for the purpose of improving my English. He asked me about the meanings behind the English terms used to describe university students: freshman for a first-year student, sophomore for a second-year student, junior for a third-year student, and senior for a fourth-year student.

At the time, I had no idea that these terms carried deeper psychological and cognitive connotations. It wasn't until I followed his advice and delved into English dictionaries that I discovered each word held a distinct meaning—one that had no direct equivalents in Arabic.

The term freshman, I learned, refers to a young, inexperienced, and lost student, often feeling lonely and out of place. For the first time, they find themselves far from home, struggling to navigate social interactions due to a lack of social skills. They are frequently the target of ridicule and bullying from upperclassmen. More often than not, they are locked in an internal battle, yearning to return to the comfort of their family and hometown. Many times, they call their families in tears, lamenting the hardships of life away from them.

The term sophomore, which describes a second-year student, has its roots in Greek and means "a wise-fool". It captures the psychological shift that occurs during the second year of university. Sophomores develop unshakable convictions that they are a know-it-all, despite their shallow understanding and limited knowledge. Hence, the term "wise-fool" arises from their overconfidence in their intellectual abilities, that is not grounded in solid knowledge.

By the third-year, a student is referred to as a junior. It describes someone who begins to feel doubt creeping into their heart, shaking their held convictions. This makes them more humble, rational, and wise, though they have not yet reached the pinnacle of intellectual maturity. They become hungry for knowledge, unsure of their beliefs and what they truly know. They are, in essence, a small wise one.

Finally, the term senior, referring to a fourth-year student who has gained knowledge and matured to the point of wisdom. By this stage, they come to understand their limitations, realizing that what they've learned is merely a drop in the vast ocean of knowledge. They reach the conviction that they have finally grasped what it means to be an educated person, and they often wish they could start their studies all over again, this time learning the right way.

Yet we, as Palestinian students, grapple with another problem—one uniquely tied to our circumstances. It haunts Palestinian university students throughout their academic years, often complicating their lives as time went on. It stemmed from the fallout of partisan conflicts, organizational affiliations, and student factions.

Typically, the unaffiliated student—who was striving to maintain their independence, preserve their autonomy, and keep a safe distance from all these factions—became a victim of this struggle. They were treated as outcasts, unwanted and unwelcome, subjected to whispers and rumors that swirled around them, framed as party secrets or organizational intelligence. At times, when tensions peaked, baseless accusations were hurled at them in an attempt to assassinate their character, especially if they possessed a charismatic personality or leadership qualities that could tip the scales in favor of one faction over another, even in relatively minor matters like student council elections.

Allegiance to any faction came at a cost. If a student leaned toward one faction over others, the opposing factions would brand them as enemies, subjecting them to interrogation or even outright aggression. This was a genuine dilemma, one I navigated during my undergraduate years at Bethlehem University. I made it a principle to maintain my independence and avoid partisan affiliations, all while fostering good relationships with the political heavyweights, parties, and factions to steer clear of their hostility. Still, I knew it was akin to walking a tightrope.

I managed to complete my undergraduate studies without falling into the exhausting pitfalls of this system. I had assumed that this dilemma would vanish during my graduate studies, especially since I was now in the United States, thousands of kilometers away from Bethlehem and Palestinian universities. However, when I enrolled at the University of San Diego, I found a relatively large Palestinian student body there, numbering over a hundred students. Unsurprisingly, they were divided into different factions, though the majority belonged to two main factions: The Habash faction and the Yasser faction.

I found that these groups had perfected their methods of recruiting members and supporters, resorting to well-known populist tactics such as offering food, operating on the principle that " The way to man's heart is through his stomach."

Shortly after my arrival, followers of one such organization invited me to a barbecue outing. The trip was to a park nestled beside the beautiful Lake Pomona, one of several lakes in the city. I accepted the invitation, and the grilled chicken they served was the most delicious I had ever tasted. Marinated with green thyme and perhaps other ingredients that gave it a magical flavor—undoubtedly, there was a distinct feminine touch in the recipe.

I could have taken advantage of the rivalry between these groups, indulging in more exquisitely prepared meals and being invited to additional outings, which were held as celebratory and recruitment rituals whenever a new student arrived. I might have even received financial support. However, I politely and tactfully explained that, due to my personal circumstances and the ever-present shadow of Arif—a sword dangling over my neck, I would maintain my independence. Especially since I have the heart of a journalist, who must never lean toward one side over the other, even while supporting everyone whose goal is the security of our land, regardless of the differing methods or interpretations they may take.

I suspect—and God knows best—that if the circle there hadn't been so wide, I might have been made to pay for the chicken I ate during that recruitment outing, which, in the end, didn't pay off.

Indeed, I maintained good relationships with everyone, though I kept a sufficient distance to safeguard my independence.

I wonder if the day will ever come when university students realize that, during their university years, they should avoid adopting rigid, partisan, and organizational stances within narrow ideological frameworks. This is especially true in light of what we know about the intellectual growth of students during their university years. After all, everyone is in a stage of learning, and we know that a student does not attain the wisdom necessary to make judgments or take firm positions until after graduation. Even then, upon reaching that stage, they realize that they have only just begun to understand the world—that there is still so much to learn. With this maturity, they may even reconsider their earlier stances.

Khalil Hamad

A party will be in Paradise and a party in the Blaze

One of the most striking phenomena I observed upon joining San Diego State University was the stark contrast in the financial and social circumstances of the Arab students attending the university.

To my surprise, many Palestinian students enjoyed a comfortable, even privileged, financial situation. Their education was funded by an official institution, and their scholarships provided more financial support than they could ever need. Most hailed from affluent and privileged families.

In bitter contrast, another group of Palestinian students toiled day and night to scrape together tuition fees and afford basic sustenance. Some worked in the most perilous corners of the city—bars, gas stations, dimly lit shops. Their primary focus was obtaining citizenship, a lifeline that would free them from financial burdens and offer a foothold in the job market, as their lives were nothing short of a real hell.

The weight of exile crushed many of these young souls. Some dropped out of university, and turned to the labor market. Among them were those who wandered adrift in the vast expanse of the world.

Meanwhile, some Palestinian students managed to carve out extraordinary success through their ingenuity. I met a young man whom the Americans paid to dispose of their junk cars. He would dismantle them and sell the parts for export, and I believe he worked alongside a group of his relatives.

Of course, this did not extend to Arab students, as most were on government scholarships. In Southern California during the early 1980s, there were thousands of Iraqi students on such scholarships, along with a considerable number of Algerians. Many of them appeared to come from privileged families, with one exception—a disheveled man I came to know who was pursuing a PhD in sociology. His unkempt appearance reminded me of a friend and colleague from Bethlehem University, specifically from the village of Husan, named Taysir.

Yet, none of them could compare to the Gulf students. This group exuded obscene wealth, though some seemed to come from more modest means, despite being on scholarships.

I discovered that many of these young men lived off the interest from bank deposits, which they would reclaim after completing their studies. These deposits could amount to as much as ten million dollars, providing a monthly income in the tens of thousands. The student would live lavishly during their studies, then return the deposit to their family after graduation.

This wealth was most visible in one Gulf student who wore a wristwatch that seemed to glisten with gold, if not precious gems. He drove the latest and most expensive cars and had befriended a strikingly beautiful university student, showering her with gifts and cash.

In sharp contrast to this affluent student, whom I often encountered on campus, were students like me—and many others, particularly Iranians whose lives had been shattered after the Imam's revolution. We lived in the hell of poverty. For me, the $250 rent alone was a constant source of anxiety, a crisis in itself.

More often than not, weighed down by debts and additional expenses, especially during the nine grueling months I spent writing my master's thesis—a period that drained me mentally and physically and forced me to stop working to focus on completing it. When my pantry ran empty, I resorted to meals of lentils mixed with pasta. This usually happened during the last ten days of the month, and I would survive on this for several days until the financial aid from my brothers in Kuwait arrived.

When the time came to buy a car, I embarked on a search that led me to a Japanese Daihatsu. It belonged to a diligent engineering student named Jamal, a young man with striking sky-blue eyes who came from one of life's less fortunate strata. But his fate took a dramatic turn when he married an American woman of Italian descent—a woman of considerable wealth. With his newfound status, Jamal decided to part ways his old car and purchase one that better suited his elevated position.

I bought the car from him for a pittance—a mere sixty dollars, the price of that scrap vehicle. That sum alone tells the story of where he had been and where he ended up after gaining citizenship and a Middle Eastern-featured American wife.

It also, undoubtedly, reflected my own circumstances. Of course, licensing such a car was out of the question, so I drove it "under the radar," so to speak. I still didn't know how I managed to ignore the ever-looming sword of Arif and evade the police for as long as I did, driving what was essentially a battered shell of a car. Often, I had to push it to get it moving. Once, while driving down a main road, a reckless young driver emerged from a side street. Though he was clearly at fault for violating traffic laws, I let him go on his way, fearing an encounter with the police and the trouble of driving without a license.

As for my friend Maher Al-Masri, from Nablus, was much like me—one of the wretched bunch, an orphan with a brother studying medicine in Russia. It was Maher who taught me to drive using his own beat-up car. I never took formal driving lessons; Maher's instruction was enough. He was with me the day we were almost attacked by a group of American youths, an incident that nearly cost us our lives were it not for the mercy of fate. That harrowing experience pushed me to finally take the driving test, and to my surprise, I passed on the first attempt—despite the examiner's abrupt stop and stern warning at one of the intersections. From then on, I drove my faded red car, often heading to the sea to indulge in my favorite pastime of fishing.

I also remember a time when I faced a financial crisis and turned to the International Organization for Assisting Arab Students. I took out a repayable loan of $300, which I repaid after returning to work in the Gulf.

I also found immense support and assistance from two Saudi students who were sponsored by 'Aramco' and lived next door to me, in the same student housing as me. Similarly, there was Maher, Al-Nabulsi, with whom I spent a great deal of time discussing the validity of my "positronic theory." As an orphan, perhaps my talk of genius intrigued him, though he remained skeptical.

But the closest person to me was Amir, an Iranian who always stood by my side. He was a supporter of the Iranian Mujahedin-e Khalq movement. Despite his difficult circumstances—thick glasses, worn-out clothes bore the marks of a life shaped by hardship—yet his smile never wavered. My bond with him, and with many other friends, was strong and unshakable.

In stark contrast to Amir was the Iranian man who lived in apartment 35, directly across from mine in apartment 36. Over a year had passed since we became door-facing neighbors, yet I never exchanged a greeting with him, let alone a single conversation. He was standoffish—'a fire that guarded its own flames.'

On the other hand, another Iranian named Abbas had shared my apartment for a time. Abbas had a peculiar habit of drinking his tea bitter while holding sugar cubes in his mouth the Iranian way, allowing the sweetness of the sugar to mingle with the bitterness of the tea. He believed that true pleasure lies in the meeting of opposites. Once, his face shone unusually bright, I discovered days later that he had been bathing with dishwashing liquid, mistaking it for shampoo.

Amid the fabric of university life, a stark divide existed among the Arab students. One group lived in the lap of luxury, basking in the generosity of wealth, while the other struggled under the weight of poverty and the harshness of life, surviving on daily meals of lentils and pasta. As for the Iranians, caught in the throes of the hostage crisis, they suffered the brunt of the crisis in indescribable ways.

Thus, the stories intertwine and multiply, including my own tale with Maher, Al-Nablusi, and that fateful day when a group of American youths nearly ended our lives. In the coming pages, I will recount these events in detail, as we explore together the American Dream and the repugnant face of capitalism.

The American Dream and the Repugnance of Capitalism

As societies industrialized in the 19th century, the exploitation of workers became a glaring issue. When Marx published *The Communist Manifesto* and raised the rallying cry, "Workers of the world, unite!" it was swiftly adopted by the working class nearly everywhere as a unifying charter against the greed and exploitation of factory owners.

As Marx theorized, the triumph of the workers and the transition of societies to socialism seemed an inevitable historical outcome. However, what transpired was quite different. The Communist Party in the Soviet Union, under Lenin's leadership, rushed the revolution before society had matured or was ready for such a shift—before it had fully transformed into an industrialized framework that could empower the working class. Consequently, a dictatorial regime, in the vein of Stalinism, became necessary to preserve the achievements of the Communist Party and the 1917 revolution in Tsarist Russia. Over time, the Soviet socialist system collapsed because, according to Marxist theory, it lacked the essential foundations for its sustainability.

Before arriving in the United States, I had been unaware that the communist movement there was one of the strongest in the world in the early 20th century. There were moments when a shift toward socialism seemed almost within reach.

But the titans of capitalism, led later by Joseph McCarthy, recognized the gravity of the situation. They devised a strategy and approach to combat communism and socialism, known as McCarthyism. This approach included several measures: increasing the workers' share of the economic pie, expanding the middle class—the so-called "swing vote" of society—and using the working class as a tool to fight Soviet communism. Thus, the Cold War was born, a conflict capitalism exploited to frame the Soviet Union as a national threat to the United States. In essence, they created an external enemy and threat to consolidate control over domestic affairs and keep them firmly in check.

They even shifted their celebration of Labor Day to the beginning of September each year, deviating from the globally recognized date of May 1st. This was just one of many ways capitalism extended its reach, not only to curb the rise of socialism and communism but also to dominate minds through media and harness psychology as a tool to achieve its aims.

From this vantage point, capitalism focused on entrenching what is known as the American Dream, planting this idea firmly in the minds of young Americans. For the vast majority—excluding the children of wealthy, dominant capitalist families who had their own private dreams—this dream boiled down to owning a house, having a wife or girlfriend, driving a car, enjoying alcohol, and indulging in nightclubs and bars.

They maintained an iron grip on people's minds, particularly the youth, confining their aspirations to this dream. When Martin Luther King Jr., the leader of the Black liberation movement, declared in his famous speech that he had a dream—a dream that was undoubtedly an alternative to the distorted American Dream—the capitalist forces worked tirelessly to impose and sustain. King's dream was one of freedom, equality, and the abolition of racism. Yet, he was swiftly assassinated, his dream aborted, to prevent any disruption to the ironclad control that capitalism held over society. Any such disruption could have spawned problems for the capitalist system.

Moreover, capitalism made the realization of this so-called dream exceedingly difficult, to the point where an American might spend their entire life chasing this distorted dream. Often, they were made to feel that their failure to attain the American dream was due to personal inadequacy rather than the harsh conditions and obstacles imposed by capitalism itself, which made the dream an elusive mirage.

The American individual is often consumed by self-interest, rarely looking beyond their immediate concerns. Their knowledge can be shallow, their culture awareness limited, and at times, this borders on ignorance—especially when it comes to international affairs.

Many American youths are shambolic, let alone distinguish Pakistan from Palestine. They have little interest in acquiring anything beyond what is necessary to achieve their American dream.

Due to the measures adopted by capitalists, the number of supporters and followers of communist and socialist parties has dwindled to a near-invisible minority. The spread of communist and socialist ideologies has become confined to university professors and the educated elite—the intelligentsia. Yet, even the exit in a harsh state of alienation, like someone trying to carry a ladder sideways.

At the University of San Diego, I met a professor named Jackie. Her passionate advocacy for socialist thought was like an oasis in a barren desert or a tiny island in an endless, turbulent ocean. Dr. Tom, on the other hand, was more pragmatic despite his deep understanding of how wealthy families control every facet of life in the United States. He shared with us, his friends, the names of the individuals—no more than twenty—who run the largest corporations. It was as if he had obtained an early copy of the secret document drafted in 1979 and revealed in 1986, which Noam Chomsky later discussed in his work *"The Ten Strategies of manipulation."* Yet, for all his insight, his thinking often felt like a dance in the dark.

Though the United States has long welcomed immigration and the influx of foreign students into its universities, as well as the significant portion of its population of immigrants maintaining strong ties to their homelands—many from Third World countries—the absolute dominance of capitalist ideology is difficult to shake. The majority of American youth, raised in this insular environment, remain captive to capitalist thought and media propaganda.

I witnessed firsthand the extent of ignorance among some students at the University of San Diego, whom I had come to know during that time.

One day, I showed a group of them photos my relatives had sent from Kuwait—images of towering buildings, bustling markets, and luxurious beach chalets. To my astonishment, they assumed the pictures were of New York. When I told them they were from Kuwait, they refused to believe me. In their minds, Kuwait was still a place where people lived in tents, traditional Bedouin houses, and herded camels.

It's hard to fathom the power of media manipulation and mental programming carried out by American news outlets on the minds of young Americans during the Iran hostage crisis, when American diplomats were held captive at the U.S. Embassy in Tehran. National television stations would begin their news broadcasts with a provocative headline like "America Held Hostage Day 444," accompanied by a running tally of the days—444 being the last number I recall.

This phrase, "America Held Hostage: Day 444," would flash across the screen and linger throughout the broadcast, often reappearing in other programs.

You can only imagine the hatred that festered in the hearts of young Americans toward anything Iranian—but that was only half the tragedy. The greatest disaster was that most of them couldn't distinguish between Arabs and Iranians. To them, every Middle Easterner was Iranian.

This ignorance put me and my friend Maher, who was from Nablus, in grave danger. One Sunday, we were at a gas station in Maher's car when a group of burly, muscle-bound American young men—clearly intoxicated—spotted us. They began shouting, "Iranians, go home!"

Given everything I had described, we knew how serious this was. We had no choice but to arm ourselves with sharp tools for self-defense, bracing for what we believed was an inevitable attack. I grabbed a yellow screwdriver, and Maher clutched a silver wrench. We were certain they would attack us, and we knew they wouldn't believe us even if we tried to explain that we were Arabs, not Iranians, and that there was a difference. But by some miracle, they held back, and we were spared.

Khalil Hamad

Creative Chaos

A conversation unfolded between me and one of my master's program professors, a visiting lecturer at San Diego University. During one of his lectures on comparative literature, he argued that the choice and direction should lean toward anarchism.

Anarchism, as a political philosophy, rejects hierarchical structures of power, which its proponents view as inherently unjust. Instead, anarchists advocate for stateless societies founded on voluntary, non-hierarchical associations.

To some, anarchism is synonymous with complete chaos, where followers of this ideology fight against the state and authority at every turn, pushing society toward disarray as a natural consequence of the absence of power.

I countered the esteemed professor's argument by asserting that we must not lose faith in the human mind, and therefore, we cannot advocate for the dominance or spread of anarchism, which is synonymous with chaos.

I shared my perspective that even in the earliest communal eras, the human mind was inherently creative, by establishing systems of values and principles through myths. These myths served as guiding constitutions and a means of passing knowledge to younger generations. Over time, this intellectual heritage evolved, with each philosophical system offering a unique way to understand and manage the world.

I further elaborated that religions provide laws and codes— not only for governing life on earth but also for envisioning what lies beyond death.

Even if philosophies and religions sometimes fail to offer effective solutions, the human mind remains endlessly inventive. It has the capacity to forge new intellectual frameworks, such as socialism, for example, which emerged after religions. Thus, there is no room for despair, no reason to lose hope, and certainly no justification for advocating the spread of chaos.

The failure of socialism and modern positivist philosophies do not mean that the human mind has reached the end of its road, rendered incapable of producing further theories and solutions. It does not justify a call to anarchism and the chaos that necessarily accompanies it. The human mind has evolved ceaselessly, always capable of innovation and creativity. So, why should it halt now? Why should it succumb to madness and disorder?

Especially when existentialism speaks of the Übermensch (Superman), a concept championed by Nietzsche, the father of existentialist philosophy, who famously declared, let your motto be to "Live dangerously! Build your cities on the slopes of Vesuvius!" Nietzsche believed that the era of the Superman was on the brink of realization.

I explained to him that the best choice for humanity is Islam faith, as it offers a comprehensive theory for both life and the afterlife, along with a distinctive economic system that aligns with the nature of human personality and their innate inclinations—something that both socialism and capitalism have failed to provide. For this reason, these man-made systems are inevitably destined to fade, while Islam has demonstrated its resilience over fourteen centuries. Not only has it endured, but it has also expanded, with its principles widely embraced, as it provides the most effective solutions. I suggested to him the necessity of holding firmly to Islam until the human mind could, hypothetically, produce a better alternative—if such a thing were even possible.

I emphasized that Islam represents the pinnacle of human thought, following the path of Prophet Ibrahim (Abraham), who arrived at his convictions not through affirmation but through negation, relying on rational evidence.

In other words, Prophet Ibrahim's approach was one of negation rather than affirmation in his quest for truth and certainty. He rejected the fire worshipped by the Magians around him was God, nor were the idols. When he found nothing on earth worthy of worship, he turned his gaze to the heavens. At first, he believed the planets were God, but when they set, he abandoned them. He then turned to the moon, but when it disappeared, he relinquished it as well. Finally, he looked to the sun, only to reject it too once it vanished. In the end, he concluded that the Creator of all these earthly and celestial wonders was the only One deserving of worship. He surrendered to the awe-inspiring majesty of creation, seeing it as proof of God's existence.

I suggested to my esteemed professor that humanity should hold firmly to the intellectual framework arrived at by Prophet Ibrahim (Abraham), peace be upon him, through his reasoning—a framework that the Quran later refined and elevated through divine revelation. This framework has been enhanced and developed to align with the progression of life on earth, serving humanity not only until the Day of Judgment but beyond.

I further posited that if the human mind cannot disprove the validity of the most comprehensive system—Islam—using Abraham's approach or any other rational methodology, and if it cannot present an alternative to Islam that is intellectually acceptable, then humanity must cling to Islam. Without it, the world risks falling into despair, hopelessness, and chaos.

It is well-known that anarchism, libertarianism, and chaos have spread widely, particularly in Europe, while capitalism embraces the idea that chaos is a source of creativity. A closer look at American society reveals countless manifestations of disorder.

Of course, I have long been aware that American society suffers from deep moral and social decay. The family, once the bedrock of stability, is crumbling under the weight of rampant divorce. Single motherhood is no longer an exception but a prevalent reality.

According to the American Constitution, American society is considered secular, though it informally maintains some religious practices. However, it does not impose religion on its people, emphasizing instead individual freedom in matters of faith.

Meanwhile, the system of individual ownership and capitalist practices generates many byproducts that fuel chaos. We see racism, unemployment, crime, the proliferation of firearms, homelessness, and countless other issues that reinforce the trend toward anarchism and disorder.

It is truly astonishing to witness the magnitude of achievements produced by a society steeped in crises, chaos, and turmoil. The streets of its major cities resemble scenes of civil war, yet it continues to give birth to extraordinary individuals like Bill Gates and Steve Jobs. This man alone is akin to an entire nation, having contributed accomplishments that propelled Western civilization forward in leaps and bounds. Through his inventions and innovations, he brought about transformative advancements for humanity. Remarkably, he was born out of wedlock and spent the early years of his life in an orphanage before being adopted by another family. It was under these circumstances that he achieved his awe-inspiring feats.

And he is not alone. Countless children, be to hell and back by family disintegration and societal neglect, have risen above their circumstances to become the driving force behind a staggering number of annual inventions and creative breakthroughs. These achievements often surpass those of more stable societies, where familial cohesion, societies untouched by the moral decay and chaos that plague the United States.

Does this civilizational progress in the United States suggest that chaos is, in fact, a catalyst for creativity? Was the professor right in his advocacy for chaos, given the apparent absence of solutions and the human mind's struggle to devise new ways to save humanity from its crises? Was Nietzsche correct in urging us to live in perpetual anxiety, perched atop a volcano, so that Superman might emerge?

Or should we hold fast to the belief in the human mind's capacity to continually innovate and find solutions to humanity's problems? Should we refuse to surrender to despair or lose hope?

I cannot say for certain what impact my arguments on this matter had on the esteemed professor, who left the university at the end of the semester and returned to where he came from. But I like to think that I planted a seed of hope in his heart.

American Universities: Beacons of Knowledge and Sanctuaries for the Troubled

Higher education in the United States is widely regarded as one of the cornerstones of societal advancement and civilizational progress. University professors are seen as the vanguard of research, innovation, and creative achievement. If we were to look at the list, names of scientists, of Nobel Prize winners from the United States since the award's inception, for example, we would find that nearly all of them were university professors who conducted their groundbreaking research and studies in the research centers, laboratories, and classrooms of these university.

Similarly, most groundbreaking inventions emerge from the halls of universities, and the same can be said for theories in scientific, economic, and humanities fields—indeed, in every discipline. It is well-known that the majority of research centers dedicated to the study of the human brain— a frontier that remains largely unexplored—are affiliated with universities.

These universities and their research centers are infused by vast sums of money, funding everything from basic research to groundbreaking inventions. The sources of this funding are diverse: federal grants, state budgets, research foundations, and private sector contributions.

These financial institutions are eager to support and fund any idea they deem reasonable, especially if it holds the potential for significant results. All a researcher needs to do is submit a funding proposal accompanied by a clear research idea, and they can obtain what they need without much effort or hardship.

These universities serve as incubators for thinkers, inventors, scientists, and writers, nurturing their ideas and ambitions. While much of the funding often comes from external institutions and entities, what truly matters is that these universities open their doors wide, welcoming ideas with remarkable flexibility. They offer every researcher the opportunity to try their luck in the realms of research and innovation, provided they meet the minimum requirements.

It is precisely because of this open and flexible policy that American universities attract the greatest minds from around the world. These individuals, in turn, go on to produce astonishing inventions that leave an indelible mark on the progress of civilization in the country.

This is precisely what happened with the Egyptian genius, Ahmed Zewail, who invented a camera capable of capturing moments so fleeting they were equivalent to one second of a 35-year-long film. Thanks to this groundbreaking invention, it became possible to observe chemical reactions, a breakthrough that earned him the Nobel Prize.

Similarly, the Nayfeh brothers, professors from the village of Shuweika near Tulkarm, leveraged research funding programs at American universities to develop astonishing inventions. While Ali Nayfeh made remarkable contributions to mechanical engineering, Munir Nayfeh conducted pioneering research in nanotechnology at the University of Illinois, achieving breakthroughs that revolutionized industrial applications of nanotechnology. In an interview, Munir Nayfeh himself spoke about the early days of his work in this critical field and how he even secured funding from the U.S. Congress, eventually becoming one of the world's foremost experts in nanotechnology.

The same can be said for most, if not all, of the researchers and inventors working in the prestigious laboratories of American universities.

Personally, I found immense support for my research on the relationship between orphanhood and literary creativity, even when it was still a general idea—something that would have been unthinkable in Arab universities. The dean of the English Literature Department at San Diego University praised my ability to propose a pioneering idea that represented a new frontier in the search for answers about one of the most essential human traits: creativity. This was a topic that none of the American students had even considered.

I received further acclaim and recognition in 1983 after completing my master's thesis, in which I presented my idea and provided a compelling study on the presumed relationship between orphanhood and creativity. By highlighting the theme of orphanhood in the works and lives of the authors I selected—with the approval of my thesis committee. The thesis, titled "Creativity and the Search for Fulfillment,"

On the other hand, despite my eventual success in presenting additional statistical evidence based on academic samples—results that transcended mere coincidence and reinforced the validity of my theory, which posits that the relationship between orphanhood and genius is one of cause and effect—I found it exceedingly difficult to convince certain institutions I approached at a national university. My goal was to obtain permission to conduct field studies to gather more robust evidence supporting the theory, such as determining the proportion and number of orphans among distinguished professors with PhDs, considering that academic achievement at the doctoral level represents the pinnacle of scholarly accomplishment.

Additionally, an initiative I proposed was rejected—a voluntary training program for a group of orphaned students from the arts faculties. The program aimed to raise their awareness that their orphanhood was a gift, not a curse, and to train them under the premise that they were projects of greatness, as outlined in my book *Orphans: Projects of Greatness*. The goal was to equip them with the tools of literary creativity, nurturing them to become extraordinary geniuses.

From the information I received, I gathered that the dean of the targeted college underestimated the idea, despite its maturity and acceptance in American academic circles. Perhaps he thought I was delusional, mentally ill, or a dreamer chasing mirages!

The role of American universities, however, does not end there. Every year, millions of graduates emerge from these institutions, feeding the job market with academically qualified young talents.

Education in American universities is taken very seriously. On one occasion, I personally witnessed an incident where a professor was late to class without notifying the students of his delay or absence in advance. The students filed a formal complaint against him for wasting their precious time without a valid excuse or prior notice. Had such an incident occurred in our Arab universities, it would have been cause for celebration and joy.

The role of universities extends far beyond what I mentioned earlier—being beacons of knowledge, research, creativity, and innovation. I have come to realize they also play a crucial social and psychological role, welcoming students of all ages and offering flexible programs that allow anyone eager to learn to enroll under accommodating conditions.

I had a classmate who was 82 years old, studying literature with a particular focus on short stories. She was a passionate advocate against wars. Another classmate, over 65, returned to university after retiring from a 35-year career in the U.S. Army, as he told me when I asked.

One of the most striking phenomena I observed was how many individuals who faced tragedies, traumas, or moments of profound distress—such as the death of a loved one, divorce, or job loss—turned to universities. They rushed to obtain new degrees or undergo training that would lift them out of the pit of despair and depression they had fallen into. This process helped rebuild their self-confidence and restore their sense of self-worth, which had been shattered by the pain and sorrow they endured.

On the other hand, when I personally considered enrolling in the faculty of law after being appointed secretary of the board of directors for a company, I encountered complications and obstacles. Despite working full-time, I was required to register for 12 credit hours. Then, when the Intifada broke out, I was forced to withdraw from the program, even though I know I would have excelled in commercial law, given my experience as a legal translator for several major corporations.

Later, when I thought about pursuing a master's degree in management, I ran into hurdles regarding the submission of my original transcripts. Although I requested San Diego University to send them directly to the register's office, the process became so cumbersome that I eventually abandoned the idea.

Now, here I am, unable to conduct laboratory research to provide further scientific evidence for the outcomes of my theory, simply because there is no dedicated neuroscience research center here—despite such centers being commonplace in Western countries.

As the relentless grind of an unjust capitalist system continued to cast people onto the streets, into wells of despair, sorrow, and loneliness, universities stood as beacons of knowledge and sanctuaries for the broken. They welcomed vast numbers of these individuals, restoring their smiles and equipping them with the tools to reintegrate into society.

Every Cloud Has a Silver Lining – A Magical Recipe for Delaying Aging

Often, we tread a familiar path in life until we stumble into a crisis or hit a bump in the road. It is then that we find ourselves reevaluating our routines, sometimes benefiting from or spurred by that crisis. What seems harmful experience at first can, in fact, become a catalyst for something better for us—a new beginning for a better life.

Yet, few among us possess the initiative to change their lifestyles or behavior without the push of a crisis, something that compels them to question what they once took for granted or considered an unchangeable routine.

This is precisely what happened to me when I faced a minor health scare after enrolling at the University of San Diego. One day, well into my studies there—sometimes after the first semester had begun, or perhaps it was already the second—I found myself completely immersed, " up to my ears," in work and studies. One day, out of nowhere, I felt a slight dizziness, which was both noticeable and frightening, as such things often are.

Since medical treatment at the university clinics was nearly free, I decided to see a doctor. When I met with the physician and explained my symptoms, he asked me about my diet.

I told him I mostly ate steak—a quick and easy meal for a student like me to prepare, whether cooked in the oven or grilled on the barbecues near the swimming pool in the housing complex. Most accommodations in San Diego had such facilities, some powered by gas, others by charcoal. All you needed was to bring the meat and the charcoal.

For a foreign student like me, it was, without a doubt, a delicious and beloved meal. I was unaccustomed to seeing such quantities of meat displayed in supermarkets back home. The steaks were exceptionally tasty and remained juicy after grilling, thanks to the way the calves were raised and fed—or so I was told when I returned to the Arab East and searched in vain for anything comparable.

No sooner had the doctor heard what I had to say, he gestured toward the walls of his clinic. To my surprise, they were adorned with drawings of chickens. He advised me to stop eating red meat and switch to chicken and fish instead, as though the health crisis I had endured was something he expected based on his experience with students like me who lived far from the care of their families.

Can you imagine? The cause of that sudden health scare was supposedly lean veal. What if it had been lamb meat, which, by the way, holds little popularity there? I've heard that even the leanest cuts of lamb contain up to 82% fat.

But the bitterest and most ironic joke of all came one day when I decided to cook sautéed pluck—a dish of fried kidneys and liver sautéed with onions and green peppers. Perhaps it was during Eid al-Adha. As I placed my purchases of kidneys and liver on the checkout counter, the cashier—a young girl—asked me, "Do you have a cat at home?"

I replied, "Yes, I have a big, hungry cat."

What she didn't realize was that I was referring to myself. It turned out that the majority of people in that country don't eat pluck at all.

The doctor also advised me to start exercising. I must have been carrying a bit of extra weight, a testament to God's abundant blessings—and perhaps to the delicious meals served at the dormitory cafeteria of Riverside University. It's possible that I had been eating without much thought or concern for the consequences, too absorbed in my master's studies.

In the end, I decided to follow the doctor's advice as best as I could. I swapped the tender, flavorful beef—enhanced with barbecue sauce—for the somewhat pungent chicken, which required more skill and time to prepare and cook properly.

That same day, I bought a set of athletic clothes and, that afternoon, set out with the intention of jogging around the residential block where I lived. The distance I planned to cover was relatively short, no more than three kilometers.

About halfway through, I passed a group of elderly people standing beside a car parked on the side of the road, chatting among themselves. As I approached, one of them called out to me with a hint of sarcasm:

"Are you sure you can make it?"

What must have prompted him to ask that question was my pitiful appearance as I lumbered along, my body heavy and unfit, gasping for breath and visibly exhausted.

Honestly, his words shamed me and sent a jolt through my body, as if he had sounded an alarm or raised a red flag based on the sorry sight of my movements.

That moment, combined with Dr. Abu Dajaj's earlier advice, became the final push I needed to make a decisive commitment to immerse myself in sports—a popular and widespread activity there. It seemed as if the entire nation, young and old, was engaged in sports, with many practicing or training for the intense sport of American football.

I began seizing every opportunity to swim or run long distances, and I joined the university's bodybuilding club. It didn't take long for me to regain my physical fitness. Along the way, I found a group of friends who joined me for runs in areas with light traffic, away from downtown, on a street called Alvarado.

Before I knew it, I was running six kilometers at a stretch. From that day on—since I was twenty-seven years old—up until this very moment, I have never stopped exercising regularly, except during times of war or circumstances beyond my control.

It wasn't until later in life that I truly grasped the immense benefits of exercise until I grew older. Through experience, I came to realize that sports genuinely delay the onset of aging. Instead of living a miserable life plagued by illness and the symptoms of old age, one can, through regular exercise, enjoy a fulfilling life and spend their later years with dignity, rather than becoming a burden on those around them.

I became even more convinced of these benefits when I later came across articles published in American medical and sports journals, written in English. These articles confirmed that exercise plays a significant role in slowing down the aging process and maintaining the health of internal organs of the human body. They also highlighted a direct correlation between the intensity of the exercise one engages in and the physical and psychological benefits gained. The more vigorous the exercise, the greater the benefits. For instance, if comparative study were conducted between a 60-year-old who engages in intense exercise with another of the same age who does not exercise at all, you would find that the physical efficiency of the athletic individual surpasses that of their non-athletic counterpart by at least ten years. These benefits diminish with lighter exercise and are at their lowest for those who limit themselves to a mere half-hour walk each day—a practice some mistakenly believe to be sufficient.

These studies also demonstrated the truth behind the ancient Greek adage: "A sound mind in a sound body." The Greeks believed that physical health protects a person against psychological ailments, and a long-standing paper published by the Mayo Clinic stated that physical illnesses often have psychological roots, and that one's mental state positively impacts the body.

Now, as I stand on the threshold of seventy, I engage in all forms of sports. I walk long distances through wilderness trails, climb mountains, and even scaled the 198 steps leading to the heart of the Qalaat Iraq Burin without hesitation. I carry mottos like "Age is just a number" and "Be strong for yourself," and I owe all of this to making exercise a lifelong commitment.

Khalil Hamad

Tip of the Iceberg – A Merciless Society

Yes, I remember that day vividly. I was living in Apartment number 42 in a modest residential complex near the university, just a ten-minute walk away on El Cajon Boulevard. I had moved there because it was more popular and, as a result, cheaper. It didn't have the same amenities as my previous building, which was more secure, with a guarded entrance system where no one could enter without permission via the intercom or a key. This complex was topsy-turvy.

The place was managed by an elderly couple. One evening, I slipped a tape of Umm Kulthum into the cassette player—a tape I had brought with me from Kuwait. As I listened, utterly engrossed, to her timeless song *Enta Omry*, I swayed to the familiar melodies that had filled my childhood. Lost in the enchanting of Eastern music, I was abruptly interrupted by the landlady, who rushed in, frantically gesturing for me to turn off the recorder. Disgust and distress were etched across her face. I silenced the music, though my explanations fell on deaf ears—that this singer was the most celebrated in the Middle East, hailed as the "Planet of the Orient" She dismissed it, saying it sounded to her like wailing at a funeral, her expression still twisted in revulsion. I didn't blame her. In fact, I understood her reaction; I'd felt the same way when I'd heard Turkish, Persian, or even Japanese songs.

Though I loved American dance music, especially the hits of Michael Jackson, whose dynamic stage performances had iconic dance moves that captivated the world at the time, I've always detested rock and roll. To me, it was sheer madness, much like the so-called "surrealist" art, which I saw as a deranged expression of the darkest corners of the human psyche.

In the same building lived a conservative Christian girl who believed in no relationships with men before marriage. Naturally, the student residents of the complex viewed her as psychologically disturbed. They punishing her for her unusual chastity in a society riddled with moral decay, as if she were a criminal. The fierce war waged against her was silent and unspoken, but she must have felt the weight of being an outcast. Yet, she stood her ground, clinging to her principles. But only God knows for how long—for there's nothing harder than swimming against the tide, especially when the current is overwhelming in an unjust society.

On another day, in the same housing complex, I encountered a young woman of fair skin, strikingly beautiful and brimming with the vigor of youth. She was in her early twenties, her charm as radiant as her distress was palpable. As I was leaving the complex, heading to the market to run some errands, she approached me by chance and asked for a dime to call her mother from the payphone installed in the building. I handed her the coin and lingered nearby, curious to understand her story, for the turmoil etched on her face was impossible to ignore. I overheard her pleading with her mother, begging for permission to return home, even if only temporarily. She had no money, no place to stay, and it seemed she had fallen behind on rent, facing the grim prospect of being thrown out onto the streets.

My heart sank when her mother refused, coldly telling her to "figure it out yourself" before abruptly hanging up.

Her plight weighted heavily on me, yet I left her to her despair, standing there at the peak of her anguish and helplessness. I never learned what became of her. Did she manage to find a way out, or did the streets become her fate?

Not far from there, another young girl, no older than sixteen, stood in the shadow of poverty. Her fair skin and beauty were no less striking than the other, but her clothes bore the unmistakable marks of sorrow and misery, not the threads of fashion that had yet to emerge in those distant early 1980s.

She stood before the takeout window of a Mexican restaurant near my residence, a window that opened onto a world of vibrant flavors where tacos were sold like small parcels of joy. She ordered just one—a single taco, its tortilla stuffed with spiced meat and drenched in hot sauce, as if she were asking for a morsel of hope. I was struck by her request; one taco could hardly satisfy even a hungry cat. When I asked why she settled for so little, she replied in a faint voice that she had only a meager of coins. Without hesitation, I quickly ordered three more for her, on me—each taco cost no more than a dollar.

The girl devoured them with a ravenous hunger that spoke of a gnawing emptiness deep within. Then, she vanished into the hustle and bustle of life, and I never saw her again. Yet, her image—her hollow stomach, the injustice of a society that had failed her—remained etched in my memory like an indelible tattoo.

In the bookstore where I worked, affiliated with the University of San Diego, there was a cardboard compactor— a machine that transformed scattered boxes into small, fist-sized blocks. I shared this oddly satisfying task with a young, blond-haired American man named Mark, a student at the same university. He was my companion in this job.

The machine, operated by a manual iron handle, demanded extreme caution and precision from its user. One wrong move, and the handle could slip from your grip, spinning out of control with dangerous force. One day, Mark took it upon himself to operate the machine—a routine task we had both mastered, though it required constant attention due to its precision and inherent risk. But this time, the handle slipped from his hand and struck his leg with such force that he cried out in pain. I rushed to him, stunned, asking what had happened and how he could have made such a mistake.

What followed was a revelation I never expected. He looked at me, his eyes welling up with tears, and after some prodding—driven by pain and hunger—he confessed that he hadn't eaten in three days. I asked him why. Did he live alone or with family? He told me he had no money, no family except for one brother, who was a member of a motorcycle gang. He had no home to return to and often slept under bridges.

It was a heart-wrenching scene, a moment that shook me to my core. I invited him to eat whatever he wanted at the nearby cafeteria, my treat. I don't know what became of him after that—how he managed to get by or whether his meager wages eventually saved him. I also don't know why he never turned to "red gold" like so many other desperate young Americans, especially since he seemed, at least outwardly, to be in good health.

All these individuals I've mentioned are victims of a merciless capitalist society, they are merely tip of the iceberg. It's a society that resembles the tombs of "the mummified," as the saying goes: "Outwardly marble, inwardly filth."

I cannot fathom what drove that mother to refuse her teenage daughter's return home, though there may have been reasons. Yet, the culture of expelling young people from their homes once they turned eighteen, forcing them to learn self-reliance, was widespread among a large segment of the white population.

Imagine, then, the plight of these young individuals—strong, healthy, and capable of work—and then consider the fate of those struck by misfortune, who suffer losses that plunge them into bankruptcy and debt. They chase mirages of wealth, only to find themselves homeless, wandering the streets. And what of the elderly, who find themselves stranded, exhausting their life savings?

Those who fall into disability and bankruptcy are trapped in a cycle of pain from which they may never escape. In that society, possessing a place to live, a residential address, and a phone number are basic prerequisites for anyone seeking employment. How, then, can someone who has hit rock bottom, living on the edge of the road, possibly manage their affairs?

These are the consequences of a ruthless, individualistic capitalist system that shows no mercy. But believe me, what troubled me most during my time in that country was something else entirely—something you might not expect. For now, I will pause here, and when I return to you, I will speak, God willing, of that which haunted me throughout my stay in that land.

The Last Resort: Acupuncture

In the early 1980s, as the twentieth century stretched toward its twilight, I packed my bags and set off for the United States, carrying with me not just my belongings but also the relentless burden of sinusitis, which clung to me like a shadow. The constant nasal drip forced me to use tissues without end, and despite consulting countless doctors in Palestine and Kuwait, the allergies refused to let go. They followed me to Riverside in Southern California and trailed me further south when I moved to San Diego. Days turned into months, and my condition remained unchanged. I was on the verge of despair in finding a cure, like a disbeliever who has lost all hope in the power of graves, resigned to living with this affliction—not as a hero, but as someone defeated and powerless.

Then, one day, I met a Native American woman, a graduate student in psychology, who was part of a diverse group of university professors and graduate students. Together, we formed a kind of League of Nations, gathering regularly in the cafeteria to discuss the pressing issues of the time. The group included a mathematics professor from India, a student of American history, a doctor of mixed heritage whose origins I couldn't quite place, a business school instructor, a philosophy professor, a green-eyed Greek psychology student, and others.

Among them was that Native American colleague, her features resembled those of the indigenous people we often saw in movies, with skin tinged a reddish hue. She noticed my constant struggle with nasal allergies and, perhaps drawing from personal experience or prior knowledge, suggested I try acupuncture. At first, I dismissed the idea outright, skeptical and reluctant. But soon, I reconsidered my stance—perhaps, just perhaps, this could be my way out. So, I decided to move forward with it, following the principle that desperate times call for desperate measures. At that moment, I was like a drowning man clutching at a straw.

I later learned that a Chinese doctor practiced traditional acupuncture at a clinic within the outpatient department of a well-known hospital called Alvarado Hospital in San Diego, not far from the university. In fact, it was close enough that I could walk there. This proximity encouraged me further, as I reasoned that a reputable American hospital would not allow a Chinese doctor to operate within its facilities unless he was fully qualified and licensed to practice traditional Chinese medicine. This reassurance eased my concerns, and I made my way to the clinic.

When I sat before the doctor, he asked me how long I had been suffering from allergies. "Twelve years," I replied, though I couldn't recall exactly when it had started. Perhaps it was triggered by the sudden blast of cold air that hit me when I opened the door to my brother's studio in the Jubeiha neighborhood, back when he was a student at the University of Jordan. I remember knocking on his door, and as I stepped inside, the room was stiflingly hot from a kerosene heater, while outside, the air was polar, with snowflakes falling gently. Or maybe it had started even earlier.

He informed me that I would need twelve therapy sessions—one for each year I had suffered from the allergy—and that my progress would be monitored accordingly.

I thought long and hard about it. I was still skeptical of Chinese medicine, seeing it as a primitive relic of the past. The doctor stared at me intently, as if he could read the doubt etched on my face. He must have sensed my hesitation, for he asked me bluntly:

"Are you convinced that I can treat you with acupuncture?" I hesitated in my reply, and he told me to leave the clinic. He said I shouldn't return unless I was fully convinced of the treatment. At that point, I assured him that if I weren't convinced, I wouldn't have come to him in the first place. I managed to embellish my lie about being convinced, hiding my anxiety well enough that he finally agreed to treat me.

He then directed me to lie flat on my back on a bed that resembled those in hospital emergency rooms. He instructed me to breathe deeply and relax, and I remained in that position for about fifteen minutes. During that time, I wrestled with my doubts—sometimes trying to banish my skepticism about his ability to heal me, and other times convincing myself that I had nothing to lose even if the attempt failed. Occasionally, my body shuddered as I imagined the needles piercing my flesh.

The Chinese doctor returned, and once he was satisfied that I was relaxed and less tense, he picked up a needle. He told me to take a deep breath and hold it, so he could insert the needle without causing me pain. I did as he instructed, and before I could blink, he inserted the first needle into the back of my hand, specifically in the area between my thumb and index finger. He repeated the ritual of deep breathing and holding it before inserting a second needle, then a third into the muscle of my right arm, just below the elbow. He did the same with my left hand.

Next, he connected the needles to a mild electric current. The needles began to dance rhythmically, such as the pendulum of a clock. As he worked, the doctor explained—in his broken English—pointing to a chart on the wall. He said the treatment plan was based on redirecting energy from specific points in the body, which were connected to the sinuses through energy lines. The goal was to strengthen the mucous membrane, making it less sensitive to irritants.

And so, the therapy session continued for perhaps a full hour, repeating the same routine over the next ten days. By the eleventh session, I found that the treating physician had changed due to the first doctor's travel. Things went smoothly during this session, though the placement of the needles had shifted—this time, they were inserted into the area above my lip, near my nose. Still, I didn't feel entirely comfortable with the new doctor.

By the twelfth session, which was supposed to be the last, the substitute doctor repeated the process, inserting needles into my face and hands. However, when he connected the needles to the electric current, he suddenly cranked the voltage to an extreme level. It felt as though I had been struck by an electric shock. I couldn't tell whether his actions were deliberate or a medical error, but judging by the look on his face, I suspected it was a mistake.

The truth is, I felt a fear akin to being electrocuted. As soon as that final session ended, I left the clinic without paying the fee—a form of protest against what had happened to me. I believe the fee was ten dollars. In the heat of my anger over the substitute doctor's grave mistake, which had shaken my body and reignited my doubts, I refused to pay.

Looking back, I wish I had paid the fee to avoid entangling myself in a maze of trouble with that incompetent doctor. In the months that followed, I received repeated demands to settle the remaining ten-dollar fee for the treatment. I ignored them all. Perhaps I should have filed a lawsuit for his misconduct, but I doubt the matter is truly over, even after all these years. If I were to travel to the United States tomorrow, there's still a chance they might have filed a case against me for that unpaid ten dollars. I wouldn't be surprised if, upon arriving in the U.S., I were arrested at the airport for failing to pay the fee for that last session—a session of terror and torture, not therapy like the ones before. Ladies and gentlemen, this is the greed of capitalism, which shows no mercy when it comes to money. The lesson I learned early on was this: always pay your financial obligations without question, especially to the government, or you'll find yourself in serious trouble—even over a trivial amount.

That said, I must admit that from the moment those sessions ended, I began to wean myself off tissues. Over time, my sinus sensitivity became nothing more than a memory, thanks to that acupuncture treatment. However, the healing wasn't solely due to the needles. The doctor had combined several elements in his treatment: instilling in me an unwavering belief in his ability to heal me, repeating the sessions, targeting the necessary energy points to strengthen the mucous membrane, and incorporating meditation exercises to promote relaxation.

I also learned the rituals of deep breathing and its importance in preventing pain. Now, whenever I undergo cupping, acupuncture, or anything that might cause discomfort, I practice those rituals. I believe they're effective in alleviating the sensation of pain.

Khalil Hamad

The Nightmare of Capitalism's Beast

To build a home in the United States, in the embrace of capitalism's monstrous jaws, is like a spider weaving its fragile web. No, in fact, it is even more fragile than a spider's web—fraught with countless, endless, and potentially deadly dangers.

One day, I was riding in the car of my friend, from Hebron, along a coastal road near the Pacific Ocean. The road was narrow, with two lanes separated by a solid white line.

At one point, it seemed my friend's tires crossed over that unbroken line—a serious traffic violation. Coincidentally, a police officer in full uniform was stationed nearby. Or perhaps it wasn't a coincidence at all. Maybe it was a deliberate trap, set by the police who knew the narrow road was a snare for drivers, one that would fill the state's coffers with hefty fines for crossing the solid white line.

In an instant, the officer signaled from a distance for my friend to pull over to the right side of the road. He approached us slowly, his hand resting on his holster. To some, this might seem routine, something that happens every day in various parts of the world. But in the United States, it is terrifying and dangerous. Here, the high crime rate means police officers are trained to assume they are dealing with a potential criminal at all times. They are prepared to shoot in response to any movement that could be interpreted as a threat to their lives. Countless police officers have lost their lives for sometimes assuming good intentions.

I remember hearing a story during my early months in the United States about a Saudi student who was pulled over in a situation similar to ours. As the officer approached, the student leaned toward the glove compartment to retrieve his car documents. The officer, assuming the student was reaching for a gun, immediately drew his weapon and fired several shots, killing him.

From this tragic incident and many others like it, I learned that the only way to survive such situations in the streets of Uncle Sam's land— and avoid the fate of that young Saudi man, who acted instinctively, thinking he was still in the safety of the East—is to freeze. You must place your hands on the steering wheel in a visible, non-threatening position and avoid any movements that could be perceived as a threat. Otherwise, your fate might be decided by bullets fired by an officer who, under the rules of engagement on the frontlines of the street, is permitted to shoot the moment they feel threatened. There is no room for mercy, hesitation, or regard for consequences—even if the threat exists only in his mind. I urged my friend to freeze and not move a muscle until the officer instructed him to do so. Those moments of waiting were agonizing. The officer moved toward us slowly, cautiously, his every step calculated. As he drew closer, I could see he was white—pale-skinned, with colored eyes. According to records of such incidents, this demographic is often the most hostile toward other races in the United States. He remained in a state of full readiness, prepared to kill.

When the police officer approached the driver's side of the car, his hand still on the trigger, he asked us in English, "Where are you from?"

I thought to myself, "Well, here we go." It seemed he suspected us, perhaps mistaking us for members of a gang he was tracking. I began silently reciting the Shahada—who knows what might happen?

When my friend replied that we were Arabs, I didn't like his answer. My tension grew, fearing the officer might interpret

116

it as a hostile act, especially since the Iranian hostage crisis was at its peak. But the officer's expression, which had been primed for violence, flipped a hundred and eighty degrees. He immediately took his hand off his weapon, and a broad smile spread across his face.

For a moment, I couldn't comprehend the reason for this sudden change—until he uttered a few broken words in Arabic. That's when we realized we were safe. He was one of us! Our joy was immeasurable. It turned out he was a police officer of Lebanese Arab descent. Relieved, I said to him, "You scared us, man! You had your hand on your gun the whole time."

After confirming that we were indeed Arabs, he warned my friend not to cross the white line again, saying, "You can't always dodge the bullet." He let us go without a ticket, and we drove away, overjoyed, as if we had stumbled upon a treasure.

In the land of Uncle Sam, under the shadow of capitalism's relentless grind, "you can't always dodge the bullet." This isn't just true on the roads—it's true everywhere. Thank God I never had to work at a convenience store or gas station; the danger from thieves was far greater than the risk of dealing with the police, whose trigger-happy instinct needed no justification.

But the dangers didn't end there. I used to go with friends to the Pacific Ocean beach, where we would surf using wooden boards pushed by the waves after venturing deep into the ocean. What a risky sport! If the sea is treacherous, imagine an ocean vast enough to hold several seas within it. They call it the Pacific, but it's often anything but peaceful. Waves could rise several meters high, making drowning an ever-present risk, one that grew more likely with the height of the waves.

It's true that I survived the tempestuous waves of the ocean, but drowning in the seas of forbidden temptation and pleasures was a very real and intense danger—far more perilous than the ocean's fury. Navigating these waters required immense strength, skill, patience, wisdom, willpower, and manhood to navigate and survive.

Of course, I could have easily become another victim of that internal, insidious conflict imposed by the clash between my conservative cultural upbringing and the need to coexist in a society marked by moral decay and boundless openness— all in the name of freedom, democracy, and other capitalist ideals. This very conflict, I observed, left behind countless victims: some psychologically scarred, others permanently damaged. I doubt anyone could emerge from the belly of the beast completely unharmed, free from scratches or wounds.

The dangers lurking in the belly of the beast were too numerous to count. Imagine, for instance, driving a rickety, unlicensed car and accidentally hitting another vehicle—or worse, a person. Picture the consequences, stranded alone in a foreign land with no support, like a branch severed from a tree.

Yet, all these risks were, to some extent, manageable and something one could learn to live with. The true monster, the one that haunted me most, was the fear of falling ill and needing hospitalization in the absence of health insurance, with the exorbitant costs of treatment.

I remember watching a famous TV program called 60 Minutes, which featured an interview with a German tourist who had arrived in the United States on a tourist visa after retiring. This is typical of foreigners who, upon reaching retirement age, set out to explore the vast world.

Unfortunately for this German tourist, who was accustomed to free healthcare in his homeland, he developed appendicitis shortly after arriving in the U.S. He was rushed to the nearest hospital, underwent surgery, and had to stay for what I believe was fifteen days. When the doctor finally allowed him to leave, he was presented with a bill stretching 72 feet long, totaling millions. He had no health insurance coverage, and I never knew how his story ended.

The nightmare of such a catastrophe was what kept me awake at night. I constantly prayed to finish my studies and earn my degree before the beast of medical expenses in Uncle Sam's land could devour me. Even something as simple as pulling a tooth became a financial dilemma. Many people made sure their teeth were in perfect condition before traveling to the U.S., or they postponed dental treatment until they could escape the beast's belly and afford the care.

Thankfully, I emerged unscathed, never facing a health crisis that could have made life unbearable. Once, I even considered getting my teeth cleaned and having gaps widened to make flossing easier. I went through with it, but after the dentist cleaned the right side of my mouth, I never returned to finish the left.

Even after all these years, I remain baffled: how can anyone escape the trap of exorbitant medical costs under such a merciless system?

Dear reader, do you have any suggestions or ideas for navigating such a predicament?

THE WELL OF EXILE

Their appointed time is the morning.
Is it not that the morning is near?

By the end of 1981, shortly after I had moved to San Diego from Riverside, the United States health authorities announced the outbreak of a deadly viral epidemic sweeping across the country.

The news sent shockwaves across the nation, plunging people into a state of panic. The health authorities, at first, were unable to pinpoint the causes or the methods of transmission. Rumors swirled, and official statements carried warnings that the virus might be transmitted through touch, saliva, or even breathing—much like the common flu. These were all speculations, but they were enough to ignite waves of fear that soon rippled across the globe, as the world braced for the possibility of the epidemic spreading beyond U.S. borders.

For these reasons, recommendations emerged: avoid public restrooms, steer clear of restaurants, and refrain from touching anything unclean.

Overnight, life in San Diego turned upside down. We became afraid of everything, avoiding any contact that might expose us to the deadly virus. However, unlike during the COVID-19 pandemic, we did not wear masks—there were no recommendations to do so. The advice was limited to cautioning against transmission through touch. Vaccination was not even a consideration—neither the technology nor the knowledge was available at the time to push health authorities toward developing vaccine, unlike what happened with the coronavirus, which was deployed without the usual extensive testing required for medications and vacations.

Our lives were thrown into disarray. We didn't know if the virus would come at us from in front, behind, above, or below. We spent hours glued in front of televisions, listening to details and bulletins about the epidemic's spread, and its toll.

Information began to spread—information we had never known before—about viruses, their nature, and the reasons behind our inability to stop a pandemic caused by viral infections. We learned of the catastrophic risks these infections could pose.

Through media reports, we discovered that advanced nations had, since the early 20th century, established massive laboratories and allocated enormous funds to discover treatments for viruses, much like what had been done for bacterial infections. Yet, all these efforts had ended in failure.

The information that began to circulate about the nature of viruses revealed that the failure to invent treatments or vaccines for viruses—unlike the success achieved with bacteria, which antibiotics could combat—was due to the unique nature of this extraordinary organism called a "virus." Its ability to mutate, undergoing changes in its genetic structure at regular intervals, meant that by the time scientists developed a treatment, the virus's nature and genetic makeup had already changed. As a result, the treatment designed for the earlier version became useless.

It was said that thousands of mutations occurred continuously in viral structures. Most of these mutations produced weaker versions of the virus, but each variant carried unique genetic properties, setting it apart from its predecessors. However, some mutations could give rise to highly infectious and deadly strains, and in rare cases, even produce a virulent version.

The secret behind the health authorities' fears in the United States, when the pandemic erupted lay in the unprecedented characteristics of the new variant responsible for the deadly outbreak. This variant had developed a structure resembling a crown, which led to the family of viruses being named "coronavirus," This variant became the first of the coronaviruses, giving rise to several other strains that emerged later, particularly in Africa, including Ebola, SARS, MERS, and finally, the coronavirus that appeared in December 2019.

The health authorities had long been aware of the virus's ability to mutate, and they warned that future variants could be far more dangerous in terms of their speed of transmission and lethality. Official estimates published at the time suggested that a highly aggressive and deadly variant could emerge within twenty years of the virus's initial outbreak in 1981.

Indeed, over the years since then, viruses had continued to mutate, up until the emergence of the coronavirus that appeared in 2019-officially named COVID-19. However, the variant that scientists had feared did not appear until approximately forty years later, rather than the predicated twenty. Although other dangerous variants had emerged in the interim, they remained confined to specific regions, such as Africa, China, and Saudi Arabia, and never escalated into a global pandemic.

What mattered most was that the health authorities, now closely monitoring the spread of the virus, began to identify its causes. Over time, they were eventually able to pinpoint the reasons and narrow them down to transmission through saliva, blood, or illicit relationships. Based on data from infected individuals and disease spread maps, it became clear to the health authorities that the disease was spreading more widely in areas with large populations descended from the people of Lot.

More importantly, they identified the symptoms and effects of the virus on infected individuals. It became clear that the virus specifically targeted the immune system, disabling it and leaving the body vulnerable to other illnesses due to the loss of its immune defenses. Based on this understanding, the health authorities named the pandemic AIDS—an acronym for Acquired Immune Deficiency Syndrome.

At the time, health authorities announced that contracting this disease could be life-threatening. Caused by the human immunodeficiency virus (HIV), which attacked and destroyed the immune system. This virus was unprecedented—the first of its kind to disable the body's defenses so completely—and its emergence fueled widespread fear about the severity of the epidemic.

As information about how the disease spread began to circulate, the expressions of healthy people softened, and the panic that had gripped people during the initial outbreak— when the causes were still unknown—began to subside. Meanwhile, the epidemic ravaged the descendants of the people of Lot, who faced a kind of mass extermination at the onset of the outbreak, much like their ancestors had. Though the method of punishment differed, it was no surprise, for divine law dictates that punishment mirrors the crime. While the people of Lot were swiftly destroyed—swallowed by the earth, their high places brought low—their descendants were afflicted by a microscopic entity, invisible to the naked eye. This entity crippled their immune systems, leaving them defenseless against disease and exposing them to suffering and death.

Amid this panic, as the AIDS virus waged war on the immune systems of the infected, I found myself gathering with a group of thoughtful friends—a kind of think tank—in the cafeteria to discuss public affairs.

This topic held particular significance due to its grave implications. When it became clear that the primary cause of infection was sexual deviance, I spoke to them about the people of Lot and how God had punished them by causing the earth to swallow them whole. I noted that it was no surprise for such punishment to return if a group of Lot's descendants continued to commit acts that warranted divine retribution, for such sins are antithetical to human nature and cannot be tolerated.

I reminded them that the prophet Lot had warned his people for defying the natural order. The noble angels sent by God to Lot and his people had declared: "Their appointed time is the morning. Is it not that the morning is near?" This warning, I argued, remains relevant as long as life persists on earth. However, my words did not sit well with some, who invoked arguments about democracy, personal freedom, and other capitalist heresies.

Now, considering the mutations that have emerged within the coronavirus family in recent years—and given that viruses possess the ability to mutate and transform into new variants—it is no stretch to imagine humanity's end brought about by a microscopic virus, invisible to the naked eye, should corruption continue to spread.

Indeed, the outbreak of that epidemic during my time in San Diego became yet another reason added to the sword of Arif, compelling me to return to my homeland.

Khalil Hamad

My Journey with the Master's Thesis

My journey toward completing my master's thesis was anything but easy. I had to meet the university's rigorous requirements to obtain a Master's degree, which included a series of demanding courses and examinations. Balancing my studies with a part-time job made the challenge even greater, requiring immense effort, discipline, and time.

One example of these challenges was a course titled "Introduction to Master's Studies." The professor assigned us five to seven novels to read within a week, followed by in-depth discussions in the next class. At times, he tasked us with researching obscure figures, sending us digging through library archives and encyclopedias for hours on end to uncover information about them. In the early 1980s, the internet had not yet become the ubiquitous resource it is today, though the first versions of university electronic communication systems were available. Training students in library research, information retrieval, and familiarizing them with scientific research methods was a cornerstone of earning a Master's degree.

Each course came with its own set of demands, from research papers to exams. Yet, despite the obstacles, I managed to navigate every task required by the faculty for the English Literature program, with a focus on Comparative Literature. After a grueling journey filled with challenges, hard work, and difficulties, I found myself facing the most daunting task of my master's degree pursuit, and indeed, the most formidable challenge of my life up to that point.

I hadn't fully grasped the magnitude of it while I was still on the shore, so to speak, and had not yet embarked on the voyage of writing my master's thesis, the task seemed deceptively simple. But as I set sail, I felt as though I were wading into the sea—a sensation that was delightful and exhilarating at first. Soon, however, I found myself in the open sea, drowning—up to my ears— in the details of the task, the demands of research and writing. I wrestled with ideas, fears, and doubts, battling feelings of isolation, loneliness, and mounting psychological pressure. I would plunge into the pages of books until I felt suffocated, only to escape my predicament by retreating to sleep, taking a walk, or a conversation with a friend. Maher Al-Nabulsi, a fatherless friend and one of my closest confidants, became my sounding board for discussing my theories and the burdens of completing this task. Though I eventually completed my thesis, I never fully convinced him of my ideas—though, over time, he became more accepting of them.

Once you find yourself in the middle of writing a master's thesis, you realize that the choices grow increasingly complex. There's no turning back once you've ventured too far into the sea. Moving forward toward the distant harbor of arrival becomes an incredibly challenging, slow, and demanding process—one that requires time, effort, and an immense amount of patience, focus, and hard work.

In my case, I was fortunate because I knew exactly what I wanted to explore—like a father who knows his child intimately. I had even defined its scope and title, and I had a clear vision of the harbor I was sailing toward—the hypothesis I had formulated at the age of sixteen, born from my personal experience with orphanhood and my early love for literature. I had noticed a striking parallel between my own experience of losing my mother at a young age and that of the great writer Leo Tolstoy. We both shared the experience of losing our mothers at an early age—

specifically at the age of two. I had never even seen a picture of my mother, which led me to hypothesize a profound connection between orphanhood and literary creativity. Over the years, I sought to prove this hypothesis, devouring every piece of literature I could find that was related to the topic.

I was particularly fortunate to receive help from the dean of the English Literature Department at the University of San Diego during my enrollment phase. He played a pivotal role in helping me clarify my choices, define my direction, and narrow down my research focus. Through our discussions, I was able to draft my thesis proposal, the most critical step for a master's student. This proposal outlines the student's core idea and serves as a roadmap for achieving the research objectives. For me, the goal was to prove the assumed relationship I had hypothesized.

Instead of narrowing the focus of the research—which had assumed that biological orphanhood was the secret to creativity—the scope was widened at the suggestion of the college dean. The professor proposed expanding the framework, making it more scientifically sound and logically compelling. The new direction shifted toward exploring the relationship between object loss and creativity—encompassing any form of loss, not just the biological orphanhood. The reasoning was simple: there were writers who had never experienced the early orphanhood, though my thesis had centered on the loss of a parent.

Next, my thesis committee was formed, chaired by a professor named Dr. Nicol, with two other members: a professor of African descent from the department and an external examiner. I began meeting with Dr. Nicol to explain my idea, present my research plan, and outline my proposal. I shared my objectives, methodology, and how I intended to achieve my goals. However, I sensed his skepticism about my topic, which filled me with anxiety. I had heard stories of students struggling to complete their theses—one had spent seven years trying to finish without success, another had written seventy pages but then lost the motivation to complete the remaining thirty, and yet another had abandoned their initial topic altogether, feeling incapable of continuing. Many others felt lost, overwhelmed by the sheer magnitude of the task. All who passed through this academic gate felt the weight of pressure and tension.

I couldn't quite pinpoint the reason for Dr. Nicol's dissatisfaction with my topic. I feared it might be because I was proposing a bold and alternative theory. It wasn't easy for a foreign student from a small village in rural Palestine to arrive on the global stage and present a universal theory attempting to explain the source of creative energy—a theory that, in many ways, challenged the established ideas of giants like Freud, Adler, and Carl Jung. Was I really bringing something new that these great minds and countless American scholars had overlooked?

I also worried about my ability to convince the committee of my approach. I wasn't sure if I could gather enough scientifically acceptable evidence, adhering to rigorous research methodologies, to make my case compelling—these doubts gnawed at me.

Over time, after relentless effort, countless meetings, and lengthy discussions, the committee finally approved my research topic. I suspect their approval was somewhat reluctant, though my unwavering enthusiasm for the subject may have played a decisive role. That approval was the starting point for the serious work of writing my master's thesis. I aspired to produce something groundbreaking, a contribution that would add value to the field, even though I knew I was embarking on a daring venture with no clear sense of where it might lead.

The End of Preparation and the Start of Work
Part Two of My Journey in Preparing the
Master's Thesis

The preparation phase had come to an end, and now the real work began—the second part of my journey in crafting my master's thesis. The supervisory committee had approved the thesis proposal, which meant we were now entering the phase of actual execution. The task ahead was to write at least one hundred pages, presenting the thesis, addressing a specific problem, and employing tools and methodologies to either prove or refute it. Afterward, a summary of the research and study would be required.

The thesis revolved around the relationship between the loss of a parent—whether father or mother—and literary creativity. I had officially begun the work, with the title, plan, and content all laid out. I had chosen three orphaned writers as case studies: Pablo Neruda, the great Chilean poet; Sylvia Plath, the American writer of German descent; and Ralph Ellison, the African American novelist. The goal was to highlight the experience of orphanhood in their lives and literature, exploring the potential connection between parental loss and literary creativity. The agreed-upon title for the thesis was: "Creativity and the Search for Fulfillment."

But before diving into the task of proving the relationship between the orphanhood of these three writers and their literary output, it was necessary to conduct a historical review of the theories that attempted to explain the source of creative energy. What had previous theories and propositions said about the origin of creative energy? Where does it come from? What is behind the creative impulse?

130

To achieve this, I turned to the library, enlisting the help of one of the librarians to conduct an extensive search using the ERIC electronic system, which connects to university libraries across the United States. The goal was to identify and compile everything written on the topic in the fields of literature and the humanities—specifically psychology, education, sociology, and philosophy—from the earliest writings to the present. The search yielded approximately 600 articles, bulletins, and books related to creativity and its origins, which the library provided, even sourcing from universities in other states.

It was essential to review all these articles, publications, and books to summarize what had been written on the subject, from the time of the ancient Greek philosophers up to the moment of my research. The focus was on what had been said before me about the source of creative energy. It became clear that there were several theses, ranging from the idea that creativity's source is unknown, to the belief that it is an innate talent one is born with. Some whimsically attributed it to jinn from the fabled Wadi Abqar. Meanwhile, leading psychologists treated the human personality as an energy system, influenced by the law of energy, which states that energy cannot be created or destroyed but only transformed from one state to another. Based on this, they developed theories attempting to explain where creativity comes from, rooted in their theories of human personality.

Freud, the father of psychology, argued that creativity is the result of a conflict between the individual's desire to fulfill their needs—particularly sexual ones—and society's refusal to allow it. The individual represses these desires, which later erupt in the form of creativity—or madness.

As for Alfred Adler, he rejected Freud's theory of deprivation and proposed an alternative theory he called compensation theory. He argued that creativity arises as a compensation for a deficiency in a person's life. While he focused on sensory disabilities, he never addressed the impact of orphanhood, narrowing the idea of deficiency to the body alone.

Carl Jung, on the other hand, believed that "there is no consciousness without pain." He envisioned humans inheriting wisdom in compartments he called "archetypes," which he saw as the source of creativity, with pain playing a key role in its emergence.

It's worth noting that many psychologists emphasize the significant role of traumatic experiences in fostering creativity. Yet, despite the widespread interest in the origins of creativity among thinkers and scientists, I found no one who explored the connection between creativity and orphanhood as a fundamental factor.

Even Cox's study from 1926, one of the most important studies on the source of creativity, failed to reach a definitive conclusion. While it ruled out heredity as a source of creativity, it also overlooked the role of orphanhood, likely due to flaws in the study's sample selection—a point I'll return to later.

Of course, this historical study required immense effort, but I completed it in record time, especially after leaving my job at the bookstore for good. I spent most of my days in the library, surrounded by books, knowing exactly what I was searching for. Financially, I relied on my brothers working in Kuwait, who sent me around five hundred dollars at the beginning of each month. This created significant psychological pressure, as relying on them for financial support was never part of my plan for this stage of my studies.

I remained in constant contact with the committee chair, updating him on my progress step by step. During this time, Dr. Nicol, the chair of my thesis committee, lost his mother and left the university for over four weeks. In his absence, I managed to draft this section of my thesis, outlining the chapter that covers what others had said about the source of creative energy. My goal was to transform abstract ideas into something tangible—a mental trick that soothes the nerves, gives form to thoughts, and creates a sense of accomplishment. This self-motivation kept me going.

I organized the first parts of my thesis into a red binder, labeling it with the title, my name, and the names of the supervision members. It looked like a finished book. When Dr. Nicol returned from his mother's funeral and saw what I had accomplished, he was astonished. He expressed his amazement with words of disbelief.

From that moment, I noticed a clear shift in his attitude. He became more enthusiastic about the project than ever before, unlike his demeanor before his mother's passing. I believe this change was largely due to the feelings of loss he experienced, which lent the research a credibility he hadn't felt before. Of course, having the completed material in his hands, presented like a book, also played a decisive role in solidifying the project's legitimacy.

Dr. Nicol's return from his mother's funeral, steeped in grief, became a new source of motivation for me to exert even more effort. This was especially important since the most challenging part of the research—proving the connection between loss and creativity—had yet to begin.

But his changed attitude fueled my enthusiasm. I dove into the most critical part of the work with passion, determination, and confidence that things were moving toward resolution and completion. There was no longer room for hesitation or fear of failure.

Khalil Hamad

The Day I Completed My Master's Thesis
March 3, 1983

Once I finished documenting the summaries of what others had said about the source of creative energy, it became clear to me that no one had spoken about orphanhood as a fundamental factor in driving creativity. It turned out that the theories of great psychologists like Freud, Adler, and Carl Jung dominated the 20th century, overshadowing all other perspectives. Years later, I stumbled upon a lone article in a journal written by a psychiatrist from New York, published in 1978, which mentioned orphanhood as a catalyst for creative achievement—though it offered no deeper exploration of the idea.

It fell to me to highlight the importance of orphanhood in the lives of the three writers central to my research—Sylvia Plath, Pablo Neruda, and Ralph Ellison. I sought to bring to light the profound impact of the experience on their literature.

Sylvia Plath made my task relatively easy, though immersing myself in her life plunged me into a state of psychological terror. Through my close examination of her harrowing experiences, which ended in her early suicide, I came to understand the depth of her pain. Shortly before her death, she wrote a poem titled *Daddy*, which, in its entirety, serves as an autobiography of her life. In it, she revealed her intention to end her life—a decision she carried out at the age of 35.

In the opening lines of the poem, Plath addresses her father:
'I was ten when they buried you.
At twenty, I tried to die

And get back, back, back to you.
I thought even the bones would do.
But they pulled me out of the sack,
And they stuck me together with glue.
And then I knew what to do.
I made a model of you,
A man in black with a Meinkampf look'

She did not live long after writing these lines, choosing instead to return to her father through death. In *Daddy* and throughout her work, there are clear references to the impact of loss, shaping her terrifying life—a life that ended in suicide. While some attribute her suicide to the failure of her novel *The Bell Jar*, despite all the personal signs she herself had expressed.

In the final lines of *Daddy*, she declares that she can no longer endure life because of this loss, which haunted her relentlessly. Not even poetry, marriage, or writing a novel could save her. She surrenders, choosing death instead:

'Daddy, daddy, you bastard, I'm through.'

As for Pablo Neruda, he was once asked by a television interviewer about the source of his poetic inspiration. He recounted a childhood memory: as a boy, he was playing in the garden of his home, holding a small white plastic lamb. He placed his hand in a hole in the garden wall, and someone on the other side stole the toy. Neruda pointed to this incident as the source of his poetry.

It was clear, of course, that Neruda was speaking about the loss he experienced in childhood—a loss that left a profound mark on him. Unconsciously, he tied the stolen white lamb to the death of his mother, who passed away before he was even a month old. This experience, though he later devoted himself to national causes, deeply influenced his poetry.

It is no surprise that his first collection of poetry, *Twenty Love Poems and a Song of Despair*, revolved around themes of love, women, despair, and death.

These lines from the end of his poem *Song of Despair* capture the essence of his grief:

'Deserted like the wharves at dawn.
Only the tremulous shadow twists in my hands.
Oh, farther than everything. Oh, farther than everything.
It is the hour of departure. Oh, abandoned one.'

Undoubtedly, the death of his mother left an indelible mark on his poetry and life, shaping him into the legendary poet who would win the Nobel Prize in 1971.

Ralph Ellison, an African American writer, authored the novel *Invisible Man*, in which the narrator is a nameless Black child. The protagonist speaks in the first person, a clear indication that the novel is autobiographical—a reflection of the author's own life.

The novel tells of a protagonist who lives his life invisibly—not by choice, but because the people he encounters "see only my surroundings, themselves, or figments of their imagination," he is effectively invisible. This invisibility, born of racism, strips the protagonist of his sense of existence and identity. He leaves the racist South for New York City, but his encounters continue to disgust him. Ultimately, he retreats to a hole in the ground, which he furnishes and makes his home. There, brilliantly illuminated by stolen electricity, he can seek his identity.

Elsewhere in the novel, he explains that he withdrew into this underground hole to write the story of his invisible life—a life in which he felt as though he had no essence, no existence in the eyes of others. He plays the song "(*What Did I Do to Be So*) *Black and Blue*" on a phonograph.

The problem is that Ellison lived in a racist society, and his story is one of grappling with that racism. His narrative is filled with events that highlight how his primary crisis was with a society that treated him as if he were nothing, as though he were unseen.

However, I believe that another equally significant reason for his feeling of invisibility was the traumatic death of his father, which he witnessed as a child. His father, who worked as an ice carrier, died in front of young Ralph's eyes when he was just nine years old. The boy had accompanied his father to the icehouse when a block of ice fell on him. A shard of ice pierced his father's abdomen, and he was rushed to the hospital with the shard still embedded in his body. He died from his injuries, and Ralph, who had accompanied him to the hospital, was left to witness this tragedy—a trauma that shattered him.

Ralph Ellison described his father's death in painful detail, and it was this very pain that shaped him into the remarkable writer he became. His novel is considered one of the finest works by an African American author.

With this, I concluded my written defense on the impact of orphanhood on the lives of the three writers, drawing from the events of their lives and the texts they wrote. This bring me to the final part of my master's thesis, which was, in essence, a foregone conclusion. It contained the findings that confirmed the role of loss in the creation of art, and how orphanhood stands as one of the most significant experiences of loss that leads to creativity, as seen in the lives of the writers I studied.

At this stage, my friend Nabil Kokaly reemerged in my life once again. He must have sensed the struggles I was facing— editing, rewriting, and correcting errors— especially since I had written my thesis as if I were narrating the story of orphanhood from memory, drawing inspiration from the lives of the writers I was researching. I had avoided the stitching together excerpts that could make the text disjointed, awkward, and forced narrative when done poorly. Nabil suggested I hand the text over to an experienced editor, and I followed his advice under the principle:

Always give your work to someone else to edit.

This is because the mind deceives us; the author often fails to see the errors that an editor can easily spot. An editor approaches the text with an objectivity that the original writer lacks, no matter how detached a writer tries to be from their work, they remain mentally attached to it. This suggestion pulled me out of a deep, dark well and relieved an enormous amount of pressure.

Later, I had my revised manuscript typed by a professional experienced in handling master's theses on a typewriter. This was back in the early 1980s, well before computer printing became widespread.

And so, my master's thesis was finally ready, awaiting the committee's approval. On March 3, 1983, the supervising committee signed off on my work, and it was filed in the library under the number 13. That date became a personal holiday for me, a day to celebrate the completion of the most important project of my life. It was especially meaningful because it lent significant credibility to my theory and arguments linking orphanhood and creativity.

Yet, even then, I knew the road ahead was still long. I needed to provide scientific evidence to support my thesis, and that became my mission in the years that followed. I continued my search for conclusive proof, driven by a relentless determination.

You might not believe the level of stress, tension, psychological exhaustion, and anxiety I endured while writing those chapters. It nearly drove me to madness. But I leaned on my friends and channeled my energy into intense physical exercise to maintain my balance. The committee's approval of my thesis marked the end of my suffering and the culmination of my efforts to earn my master's degree. It filled my heart with joy and etched that day into my memory as a permanent celebration.

However, graduating with a degree in English literature plunged me into the labyrinth of "What next?"

Khalil Hamad

The Homeland Calls Its People

Yes, yes. Despite the scales of return gradually tipping in its favor, and the fierce internal struggle beginning to lean toward the triumph of conscious rationality—rooted in national belonging—over the temptations of the self, pushing me closer to the decision to return.

The fading desire to complete another master's program, this time in Mass Communication at the College of Media, added further weight to the decision to return. Yet, the matter was far from simple. Leaving behind a society in which I had been immersed for over three years was no easy feat, even if those years had sometimes felt like being trapped in a dark and deep well. Even if you find nothing to yearn for in such a place, you might still long for its oppressive darkness. So how could I leave a society brimming with temptations, pleasures, and opportunities? A society where I had lived, learned, acquired new knowledge, and experienced countless life lessons? A society where I had achieved the most significant accomplishment of my life—one that would have been impossible without the opportunities it provided! This was a society that embodies hope and dreams for every aspiring individual seeking success and wealth.

The difficulty, as sociology explains, lies in the fact that when a person moves to a new society, they begin at point (A). Over time, they progress to other points (B, C, D, E, etc.) through intellectual growth and the accumulation of new experiences. They may delve deeper and deeper into the richness of their experiences in this new society. If they then decide to return to their previous society, they can never truly return to point (A), no matter how hard they try. The layers of knowledge and experience they have gained transform them into a new person, fundamentally different from who they were at the starting point.

From this point onward, the ability to uproot oneself from a new society becomes a task more daunting than impossible—especially when that society is open and welcoming, and you have been deeply embedded in it for a significant period of time. It has provided you with opportunities to realize your potential and achieve remarkable success, granting you a sense of self-worth. Yet, you know that returning to your homeland means stepping back into a vast prison, one filled with endless stations of oppression, humiliation, and degradation—perhaps even arbitrary death. Merely thinking about return awakens memories of bitter experiences you may have endured: the midnight raids by intruders, the checkpoints, the crossing of the bridge of return, demeaning labor, poverty, fear, and the suffocating loss of hope.

For all these reasons, I became a prisoner to my anxieties, fears, the temptations of capitalism, the whispers of the devil, and the inclinations of my own sinful soul. I was paralyzed, unable to make a final decision to return. Because my travel permit still granted me some leeway, I continued to play the game of procrastination and delay until mid-1984. It was then that I decided to try my luck by enrolling in a doctoral program—this time in Education, specifically Teaching English as a Second Language (TESL).

This program, as I learned, was a joint initiative between San Diego State University, where I had already been enrolled, and the University of California, San Diego (UCSD). Admission to the program seemed relatively straightforward. I even registered for one course as a trial, hoping to get a closer look at the program.

142

However, I ultimately decided to withdraw from the idea, despite the encouragement of the course instructor, who appeared to be of Arab descent but was not. My reasons were the same ones that had led me to abandon my master's program in Media: a lack of enthusiasm, financial constraints, the call of my homeland, the restrictions of my travel permit, the ever-looming specter of Arif, and my burning, insatiable desire to continue my research on the source of creative energy and the relationship between orphanhood and creativity.

It seems I had underestimated the importance of that specialization at the time. When I returned to Kuwait later and applied to teach in its schools, I was called for an interview at the Ministry of Education. The official there was enthusiastic about appointing me as a supervisor for the English language teaching program. However, when she noticed that I had only taken one course within that program, she informed me that I was, in fact, the only person in Kuwait in 1985 with any knowledge of that rare specialization. She even hinted at the possibility of sending me on a scholarship to complete the program under a contract with the Ministry. But back then, I chose to work in the translation department at the Ministry of Information instead, swayed by rumors of student rebellions and unruly behavior, and lured by the prospect of higher financial rewards in the private sector—corporate world.

Let me take you back to San Diego to continue the tale of that fierce internal struggle—the tug-of-war between the voice of reason, which grew increasingly insistent about returning home, and the overwhelming desire to stay.

As my enthusiasm for completing the joint PhD program in Teaching English as a Foreign Language began to wane, I found myself searching for additional justifications to tip the scales further in favor of returning—making the decision easier to accept.

I crafted a personal philosophy of justification, convincing myself that returning to Kuwait was the better choice—primarily because of the strength of the Kuwaiti dinar, which at the time was equivalent to three dollars. This meant that a salary of 1,000 Kuwaiti dinars would translate to 3,000 dollars in U.S. currency—a compelling argument.

I also reasoned that my specialization was ill-suited for a society already saturated with native English speakers, where competition would be fierce and futile. In contrast, based on my previous experience in Kuwait, I believed the job opportunities there would be a thousand times better than anything I might find in a foreign job market. There, I feared, I might end up in manual labor, working under harsh conditions, navigating dangerous streets plagued by violence—a place where the murder rate rivaled that of war zones.

But the real reasons that ultimately sealed my decision to return were twofold: my refusal to relinquish my Palestinian citizenship and my determination not to let my father down. He worried deeply about the impact of Western culture on my Eastern upbringing, and even more, he dreaded a repeat of the tragedy of Arif, the son of our village who had left home, vanished without a trace. Arif never returned to his birthplace, and his story had become a cautionary tale, a proverb whispered in the wind.

I began to imagine the overwhelming joy that would wash over my father when he saw me return from the depths of exile, my head held high, clutching a master's degree. I pictured the pride and honor swelling in his heart. It felt like the least I could do for a father who had loved me so deeply and waited for this moment with bated breath, his hopes pinned on my return.

And so, whenever I was asked about my plans, I would reply, "The homeland has called its people back," leaving no room for retreat, delay, or hesitation in my decision to return. I began to prepare myself for the moment of emergence— stepping out of the belly of the whale, boarding the plane, and crossing the bridge into the vast prison—the homeland, my family, my loving father, and the place where my life story had first begun.

The Struggle Between Returning and Staying

The signing and approval of my master's thesis by the supervisory committee on March 3, 1983, marked the completion of the requirements for my degree in English Literature, with a focus on Comparative Literature. However, I still had to wait for the printing process and routine administrative procedures to be finalized. These were completed by the end of the second semester of 1983.

Despite being as alone as a tunnel, as Pablo Neruda once described—with no family, relatives, or anyone to share in the joy of my graduation—I was determined to don the black graduation gown and the tasseled cap, and to participate in the solemn graduation ceremony held in the vast sports arena of San Diego State University.

I tried to fill all my heart with joy, even as feelings of loneliness and alienation intensified during such social occasions, especially when most graduates were accompanied by family members or relatives. Meanwhile, I knew that no one in the audience cared to hear my name called, to take my photo, or to applaud or cheer for me as I walked across the stage to receive my diploma. Nor did anyone care as I sat proudly among the rows of graduates, wearing my robe and holding my head high.

Truthfully, I was incredibly fortunate during my time in San Diego. Unlike many expatriates, I did not suffer the harsh pangs of loneliness, which can sometimes become deadly, as it did for Sylvia Plath. This was especially true during social occasions when such feelings intensify, far from family and loved ones. And the reason for my fortune was something I never expected.

At the university, I met a professor in the English Literature department named Professor Mines Savas, a man of Greek origin who loved Palestine with all his heart and soul. He adored everything connected to Palestine and defended the Palestinian cause with such fervor that I sometimes thought he was more Palestinian than the Palestinians themselves. Although I never took a class with him, I learned a great deal from him and grew close to him. I often visited him in his office, where we would discuss a wide range of topics, especially academic and Palestinian issues. He became my most trusted advisor in academic matters.

But the role Professor Savas played in my life during my exile, and the way he eased my burdens, went far beyond academic support. He embraced me as a surrogate family member, welcoming me into his home during times when feelings of loneliness were at their peak. Not a single one of their traditional holidays passed—especially Thanksgiving, the holiday when family members reunite despite being estranged for most of the year—without him inviting me and another mutual friend, an Iranian man we called Samad, likely short for AbdulSamad. We would spend the day in his home and spacious garden, with its trees and swings, and then share a meal of roasted turkey, the traditional dish prepared specifically for the occasion as part of their Thanksgiving rituals.

But the life of that remarkable man turned upside down, transforming into profound suffering and unbearable pain. He had left behind all the women of the world—blondes, brunettes, redheads, the fair-skinned—and married a Greek woman, a relative of his. Together, they had a child named Peter, born around the time I completed my master's thesis. However, Peter was born with a milk allergy and other hereditary illnesses. Later, I received the heartbreaking news that he had passed away at the age of eighteen due to those incurable diseases he had carried since birth.

Just as the life of my friend, the Greek Professor Mines Savas, was upended by the birth of his firstborn, Peter, my own life took a sharp turn after I received my master's degree in English literature. There was no longer any reason—or justification— for me to remain in the land of exile and estrangement. The noble goal that had brought me to the back of beyond had been achieved.

Yet, I found it incredibly difficult to accept the idea of leaving the land of Uncle Sam. The thought of abandoning a life of comfort and the American Dream—a dream coveted by people across the globe—seemed almost insane. How could I return to a burning Palestine, like a fish tossed into the flames of fate? Or even to Kuwait, with its raging dust storm, and its scorching heat and suffocating humidity, despite the financial allure I had once known?

I began concocting excuses to stay in the land of Uncle Sam, even though I was now without work or studies, aimlessly wandering the streets. An overwhelming sense of guilt consumed me for my inability to pack my bags and return home triumphantly.

My inner self, prone to weakness, won out. I concocted the idea of enrolling in another master's program, this time in media studies, especially after facing difficulties in gaining acceptance for a PhD in comparative literature. The latter required mastery of another foreign language in addition to my native tongue, which meant learning Spanish, French, or even Hebrew as a prerequisite for admission.

But I was utterly exhausted and impoverished, with no reserves of money, enthusiasm, or energy left to propel me into such an intensive academic program. Deep down, I knew there was no real justification for it other than escaping the bitter truth: that it was time to pack my bags and return to where I had come from.

During that time, I was consumed by feelings of guilt. It never crossed my mind, throughout my years abroad, to seek American citizenship through a sham marriage, as others had done. Nor did I consider finding a job outside the university campus to justify staying after graduation and secure a residency permit, which was no longer valid once my master's program ended.

Defeated by the temptation to stay unjustifiably in the land of Uncle Sam, I enrolled in the core courses of a Master's program in Mass Communications. Yet, I attended lectures without enthusiasm, passion, or the high spirits that had once fueled me during my studies in Comparative Literature and the preparation of my master's thesis in that field.

In this program at the college of media, I was physically present but mentally absent, even though I had always been passionate about journalism and saw myself as a journalist. Instead, I was weighed down by guilt for betraying the promises I had made to myself—to return home after graduation without hesitation or delay.

More importantly, I was acutely aware that the six-year period permitted for staying abroad was nearing its end. Exceeding this limit would mean forfeiting my sacred right to reside in Palestine—a prospect that would neither please nor be acceptable to my father, who awaited my return with bated breath, his heart consumed by fear that I might meet the same fate as Arif, his contemporary, who had left and never returned, becoming a cautionary tale.

To make matters worse, I had stopped working even at the bookstore. During this period of aimlessness and confusion, I relied entirely on the financial support of my siblings—a dependency I found deeply unethical.

When the semester at the College of Media ended, my academic results were far from satisfactory. I realized that my pursuit of a second master's degree had been derailed and was nearing its end, especially after heeding the advice of several friends who argued that another master's degree would neither improve my job prospects nor serve any real purpose. It would only be a waste of time. If anything, they suggested, I should consider pursuing a PhD.

Despite these developments, which tipped the scales in favor of returning home, the internal conflict between my desire to stay and my obligation to return raged on. I continued to drift, wasting more time and money, and concocting feeble justifications for my indecision.

Returning to Kifl Haris

The countdown to my departure from the United States had begun, and with it, the psychological preparation for my return to my hometown, Kifl Haris. After six long years of exile and estrangement—years filled with movement, adventure, learning, work, exploration, disappointment, joy, and relentless activity—I was finally going home.

I did everything a person leaving for good would do: closing my bank account, selling my old clunker of a car, packing my suitcase, settling my rent, and securing a one-way ticket from Los Angeles Airport, with a layover in London, then Amman, Jordan. From Amman, I would drive to Kifl Haris after a brief stop with relatives in Awajan.

During this tense and uncertain time, I happened to meet someone who offered me a job as a lighting technician's assistant for an astonishing fifteen dollars an hour. To put this in perspective, the highest wage I had ever earned while working at the university bookstore was three dollars and fifty cents—the minimum wage at the time, in the early 1980s. Had this offer come before I had mentally prepared to tighten my belt and leave, it might have changed the course of the wind and altered my destiny.

As I bid farewell to my friends, I was in a pitiful emotional state, consumed by despair. I confided in my friend Dr. Lou, sharing my anxieties and fears about the moment of crossing the bridge back home. I couldn't shake the harshness of the scene, its gloom, the potential dangers, and the dread of what awaited me after such a long absence. He tried to comfort me, suggesting I should imagine myself as a refrigerator during the crossing—to approach the situation with simplicity and cool composure. I told him I would try, but deep down, I knew no spell could ward off the shadow of melancholy or make you feel good about stepping into a prison, no matter how spacious it might be.

Before completing the multiple checkpoints and leaving Jericho, which had, over time, replaced the Karameh crossing, I couldn't help but feel that the ground beneath me was unstable—as if the high and low had merged into one.

Those negative feelings could cling to you for days, leaving a mark so deep it felt etched into memory, never to be forgotten. One image that stood out in my mind was that of an elderly man I had seen years earlier, forced to exit the inspection checkpoint barefoot after forgetting his shoes in the inspection bin. Yet, he had remembered to retrieve his igal—the traditional headband—from the same bin.

Every time I crossed the bridge to leave, I felt the joy of a bird escaping its cage the moment I heard the clatter of the bus wheels on the iron bridge. But each time I crossed it to return, I was overwhelmed with a sense of anguish and melancholy, as though heading back to a vast prison—even if my absence had only lasted a few days. So, how would it feel now, after an absence of nearly six years?

This thought filled me with deep anxiety and dread. I had to leave San Diego for Los Angeles to be closer to the airport and ready to board the plane according to my scheduled departure.

Strangely, I don't recall how I left San Diego, who I was with, or how I traveled from San Diego to Los Angeles. It was as if that painful moment had been entirely wiped out from my memory. What I do remember is arriving at the home of a Palestinian student named Naeem, from the village of Hajjah, who was pursuing a PhD in Political Science at the University of Southern California. He hosted me warmly and provided much-needed moral support during those critical hours leading up to my flight—hours filled with overwhelming turmoil. And how could it not be? I was transitioning from one kind of hell, where pleasure and estrangement coexisted, to another, a raging inferno of events whose paths and outcomes no one can foresee.

I spent a pleasant time with Naeem Al-Hijjawi as we waited for my departure. During that time, I visited the University of Southern California and strolled through the streets of Los Angeles. I didn't witness or hear about the violence I had been warned was rampant there. Still, I had taken precautions: I wore short, frayed denim shorts and a shabby blouse, aiming to look like a homeless hippie living on the streets. After all, it's either eat or be eaten.

Fortunately, everything went smoothly, and the time came for my flight to depart. My friend Naeem drove me to the airport, and soon the plane was airborne, heading toward London. This time, the winds were in our favor—unlike the journey from Amsterdam to New York. We reached London in just nine hours instead of the twelve it had taken on the outbound journey.

The plane landed safely at London Airport, where we spent some time waiting for our Royal Airline flight. As scheduled, we took off, and five hours later, the plane touched down peacefully on the tarmac at Amman Airport. Upon arrival, I headed straight to my aunt Umm Rida's house in Awajan, where I stayed for two or three days, recovering from the fatigue of the long flight and mentally preparing myself for the next leg of the journey: crossing the bridges.

On the second day of my arrival, I visited Amman, a city I had always loved. In those days, I enjoyed taking the Zarqa-Russeifa-Amman bus, wandering through the streets of Amman and spending time in the Hashemite Plaza, as I had always done. On my way back to the bus terminal, just as I was passing in front of the Amman Municipality building, a heavy truck rumbled down the street in the same direction. The driver of the truck unleashed his horn—a terrifying sound that made me jump in place, convinced for a moment it was the blowing of the trumpet blast heralding the Day of Judgment. It took me a few seconds to remember that I was no longer in the quiet city of San Diego, where I couldn't recall ever hearing a car horn.

The next day brought the most challenging part of the journey: crossing into the West Bank via the bridge. On the Jordanian side, the departure station officer handed me a green card. To be honest, I had no idea about these cards—green and yellow—or what they meant. After learning the implications of this administrative procedures inside the hall, I tried to persuade the officer to reconsider his decision. I argued that I had been working in Kuwait and showed him my residency permit there, explained that I was returning to work after a short vacation to renew my permit. However, he dismissed my plea, directing me to consult the administration in Amman and classified me as a student returning from university studies. That simple administrative decision would later cost me dearly after the invasion of Kuwait and our forced departure, as I was married to a Jordanian woman who did not hold a West Bank ID. A situation I will elaborate on what happened later and how, after several years, I managed to replace the green card with a yellow one through a simple administrative procedure—though it took several years and was ultimately swept away with the wind.

We crossed the bridge, and as usual, we were ordered to disembark from the bus at the first inspection point, just a few meters from the iron gate. Then, we got off once more in front of the arrivals hall. As I was stepping down from the bus, carrying my Samsonite suitcase filled with my certificates, a soldier standing near the bus door gestured for me to follow him. Frankly, not knowing why I had been singled out in this way, I felt a surge of fear. I thought to myself, "I've been caught." But he simply pointed for me to climb down into a deep pit, where he instructed me to open my suitcase. I complied, showing him my certificates and some graduation photos from a distance. After a brief inspection, he let me climb out of the pit and rejoin the line of passengers to complete the baggage inspection, body search, and entry procedures. Everything went smoothly, and once the process was complete, I stepped out into the Jericho rest area, feeling as though a mountain had been lifted off my shoulders. I hurriedly left Jericho and made my way back to Kifl Haris.

THE WELL OF EXILE

A Bitter Homecoming

One might assume that joy and celebration would mark my return to Kifl Haris after such a long absence. Instead, it was a homecoming tinged with bitterness.

I had left Kuwait for the United States on January 1, 1980, with the goal of improving my qualifications to secure a better job and, consequently, a higher income in Kuwait, where I had worked as a bank employee for a year and a half after graduating from university. At the time, I believed my bank salary would never be enough to sustain me, so that's why I decided to pursue a postgraduate degree. I hoped it would open doors to better opportunities and income, assuming that Kuwait would remain stable as long as oil kept flowing. It never crossed my mind that the theory calculations did not match field calculations.

Now, in early 1984, I returned, emotionally and financially drained, approaching my thirties. I had missed the chance to obtain American citizenship, which in modern terms is akin to Ali Baba's magical incantation, "Open Sesame." The opportunity had been within my grasp, and perhaps the risks were far less for me than they were for others. But a lingering sense of patriotism held me back. I cast Aladdin's magical lamp into the well and ignored Ali Baba's enchanted spell, captivated instead by my degree and my national pride. I believed they combined the power of both magics and would unlock every closed door, fulfilling wishes even the mightiest of Solomon's jinn could not achieve.

On my way back, while renewing my travel permit—a requirement imposed by the occupation, valid for only six years—I was careful not to overstay by even a single day, as doing so would strip me of my right to reside in or claim identity from my birthplace. Determined not to lose my fundamental right to live in the land where I was born, I renewed the permit and prepared to set off for Kuwait to chase my dreams of employment and wealth. But during this return, I was blindsided by what seemed a trivial administrative procedure—superficially mundane but deeply painful in reality, with catastrophic consequences that would unfold over time.

It's true that the joy at my return was overwhelming. I was swept up in the euphoria of reuniting with my homeland, and I swelled with boundless happiness seeing my eighty-year-old father's eyes light up at the sight of me, dispelling the nightmare of Arif the Legend. His joy, usually concealed and hidden deep within his chest, was now unmistakable and unrestrained after all those years of absence. My aunt, the rest of my family, and the beloved people of my village shared in this happiness.

But the news from Kuwait struck me like a thunderbolt, shattering my peace. I discovered that the impossible had suddenly grown to fourfold, with the fourth being entry into Kuwait itself. I learned that the country had closed its doors following a brutal and sinful attack it had endured, and many things had fallen apart, including Souk Al-Manakh, which had plunged Kuwait into an unprecedented financial crisis. Securing a job there had become the most impossible of all impossibilities.

This news pushed me to hasten my journey to Kuwait, even though obtaining a visit card from there now felt like the devil dreaming of paradise. Finding a job seemed equally far-fetched, but my options were severely limited.

And here I am, unable to fully piece together the reel of memories from that brief visit to my hometown. Perhaps it was the flood of emotions—regret, sorrow, and the gnawing fear of a dark, uncertain fate that now hung in the balance—or worse, the looming threat of returning to the backbreaking labor of construction, building the soulless houses of others, work that could only be classified as grueling. Except for three moments, etched deeply into my memory, which I still remember with vivid clarity.

The first moment was when I knocked on the door of my sister Aziza's house. She was married and living in Nablus, and I had come to visit and greet her. When she opened the door, I greeted her with the traditional peasant greeting:

"Hello, sister! How are you?"

She stared at me and replied:

"This can't be you! You're speaking peasant Arabic too? As if you never traveled and lived among foreigners!"

The second moment was when I stood with my father in the town garage, waiting to return to the village after our visit to Nablus. We were waiting for the only public transport van at the time, which made shuttle trips to and from Kifl Haris. The driver was my father's friend, Abu-Arif, whose name was Saleh Al-Arif. He was the son of that legendary man who had traveled to America at the beginning of the 20th century, when his son Saleh was only forty days old—or so the story goes. As we waited for more passengers, Abu-Arif suddenly pointed toward the mountain and shouted:

"There he is, there he is!!"

At that moment, I was overcome with the same feeling I had when I jumped out of the large transport van in front of the Amman City Hall. My mind raced with countless possibilities, all tied to the electrified atmosphere of life under occupation. These thoughts, mixed with my swirling emotions, must have reflected on my face as confusion and fear. Then, Abu-Arif burst into heartfelt laughter at my expression, as I realized I had fallen victim to a prank—a hidden-camera-style stunt, orchestrated and executed by Abu-Arif, my father's friend, who was present for the entire scene.

When it finally dawned on me that the whole matter was nothing more than a heavy-handed joke—a comedic prank by my father's friend, who perhaps sensed my confusion and the deep-seated fear I was trying to hide—I felt a twinge of embarrassment. I smiled at him and said:

"May God forgive you, Abu Arif." I almost crossed the line and said to him, "Man, hasn't your father done enough for me?! Didn't I return to this country because of his sword, which remained unsheathed and hovering over my neck throughout my stay in the United States? And now you're here to mock me and embarrass me in front of my father and everyone else?!"

Instead, I simply smiled at him gently and repeated, "May God forgive you, man. You scared me to death."

The third incident was a visit I made to Bethlehem University, where I presented a copy of my master's thesis to the library and greeted my former professors, expressing my pride and gratitude for the new achievement that would not have been possible without what I had learned from them.

Truthfully, I found little interest, except from Dr. George Rashmawi, with whom I spoke at length. When I read him some of my poems written in English, he asked for a copy and told me he would include them in the Romantic literature curriculum he was teaching. I don't know if he actually did so or if it was merely a kind gesture on his part.

I left the university convinced that applying for a job there would be futile. Soon after, I departed the West Bank for Jordan, despite knowing how difficult it would be to obtain a visit visa to Kuwait. But I wanted to throw my full weight into my brother's court—he was striving to achieve what seemed beyond impossible. There, I sat waiting for God's help and the arrival of the visit visa to Kuwait.

Khalil Hamad

As If You, Khalil, Had Never Conquered

The most compelling reason for my departure from the United States was my desire to return to work in the richest country in the world—the only nation whose dinar was worth three dollars. These financial indicators were significant justifications for my decision to return to Kuwait, especially since the image of the economic boom that had flourished in Kuwait in the late 1970s, and which I had personally reaped some of its blessings through my job at Burgan Bank, still lingered in my mind. It was a vision that made every ambitious soul salivate at the thought of a respectable job and wealth.

However, upon arriving in Jordan, news began to trickle in about the situation in Kuwait. It soon became painfully clear that the reality there had completely changed. A series of events had swept through the country, and the wheel of time had turned, grinding away the blessings that once seemed universal and abundant. That wheel had shattered the economic prosperity and financial stability I had known, plunging the nation into a crisis that affected many aspects of life, particularly the laws governing expatriate workers. It was as if the old saying had come to life: "Live a rough life because favors do not last forever."

This news left me deeply unsettled. The harsh reality crushed my beautiful dream of returning to complete what I had started there, of making a significant leap forward with my additional university qualifications. But now, even the possibility of entering Kuwait felt uncertain, hanging by a thread.

For all these reasons, I hurried to leave the West Bank after fulfilling the purposes of my visit—chief among them, bringing joy to my father and delighting my own eyes by seeing him again, as well as renewing my permit to maintain my identity.

Although there was no guarantee that a visit visa to Kuwait would be issued, I left for Jordan to begin a waiting period for "Godot"—this Godot being the visit card that would grant me entry to Kuwait. Only then would another battle begin: the battle to secure a job and obtain a work permit, which I had heard had become nearly impossible.

During this period of instability, I stayed at my aunt Umm Rida's house in Awajan. Her home had always been a resting place for us during our travels, and she delighted in hosting us, growing upset if we even considered staying elsewhere.

This aunt was the only one in the village who had defied my father's orders not to relocate after the setback of 1967. She and her family paid dearly for that decision, enduring years of grinding poverty and hardship. Had it not been for her resilience, resourcefulness, and ability to navigate crises, the family's situation would have been far worse.

Despite the dire circumstances following the setback, she managed to buy land, build a house, and cultivate a garden— she was, after all, a lover of gardening.

During this stay, something in her garden caught my eye: the skeletal remains of an almond tree. It had withered completely, perhaps standing there in that pitiful state for years, untouched by human hands. At the time, I was in a state of waiting for "Godot," and grappling with a sense of emptiness. I convinced my aunt that the presence of such a barren, lifeless tree was casting a shadow of negativity over the family, hindering their progress. I even linked it to the delayed marriage of her son, Rida, who worked at the Arab Bank. I told them that cutting it down would turn their fortunes around for the better. With an axe in hand, I set about breaking and shattering the branches of that dead tree, uprooting it entirely. It felt as though I were Abraham himself, smashing idols and purging evil from the land.

And as if by magic—or the flutter of a butterfly's wings that sets off a chain reaction. The very next day, my cousin Rida told me he had seen a girl on the bus who had caught his eye. He thought she might be from our village. Based on his description, I suggested we visit a relative of ours, Mustafa Al-Sharif, who had good connections with the girl's family. They were neighbors in Jabal Faisal. We asked him to be our intermediary, explaining what we needed, and he agreed to help. Before we left, he invited us to share a meal of moghrabieh. This took place in May 1984. The wheels of fate began to turn, and after what seemed like the impossible, I received permission to re-enter Kuwait and left once again. Miraculously, the knot in my cousin Rida's life unraveled, and he married that very girl in July of the same year—just two months after I had cut down that withered almond tree.

I still believe that cutting down that tree stirred the stagnant waters, ushering in an atmosphere of joy, ease, delight, and positivity, replacing the gloom of sorrow, misery, despair, hopelessness, and negative thinking.

I remember how, the very next day, we planted a Kenya sapling in the no-man's-land between the railway track and the wall of my aunt's house, perched on the edge of the cliff just above the tracks. It stood opposite the site where the statue of the Arab Revolution would later be erected. This evergreen sapling we planted there was meant to bring an aura of happiness and positive energy, replacing the withered almond tree. I had insisted on tying my cousin Faraj with a rope that day, fearing he might fall while planting it. Faraj, born just days after the setback (the 1967 defeat), had been given his name in the hope that God might relieve people's sorrows. Over time, that sapling grew into a massive tree, becoming a landmark of the area.

We also cultivated a plot of land in front of my aunt Umm Majid's house, next to my aunt Umm Rida's home, planting it with various vegetables. Never in my life had I seen such an abundant harvest—both in quantity and quality. I don't believe the cutting of the withered almond tree was the sole reason for that abundant yield, but rather it was the high phosphate content in the soil, owing to its proximity to the Russeifa phosphate mines, that played a crucial role.

Amid this positivity, I visited the library at the University of Jordan and donated a copy of my master's thesis. A few days later, I received a letter from the library director thanking me for the gift. This gesture brought me immense joy, and I saw it as a sign of recognition for the effort and achievement I had poured into my work.

It seemed the butterfly effect of cutting down that almond tree extended far beyond its immediate surroundings with its positive influence. It even reached Kuwait, where my brother Mustafa, who held a prestigious position, managed to secure a visit permit for me. This ended a period of uncertainty and fear, as the door of hope, once closed, now swung open. I left Jordan in haste, chasing dreams of wealth that now seemed within reach.

But my stay there was short-lived. I soon realized I was like someone who "fasted and fasted for six full years, and then breaks his fast with an onion." Or, as the saying goes, "You returned as you went." In fact, the situation had become far worse than before.

Khalil Hamad

Breaching the Wall of Impossibility

My ability to reach Kuwait under such tense circumstances and through extraordinary measures felt like breaching a wall of impossibility—a fleeting glimmer of hope. Yet, the reality I encountered on the ground was far more challenging. Achieving another breakthrough, this time in securing my dream job, would require immense effort, luck, and hard work—perhaps even more than that.

Truthfully, I don't recall how I traveled, by what means, or even the circumstances of my arrival in Kuwait this time. This lapse in memory points to one of two things: either the event was so joyous that it blurred into a haze of happiness, or so tragic that my mind shielded itself from the pain. In either case, it hasn't clung to my memory, thanks to the blessing of forgetfulness that stepped in, protecting me from the weight of pain and the loss of balance.

What mattered was that I had arrived in Kuwait on an impossible mission. The first thing I remember doing was visiting Burgan Bank, where I had worked before leaving for America. I went to greet my former colleagues, to gauge their news, and to catch up on the latest news about the country, work, and residency permits. Naturally, my first attempt at finding a job was to return to my old position at the bank. However, I soon discovered that their internal policies prohibited rehiring anyone who had left the job through official channels—let alone someone like me, who had left without formally resigning. I had traveled under the assumption that I was on annual leave, holding onto my residency permit as a safety net in case the winds blow counter to what ships desire.

A friend from the auditing department quietly informed me that the bank had processed my end-of-service benefits, which were still sitting in my account despite my absence of nearly three and a half years. This was a pleasant surprise, providing me with some pocket money—a small treasure I hadn't anticipated, though modest in size.

The deafening surprise—the one that left me utterly stunned, stirring a storm of regret and sorrow within me, and making me wish my journey to America had been nothing but a dream, that I was still an employee at that bank—was this: I discovered that a colleague of mine, someone who had been hired at Burgan Bank around the same time as me, earning the same starting salary of 150 Kuwaiti dinars—a salary I had once thought insufficient even to buy bread—was a shambolic person. I had believed he knew nothing of value. One day, his Volkswagen Beetle—the tortoise car—nearly caught fire because he didn't know it needed oil. I had often mocked him, treating him with disdain for what I saw as hid shallow thinking and peculiar logic.

But here was the twist: during my absence, his salary had risen to 750 Kuwaiti dinars, not including bonuses. While I was busy writing about the book of the *Dead* and the secrets of their creativity, this man—the owner of the tortoise car— had married, fathered children, boys and girls, and now drove a car of the latest model. Meanwhile, I, the eloquent one, the man of degrees, owned nothing. I had no job, no wife, no children—they were but a distant dream—and I was threatened with deportation if my visit visa expired before I found work. The prospect seemed harder than the devil's dream of entering paradise. Even if I did find a job, it would be in the government sector, a soul-crushing position with a salary that, at best, wouldn't exceed 250 Kuwaiti dinars. There was no hope of it doubling, as it might in the private sector. This meant I was back to earning a salary that couldn't even buy bread—a salary I could have earned as a janitor in the same ministry, without even needing a birth certificate.

By the end of that day, I was certain that the doors to lucrative jobs in the private sector were firmly closed to someone like me, an outsider, due to the newly imposed emergency laws. My only option was the government sector. But I held on to a sliver of hope; after all, I held a master's degree in a rare specialization. I poured all my energy into finding a job, mobilizing every connection and friend I had. My efforts bore fruit when a glimmer of hope appeared: potential positions at prestigious institutions like the university. On a friend's advice, I applied to Kuwait University and was granted an interview with the selection committee. But the opportunity faltered for a reason I found utterly absurd. One of the committee members asked me, in English, for the title of my master's thesis. The entire interview had been conducted in English, so I replied: "It is entitled 'Creativity and the Search for Fulfillment.'"

He asked me, "'Entitled' or 'titled'?"

I didn't know the difference between the two—and honestly, I still don't, even though my specialization is English literature, not linguistics. At that moment, I felt the university job slip through my fingers like smoke. I didn't even bother to ask further or follow up with the university.

A few days later, a friend arranged an interview for me to work as a broadcaster at the BBC. I went to the embassy building, where someone recorded my voice to see if it was suitable for broadcasting—and, by God, I can't even begin to describe how awful my voice sounded terrible in that recording. I even told him, "My friend, I'm not cut out to be a broadcaster, but I'm an excellent translator if you need one." But he never called me back.

Days passed, and my visitor's permit was about to expire without any prospects of securing a job. The possibility of leaving Kuwait empty-handed grew more likely by the day. I realized that a government job—low-paying and far from the dream I had envisioned—was the only lifeline I could cling to at that moment. I hoped it might eventually become a bridge to the private sector, though nothing was guaranteed.

I surrendered to the bitter reality, disappointment, and betrayal, and turned my attention to securing a government job. As the saying goes, "When you have no choice, you make do with what you have." The options were either working as a teacher at the Ministry of Education or as a translator at the Ministry of Information. I leaned toward the Ministry of Information, where I was appointed as a translator at the Information Center in the old building.

I disappeared into the depths of that ministry for over a year. During that time, I received help from a colleague who had graduated from Bethlehem University. He worked as a recruitment manager at the SAS Hotel in Kuwait, and I took on a part-time evening job there to supplement my income. Then, another lifeline came from a fellow Bethlehem University graduate, who became the reason I was pulled out of the abyss of the ministry. She helped me move to a job in the private sector, allowing me to escape the shadows of that ministry and begin pursuing the dream I had put on hold.

Khalil Hamad

Lean Years

The period following my joining the staff of the Ministry of Information in Kuwait—marking the beginning of my second exile in that wealthy country—and my decision to leave the private sector there, turned out to be lean years for me. They were among the hardest phases of my life. I had fallen into a pit of disillusionment, consumed by feelings of depression, failure, regret, and an endless sense of sorrow. How could it be otherwise? I had traveled to the ends of the earth, relinquished what felt like a paradise, endured countless sleepless nights, and faced immense hardships to improve my professional, financial, and, by extension, living conditions. Yet, when the time came to reap the rewards of all that effort, I found myself in a worse position than before I had left. Despite the additional academic achievements I had earned, they seemed to hold no value or impact whatsoever.

My dreams of wealth and a prestigious career evaporated, and all my plans were postponed indefinitely. The income from my government job was meager, barely enough to cover basic necessities and rent.

And what a dwelling it was! I had imagined it would be akin to my dream home on the shores of the Pacific Ocean. But reality revealed the ugly face of bachelor housing in Kuwait, even if it was located on the most beautiful beach of the Arabian Gulf—the Salmiya beach. It reminded me of the saying, "Marble on the outside, filth on the inside."

On one hand, the bachelor accommodations were unbearably overcrowded due to skyrocketing rents. Spacious rooms were divided by temporary wooden partitions, non-soundproof and flimsy, to cram as many bachelors as

169

possible into each apartment. This came at the cost of cleanliness, privacy, peace, and peace of mind. In many cases, a sheep pen would have been less crowded than these bachelor quarters.

These accommodations resembled military barracks or ill-reputed refugee camps. The tenants had to coexist with people of various nationalities, each with different backgrounds, cultures, and temperaments. As for the health impact of these dwellings, words fail to describe it.

If the conditions of bachelor housing were difficult— extremely difficult—no matter how vividly I try to describe them, I might still fall short of conveying the full picture of the suffering bachelors endured at that time, then the way society viewed and treated bachelors was even harsher and crueler.

A bachelor found himself drowning in misery and gloom alongside his fellow bachelors, all of them grappling with feelings of loneliness, alienation, isolation, and disgust. Yet, as painful as these emotions were, they paled in comparison to the negativity inflicted by society's unjust treatment of bachelors.

I can say with certainty that bachelors in Kuwait in the mid-1980s were treated worse than the "untouchables" in India— the lowest caste in the four-tiered social hierarchy there. A bachelor in Kuwait wasn't just an outcast; he was often treated as a criminal or a dangerous contagion, which only deepened his misery and turned his life into an unbearable hell.

Landlords, for the most part, refused to rent apartments to young bachelors. It was common to see signs that read, "Families only," a phrase that implied bachelors and dogs were equally unwelcome.

Given the circumstances, I found myself escaping the bleakness of my bachelor's quarters during those lean years, returning only to sleep. At first, I bought fishing gear and spent long hours by the seashore, attempting to catch fish. But my true aim wasn't the fish—it was distraction, an escape from the crushing loneliness and the oppressive atmosphere of dreary bachelor's lodgings.

To make matters worse, my bed in the shared lodging was next to that of an Egyptian artist, a painter who, as I later learned, had once been a soldier in the 1973 war. He was often somber and withdrawn, as if he lived on another planet. I suspected he was haunted by nightmares and the lingering scars of post-traumatic stress, common among those who have endured the horrors of war.

One of the most striking signs of his melancholy was that he spoke only when spoken to, and his diet consisted solely of fava beans— morning, evening, and at any hour in between. I never once saw him eat anything else in the lodging.

Fishing by the sea wasn't my only escape. I also spent a great deal of time tutoring my brother's children in English. In those early days, I was so idealistic to the point of considering never marrying, content instead to dedicate myself to educating and supporting my nieces and nephews. But life had other plans, and events later would upend this way of thinking, and I'll share those stories in due time.

Having grown accustomed to regular exercise during my time in the United States, it had become an inseparable part of my being—a necessity I couldn't live without. Even in the early days of my arrival, amidst the frantic search for work, I never stopped walking. Despite the bouts of melancholy and despair that sometimes paralyzed me, making it hard to muster the energy for exercise, it remained another refuge from the bleakness of bachelorhood.

During this period, when feelings of hopelessness, desolation, loneliness, disappointment, and melancholy threatened to overwhelm me, a glimmer of hope emerged— a spark that revived my spirit and, even if only partially, lifted me out of the suffocating gloom I had sunk into. It made the harshness and pain of exile feel even more acute, but I will save the details of this turning point for the next chapter.

Khalil Hamad

A Glimmer of Hope

The reality I found myself in was unbearable. After returning to Kuwait for my second stint of exile, even the nature of my work at the Information Center in the Kuwaiti Ministry of Information required no real mental effort. There was no clear plan or direction for the center where I had been assigned, as if we were running in circles—a futile, endless loop. Our tasks involved translating articles from foreign magazines and newspapers, focusing on news relevant to Kuwait. Yet, the center lacked a hands-on manager. Instead, we were a loose group of employees, free to do as we pleased during the short working hours. Government offices and ministries closed by 2:00 PM at the latest, operating within a soul-crushing routine that demanded neither brains nor expertise.

Amid this suffocating darkness and emptiness, my friend and colleague at the Information Center, Mohammed Kameel, believed I hadn't fully captured the depth of our predicament. He insisted there was much more to say about the injustices faced by expatriates—like being denied a driver's license despite the brutal summer heat, which made owning a car not a luxury but a necessity. He reminded me of the torment we endured together, waiting for public buses in unbearable temperatures to take us back to our homes.

It was in the midst of this bleak atmosphere that I received word from a colleague, Saad Eldin Shehadeh, a graduate of Bethlehem University. He was working as the personnel manager at the SAS-Kuwait Hotel, a foreign-managed establishment located directly on the beach in the Salmiya district.

I saw this as an opportunity to leverage my acquaintance with him and secure a part-time evening job at the hotel. Not only would it supplement my income, but it would also fill the void of idle time, provide valuable experience in the hospitality industry, and—most importantly—allow me to save on food costs by eating meals at the hotel. This would spare me the ordeal of cooking in the filthy kitchen of my bachelor's apartment, a place I had never dared to enter.

And so, I turned to my colleague, Saad Eldin Shehadeh, and asked if he could help me find a part-time job at the hotel. Without hesitation, he appointed me to the sales department under the hotel's reception management. My primary task was to type correspondence for the hotel's foreign clients using a telex machine—a relic of a time before the internet and social media, which had yet to emerge in the mid-1980s. This part-time job became a glimmer of genuine hope, a window out of the dark well of despair I had been trapped in. Working there presented a positive challenge, a stark contrast to the monotonous routine of my ministry job. Not only did it boost my monthly income, but it also solved a host of personal problems. It pulled me out of the suffocating atmosphere of regret and melancholy, breathing life back into my spirit.

I quickly began to rely on the lavish free meals the hotel provided for its staff. We could choose whatever we craved from the menu, and I often gravitated toward the Chinese dishes prepared right before my eyes by the Nepalese chef. I frequently indulged in calamari, shrimp, and an array of fish dishes, all of which were abundant in the Arabian Gulf.

As for the job itself, it taught me the fundamentals of public relations and customer service. The management paid attention to the smallest details, even forbidding us from dousing ourselves in cheap perfumes or any unpleasant odors. They posted a sign in the changing room that read: "No bad odors."

I also learned typing and became both fast and accurate, though I could never match the lightning speed of my Indian colleague in the department. Later, I would share a wild adventure with him involving an American client—a near-death experience in the Arabian Gulf that I'll recount in detail later.

During that job, we dealt with all kinds of people, each with their own temperaments and moods, all under the golden rule that "the customer is always right." One particular Swiss customer posed a significant challenge for us. No matter how meticulous or diligent we were, he was never satisfied with our work or service unless the reception manager personally reviewed it. Often, he would raise a fuss over the smallest details—like noticing that the period at the end of a line in his Telex message to his company in Switzerland was two spaces instead of one from the last word.

Once, Mr. Ackermann, the reception manager at the SAS-Kuwait Hotel, gathered us for a training session. He explained the different types of customers, gave examples of each, and outlined how to handle each one.

He told us that customers could be divided into four categories. The first category was the perfectionists—people who would express dissatisfaction and frustration over the tiniest issues and often escalate their complaints to management. He pointed to that Swiss customer as a prime example of this demanding and nitpicking type.

On the opposite end of the spectrum was the simple, laid-back, and somewhat disheveled type. These customers often carried their own luggage in their hands. They might walk into the hotel in shabby clothes, their requests always minimal and straightforward. Treating them with the same formality as a perfectionist could make them uncomfortable. Mr. Ackermann pointed to an Italian customer as an example—a man who frequently entered the hotel with his shirt untucked, no tie, and a bag slung over his shoulder.

There was also a category that fell somewhere between the perfectionist and the casual, easygoing types. I found this classification incredibly useful in dealing with customers, as it helped me better understand customer personalities and tailor my approach to win their satisfaction.

One day, a large, burly American customer came to us. We exchanged a few words, and it turned out he was a consultant for a company. He invited me and my Indian colleague, Santan, to join him on a sailing trip aboard his wind yacht. It sounded exciting and fun, so we agreed. We ended up accompanying him on that trip, which started wonderfully, but it nearly ended in disaster.

I'll share the details of that adventurous journey, God willing, along with the immense struggle I endured to obtain my driver's license.

Khalil Hamad

Like Hell Itself

No one can truly grasp the importance of owning a car in Kuwait unless they have lived there and experienced firsthand the brutal weather conditions that sweep across this small emirate, especially during the summer months. The climate is unpredictable and unforgiving. At times, sandstorms sweep across the country, raging for days or even months on end, creating a phenomenon known locally as "Al-Tooz." This is a dense haze of fine sand that engulfs the horizon, veils out the sun and erases the blue from the sky. In its place, a suffocating yellow—the color of death—dominates every direction, sometimes leading to deadly cases of suffocation.

At other times, the temperature soars, surpassing 50 degrees Celsius in the shade and reaching up to 70 degrees in exposed areas. Living without air conditioning becomes a futile attempt at survival.

There were moments when the steering wheel of my car burned so intensely that I could barely keep my hands steady on it. Without the car's air conditioning, driving would have felt like descending into the depths of hell itself.

Occasionally, Al-Tooz and the scorching heat collide, creating a true vision of hell itself. Escape and seclusion, even into the depths of a well, seemed like the only refuge.

For all these reasons, a car in Kuwait is as essential as water and air. My story of obtaining a driver's license there feels like a tale straight out of One Thousand and One Nights. For an expatriate, getting a license after Kuwait entered its era of crises became more arduous than earning a doctorate—a fact attested to by many who endured this ordeal.

And this is my story...

When I first arrived in Kuwait as an expatriate in mid-1978, the thought of obtaining a driver's license never even crossed my mind. My life was marked by instability, plans for graduate studies abroad, poverty, meager income, and the stringent laws that made it nearly impossible for an expatriate to secure a license.

When I returned as an expatriate for the second time in mid-1984, obtaining a driver's license topped my list of priorities—especially since I had already acquired a license in California and driven there for over two years. It's well-known that most countries readily exchange an American driver's license for a local one without any hurdles. However, in Kuwait, I discovered that the law did not recognize an American license and required expatriates to take—and pass—a local driving test. According to the law, or perhaps specific regulations for foreign residents—anyone applying for a driver's license had to complete practical training at a registered and officially recognized driving school.

On top of that, applicants were required to complete thirty hours of training before being allowed to take the driving test. And so, I found myself in exactly that situation. I arranged lessons with a Palestinian driving instructor, who I believe was from Dayr Dibwan or a nearby village, even though I had already passed the driving test in the United States and had driven there, even on crowded highways.

Naturally, I opted to go for an automatic car license in Kuwait. Such cars were as common there as grains of sand, and they were much easier to handle. In a flat, desert country like Kuwait—spread out like the palm of a hand—there was no need for a manual transmission car, with its endless gear-shifting. More importantly, avoiding the alternative system—the manual transmission—meant sidestepping the hefty costs and the added difficulty of passing the driving test.

Despite the law prohibiting expatriates from obtaining a driver's license during that critical period following the series of crises that had struck the country since 1982, it did allow those with foreign licenses to apply for a local one. However, behind the scenes, people whispered that you wouldn't get the license without connections. End of story.

People joked about the situation, trading sarcastic quips and swapping stories, rumors, and tall tales. One such story was that if the instructor asked you who had the right of way at a roundabout, you had to answer, "The Kuwaiti," without hesitation—whether the Kuwaiti was descending from the sky or emerging from the ground. After my first lesson, the instructor seemed to think I didn't need much training. Instead, he focused on reminding me of traffic signals and the optimal way to behave to pass the driving test. Looking back, I suspect he was withholding some crucial information from me.

I completed the required hours of driving lessons, though it felt like a waste of both time and money to me. True to form, the instructor arranged the driving test according to protocol, though I suspect he already knew the outcome would be failure, based on his experience and familiarity with how things worked in that system. And indeed, that's exactly what happened, forcing me to return for yet another round of training, with the same number of hours.

This process repeated itself perhaps two or three times. Each time, I went back for more lessons, and each time, the instructor swore that I was a better driver than he was. But, as he reminded me, the final decision lay with the traffic department.

It never crossed my mind that failing foreign applicants might have been a deliberate ritual, a premeditated strategy to control the number of expatriates permitted to drive.

Each driving lesson cost ten Kuwaiti dinars, and by the time I finally passed the test, I had spent nearly a thousand dinars on training fees alone—not to mention the additional costs of lost time, the test fees, and the toll it took on my morale. What made it worse was that no one had advised me to stop wasting my time and energy on what was clearly a foregone conclusion, nor had anyone suggested I seek a connection to ease the process.

It wasn't until after repeated failures, and the near-shattering of my self-confidence, that I finally sought help. I had begun to feel utterly incapable, even defeated, by what should have been a simple driving test. If I hadn't already passed a driving test on my first attempt in the United States, my self-esteem would have completely crumbled.

After spending all that money, someone finally pointed me to a dark-skinned man—perhaps a cook or a security guard for some important figure—who handed me a sealed white envelope. He instructed me not to open it and sent me to a specific individual. There, I stood before him like a beggar pleading for salvation. And indeed, the envelope worked like a charm, breaking the spell that had doomed me to failure.

Finally, thanks to the connection of that kind, dark-skinned man, I obtained my driver's license. I couldn't help but wish I had gone to him earlier, sparing myself the endless loops of failure, the financial losses, and the wasted time, not to mention the negative impact that repeated failure had on my sense of self-worth. But as the saying goes, "One man's trash is another man's treasure," or, as another proverb puts it, "God breaks a camel's back to feed an ant." Perhaps my struggles were tied to the driving instructor's livelihood.

When that bitter ordeal of obtaining a driver's license finally came to an end, it felt as though I had earned a PhD. I was now qualified to live with dignity.

As soon as I got the license, I bought a white Japanese Daihatsu—a real car this time, not like the junk car I had driven in San Diego.

THE WELL OF EXILE

Come back, O sea—bring them home, O sea

The part-time evening job at the SAS-Kuwait Hotel marked a turning point for me. It lifted my spirits, brought joy to my heart, and freed me from the drudgery of cooking and daily chores, even though it fell short of my ambitions—both in terms of income and the nature of the work itself.

Yet, the atmosphere of the hotel, buzzing like a beehive, the sense of belonging to a work family in that beautiful seaside building, and the opportunity to interact with a wide array of foreign businessmen—all of this was enough to pull me out of the well of despair I had fallen into after a series of crushing events. It began with my near-forced return from the land of Uncle Sam, followed by a cascade of disappointments, losses, and hardships that nearly drove me to the edge. Then came the reluctant acceptance of a lackluster government job, both in mundane nature and meager income, a consequence of the emergency laws in place at the time. Those laws stifled my dreams of a prestigious career and achieving wealth, even if only temporarily.

The truth is, the difference between the atmosphere of my morning government job and the evening work in the hotel's service sector was, for me, like the difference between stagnant water and a flowing river—or between the earth and the stars.

What added to the beauty of the hotel's environment and further lifted my morale was its location on the shores of the Arabian Gulf in the picturesque Salmiya district. The hotel had several recreational and tourist facilities that we were allowed to use outside working hours, including a soft, clean sandy beach free of jagged rocks, perfect for swimming in the Gulf waters—a stark contrast to the rough, rocky, and dangerous public beaches.

The hotel had also repurposed an old fishing vessel, anchored at its waterfront, into a restaurant serving luxurious seafood meals. That ship become a window into an important part of Kuwait's pre-oil boom history, when the society revolved around fishing and pearl diving.

Those fishing expeditions and long, perilous voyages across the Arabian Gulf gave rise to folk rituals. As the day of the ships' return approached, women would gather on the shore to perform celebratory rites, expressing their longing for their husbands and sons, the sailors. They would chant traditional songs, including this one, pleading with the sea to bring their loved ones back safely and victoriously:

Turn back, O sea, turn back, O sea,
Four have passed, and the fifth... the fifth has come.
Four have passed, and the fifth month,
Bring them back, bring them back.
Turn back, O sea, turn back, O sea,
Do you not fear God, O sea?
Do you not fear God, O sea?
O sea, bring them back,
O sea, bring them back.
And turn back, O sea, turn back, O sea.

So, when that American client—a consultant for one of the companies who spent much of his free time at sea after work and holidays—offered to join him on a sailing trip from the SAS Hotel area to the nearby island of Failaka, I didn't hesitate to agree, despite sensing the journey might be risky. But the moment I found myself on the boat, swaying violently amidst the waves, I realized I had gravely misjudged the situation. I hadn't fully grasped the peril of being on a sailboat made of a few wooden planks, ropes, and no solid base—no seats to sit on, just a fragile structure pulled by the wind and pushed wherever it pleased, guided only by the sail.

My Indian colleague, San Tan, also agreed to join the adventure, and together we met the adventurous American sailor at the appointed time. The first thing he did was explain our tasks before setting sail, while we were still on the sandy beach. The instructions were simple: tighten the sail ropes to steer the boat according to the captain's commands—nothing more.

But once we ventured onto the waves, it became clear that this was no simple or safe endeavor. It demanded more than mere effort—it called for an immense courage, skill, strength, balance, agility, experience, and quick thinking.

I soon realized that San Tan and I had been too hasty in agreeing to this trip. Our decision was impulsive, based on a misguided assumption that we'd be sitting on chairs, perhaps even fishing, imagining the American's boat to be a proper vessel like the fishing boats converted into restaurants near the hotel. Instead, we discovered there was no space on the sailboat except for a narrow spot to place our feet. It wasn't even a boat in the traditional sense—just a collection of planks assembled in a way that allowed a sail to be attached, moving those planks in the direction of the wind.

As we took our positions on the sailboat, the weather was beautiful—the sky a clear blue, the sea calm, and the waves gentle. Despite the shock of the trip's nature, the boat's rudimentary design, and the growing fear of what might go wrong, I tried to convince myself that this would be a thrilling adventure worth experiencing.

Then came the moment of truth. The burly American gradually raised the sail, and the boat began to glide slowly into the water, then picked up speed, racing with the wind toward Failaka Island in the open sea. He issued instructions every minute, directing San Tan and me on what to do. We struggled to carry out our tasks, which felt urgent and critical, with no room for error.

Just a few miles into the sea—a distance we covered in mere minutes—my Indian companion began to show signs of seasickness. He gradually deteriorated, losing control of his digestive system and vomiting overboard. The situation escalated from dangerous to downright dire—and frankly, disgusting.

Once that happened, San Tan became a limp rag, leaving the captain and me stranded in the depths of the sea to manage the boat with half our workforce gone. Suddenly, I had to perform not only my tasks but also San Tan's, all while keeping an eye on him to ensure he didn't fall overboard as he clung desperately to the side of the boat.

The captain moved about the boat like a monkey swinging through tree branches, tugging at one rope, then another, steering the vessel toward the island. He barked orders at me to assist with tasks he couldn't manage alone, which I carried out with one eye on my duties and the other fixed on my companion, San Tan.

The problem was, despite San Tan being incapacitated by seasickness, the captain continued to sail farther from the shore. I thought we ought to turn back immediately, but he pressed on, guiding the boat deeper and deeper into the open sea, closer to Failaka Island.

Then, in an instant, the weather turned a hundred and eighty degrees. The blue sky vanished, swallowed by a swirling blend of gray clouds and desert sand carried by the wind. The waves grew fiercer, and I waited anxiously for the captain to decide to return.

Finally, he performed a deft maneuver, flipping the sail's direction, and we began our journey back to shore. I was gripped by genuine terror, imagining all the worst possibilities, but I held my ground—steadfast, resolute, and composed. I followed every instruction to the letter, doubling my efforts, all while keeping a watchful eye on poor San Tan, poor and trembling, clutching the edge of the boat with both hands, utterly helpless.

I still don't understand how a sailboat could move in two opposing directions without the wind changing course. It remains a mystery that baffles me to this day. But I never asked about it, for I had already vowed never to set foot on a sailboat again.

Our struggle against the waves raged on—just me and the American captain. The boat was being driven toward the shore by the relentless force of the wind, yet still under the captain's steady control. His mind remained sharp, alert, carefully adjusting our course as the sky grew heavy with Tooz—those dense, foreboding clouds—warning of an approaching storm.

The captain single-handedly took on most of the work required to steer the boat and keep it balanced. He didn't utter a word, nor did his face betray even a hint of fear or apprehension, despite the sudden and violent shift in the weather. Nor did he seem fazed by the Indian's condition, who had now collapsed into a lifeless heap, becoming a burden rather than the helping hand we so desperately needed.

It became clear that this captain, who stood like one of Sparta's towering warriors, possessed a deep expertise in sailing. Perhaps he had faced far worse situations in the past, which explained his calm, unshakable composure and ironclad nerves.

In the end, we made it safely to shore, thanks be to God. What began as a thrilling adventure had turned into a harrowing ordeal, etching itself into the pages of my memory as an unforgettable experience. As my feet touched the sand, I was reminded of the women who would go to the sea, pleading with them to return their loved ones, chanting: "Bring them back, O sea! Turn back, O sea!"

Yes, that sea voyage, which we had embarked upon for adventure, pleasure, and relaxation, had turned into a terrifying nightmare in the open waters. It nearly ended in disaster, and to this day, I still find myself murmuring, "Turn back, O sea."

The book of memories is still filled with monumental events, so stay tuned for the next chapter from The Well of Exile.

THE WELL OF EXILE

Life Narrowed When It Entangled Her Rings

And so, my days settled into a monotonous routine. Each morning, I dragged myself reluctantly to my job at the ministry, housed in an old red-brick building that belonged to the Ministry of Information. The building stood near the heart of Kuwait City, and within its walls, alongside the Information Center, was the headquarters of *Al-Arabi* magazine—a prestigious cultural publication that we, as children, had eagerly competed to get our hands on. And now, here I was, in the very place where that magazine was published, the same magazine that, in my childhood, had felt like the embodiment of a beautiful dream.

The building also housed a library managed by a blind Kuwaiti writer named Abd Al-Razzaq Al-Basier. I visited the library often, and it was there that I got to know Al-Basier closely. He was assisted by a man from the Salama family, hailing from Biddya—a village near my own hometown, Kifl Haris. Over time, through these visits, I began to see Al-Basier as a living embodiment of Alfred Adler's psychological theory of compensation. Despite losing his sight at a young age, he had become a brilliant and widely cultured writer, deeply knowledgeable about literature and its history.

The ministry also had a public relations department, which I became aware of when the Ministry of Information hosted the famous actor Duraid Lahham, known for his iconic role as Ghwar al-Tousha. I met him in person in the corridors of the PR department, surrounded by a crowd of employees. This was during the peak of his fame, following the success of his plays like *October Village* and *Kasak Ya Watan*, as well as numerous other artistic and theatrical works with a nationalistic bent. I remember him wearing his signature black trousers and red fez, embodying the character as Ghwar al-Tousha, the beloved artist who had captured the hearts of the people.

Despite the passage of time, my job at the ministry remained dull and unfulfilling. I never felt like I was contributing anything meaningful or worthwhile. My colleagues and I in the Information Center would sit together in a single room, like students in a classroom or participants in a roundtable discussion. Most of the time, we passed the hours engaged in cultural and philosophical debates, killing time until the clock struck the hour of our release, allowing us to escape the bleak, autumnal atmosphere that hung over the place.

The only exceptional event I experienced during my time at the center was joining my colleagues in a protest movement against the consultant tasked with establishing the center. The aim was to improve the work environment, develop its tools, and define its direction and goals. However, the protest achieved little beyond harming the consultant, who, as far as I know, was forced to resign after being made the scapegoat for the center's lack of direction. I recount this incident here with regret, ashamed of my participation in what was ultimately a futile endeavor—one that, within the existing system, could only result in the downfall of that consultant.

When my morning shift at the ministry ended, I would hurry to my second job at the SAS Hotel in Kuwait after a brief rest. This evening job transported me to a world entirely different from the monotonous atmosphere of my mornings. It was a lively, bustling place filled with constant motion and people. The two jobs were like night and day, autumn and spring. In this evening role, I felt more like myself, able to fully stretch my capabilities and potential. It filled me with a sense of fulfillment, and I carried out my duties with enthusiasm, vigor, and even joy, which helped forget some of the accumulated disappointments weighing on me.

Though my time at the evening job was fulfilling and allowed me to experience a five-star lifestyle, where I met many foreigners who frequented the hotel and learned a great deal about the intricacies of public relations, sales, and hospitality, it was rewarding in many ways. Yet, a smoldering fire burned beneath the surface of my chest fueled by my meager income, the lack of prospects, and a profound sense of loss for what I had left behind. Adding to this were the social pressures from acquaintances and friends, who constantly reminded me and blamed me for what they saw as a lost paradise—a paradise I had willingly abandoned in my pursuit of the illusion of wealth in an oil-rich nation, choosing an Arab exile over the foreign exile I had experienced in the United States.

Alongside this burning fire in my heart was a fierce internal struggle, filled with pain, regret, and turmoil. I found myself mourning the comfortable life I had once lived in the land of Uncle Sam, lamenting the opportunities I had squandered there and lost forever upon my return—a decision I had believed at the time to be the right one. I had left it all behind so easily, for reasons that now, with the passage of time, seemed flimsy and misguided. I had returned to a country floating on a sea of oil, a place where every indicator suggested it was the richest spot on earth, dreaming of prestigious jobs and wealth.

But after enduring hardship, anticipation, and the struggle to settle in, I found myself in a barren, desolate desert—a country far removed from the one I had left in the early 1980s to pursue my studies. The circumstances here were starkly different, drying up my dreams and shattering my ambitions. I was living a life without horizons, drowning in regret and sorrow, my hope for change in the foreseeable future all but extinguished. The days raced by, and despite my advancing age, marriage remained a distant dream, elusive and out of reach.

Amid this inner turmoil, this raging fire within me, and despite losing hope of making a leap that could change my bitter, hellish reality, the thought of returning to the land of Uncle Sam crossed my mind. Without consulting anyone or revealing my intentions, I sought an escape from the deep well I found myself in, a well with no visible way out. I wrote to the University of San Diego, requesting a student acceptance letter (I-20) to resume my master's degree in media studies—a program I had abandoned in an unceremonious manner, convinced I would never return to it or need it again.

Truth be told, I had no intention of going back to study. Instead, my thoughts were focused on returning to work as a masseur or any job that would provide a decent income and offer me a dignified human life. Here, I was trapped in a life of exile, misery, and poverty—imposed by the harsh realities of security and the ravages of a brutal Gulf War that cast its shadow over every aspect of life. There, in the land of the greenback, lay the promise of alienation and exile, yes, but also greater opportunities for wealth and stability.

It wasn't long before I received a response—a rejection and apology from the University of San Diego, with no explanation given. This rejection was another blow, slamming shut the doors to the United States and crushing my hopes of escaping this wretched, hopeless, miserable existence. The one window of hope I had secretly kept open, the one I had bet on, was now firmly shut. The world seemed to close in on me, and the cycle of despair tightened its grip. I withdrew into myself under the weight of this new, harsh blow, keeping the rejection to myself. I sank deeper into the well of depression and estrangement, surrendering to the painful, bitter reality that had imposed itself on me.

I didn't know what would become of me, but as they say, "A glimmer of light never fully disappears, no matter how intense the darkness." It wasn't long before a phone call pulled me out of the anguish, depression, misery, and despair I had been drowning in. Wait, and you'll learn the secret of that call—how it rescued me from the depths of that deep well.

Khalil Hamad

After Black Clouds, Clear Weather

Returning to the United States represented my only flicker of hope. The economic and, consequently, the job market had deteriorated after the ominous bombings that shook Kuwait in the early 1980s, just before my return. Those events led to regulatory laws that tightened the noose around job seekers, making opportunities scarce. To make matters worse, the University of San Diego, where I had earned my master's degree in English Literature, refused to issue a new acceptance letter I-20 for a program in media studies, that door slammed shut. I was plunged into despair, regret, and a profound sense of hopelessness.

Despite working two jobs—one in the morning and another in the evening—I was far from satisfied with how my life had turned out. My master's degree had brought me no tangible benefits, neither improving my professional standing nor boosting my income. There were moments when I drowned in regret and sorrow for leaving my bank job in Kuwait, all in pursuit of a higher degree from America. I had believed it would be my salvation from poverty, a key to wider doors and better opportunities. But the developments in that region had imposed a new reality—one that was shocking and painful.

In the shadow of this bleak and bitter reality, I often blamed myself for lacking the courage, during my time in the United States, to venture into the twisted paths others had taken to obtain a Green Card. Time had proven that a Green Card was more valuable than the highest academic degrees. It was the master key to borders, airports, and closed doors—the ultimate qualification for a rewarding job. It was, in essence, the modern-day "Open Sesame" to Ali Baba's cave.

193

Amidst the misery, despair, and fading hope for change, I received a phone call from a man named Moeen Khoury. He was the owner of a well-known advertising company called Impact and Echo, which provided services to Yousef Ahmed Al-Ghanim Company

Yousef Ahmed Al-Ghanim Company was one of the largest companies in Kuwait at the time, if not the largest. It operated in multiple sectors: besides being the dealer for luxury American cars, it had divisions for shipping, travel agency, car parts, garage services, and electrical appliance sales. It also held agencies for several major international companies.

It turned out that the company in question had asked Mr. Moeen Khoury to help recruit a translator to replace their current one, who had decided to resign and move to Jordan. The outgoing translator was facing difficulties in bringing his only son, who had traveled there to study, back to Kuwait. Due to sudden changes in residency laws, he had lost his right to stay in Kuwait as a dependent, as he personally explained to me when I asked him why he wanted to leave the job.

Mr. Moeen Khoury then reached out to a former colleague of mine from Bethlehem University, a woman named Hanan Demo, who worked as a translator at a bank there. She recommended me for the position, and based on her endorsement, he contacted me and offered me the job at Al-Ghanim Company.

Despite the staggering surprise of such a grand offer, and the fears that arose in me about transitioning to a role of that magnitude in a prestigious, multifaceted company—the largest in the market—I expressed tentative agreement after he assured me that transferring my residency would not be an issue, given the company's esteemed standing. The offer represented a glimmer of hope, a chance to escape my current situation and, for the first time, step onto the right career path I had always dreamed of—one where I could utilize my qualifications, improve my income, and finally find my footing. Before the call ended, I secured an interview appointment with the company's officials.

The leap from my barely noticeable position at the Ministry of Information's data center to working for the largest company in the market, with no real commercial experience in translation and at such a high level, felt like climbing from the depths to the summit. It was an adventure without limits, but it also filled me with dread, anxiety, and hesitation. I wasn't sure I was capable of handling such a daunting task, which, at first glance, seemed impossible. I would be the sole translator, with no one to fall back on or share the responsibility. This meant I would have to handle translation, proofreading, typing, and ensuring the accuracy of texts—whether legal, technical, or otherwise—with no room for error in a company of such stature and scale.

Later, it became clear that my apprehension was largely justified. I learned that the bulk of my work would involve highly precise legal translations, to and from English, for the company's legal department. This department was staffed by a team of seasoned, professional lawyers, headed by my point of contact, the Lebanese attorney Mr. Ramzi Samaaha. I found myself in a quandary—torn between accepting or declining the offer, as the job stirred deep fears and anxieties within me. As the interview date approached, and on my way there, I decided to seek advice from my older brother, Mustafa Hamad, who worked as the manager of Al-Watan Printing Press, located near the Al-Ghanim company headquarters. I went to see him, and while waiting for him to finish his tasks at the press, an Egyptian employee sitting at the reception counter noticed my unease. He asked why I seemed so anxious and troubled. I explained the situation, sharing my fears about accepting the new job offer.

The young man broke into a wide, almost mocking grin and asked, "Haven't you heard what the poet said?"

"What did the poet say?" I asked, intrigued.

He replied:

The daring soul reaps joy, while the cautious one dies of regret.

Take the leap, my friend, and do not hesitate.

Truth be told, his words struck me like a thunderclap, tipping the scales in favor of accepting the offer. His profound advice cut through all my hesitation, and I made up my mind, setting aside all thoughts of consequences and possibilities. Armed with that earth-shattering advice, I resolved to move forward, no longer needing further consultation or reassurance.

And so, I walked into the interview with newfound courage and determination.

Fate smiled upon me, and I found myself on the brink of climbing out of the deep well I had been trapped in. Indeed, I secured the prestigious position without facing any significant competition from other candidates or hardship.

However, my joy was short-lived. I soon discovered the company's hidden motives for replacing the resident translator and the true nature of the offer they had presented to me.

Stay tuned to uncover the secrets that soured my happiness and dashed my high expectations.

Khalil Hamad

Oh, Joy Unfulfilled!

And so, I plunged headlong into the adventure, pushing aside the discouraging thoughts of the challenges that came with transitioning to a highly demanding job—far beyond what I had been doing. I resisted the fears that typically accompany the desire for change, fueled by a sudden surge of courage that came from the advice of that young Egyptian man and the stirring words of the poet, which seemed to awaken the reserves of bravery hidden in my heart. I walked on foot to the headquarters of Yusuf Ahmed Al-Ghanim Company, located very close to the *Elwatan* Newspaper office where I was at that moment, just a kilometer away.

At the reception of Yusuf Ahmed Al-Ghanim Company, I was directed to the Administrative Affairs Department, where I learned that the Translation Division operated under its umbrella. There, I met the assistant manager of the department, a handsome, tall, and slender Lebanese man from the Saadeh family. Next, I was introduced to the resident translator, who was still at his post, and finally, for a few minutes, I met the Kuwaiti department manager himself, Mr. Sorour Al-Samarrai. Everything went smoothly.

I must have been convincing in presenting my qualifications, experience, and eloquence during the interview, for I left the department with an offer from Mr. Saadeh, the assistant manager. The salary was set at 450 Kuwaiti dinars, with no additional incentives. While this amount was more than what I earned combined from my morning job at the ministry and my evening job at the hotel, it still fell short of what one might expect from a major company.

Nevertheless, I was thrilled by the offer and what the new position represented at one of the largest companies operating in the Arabian Gulf. I was overwhelmed with joy at the prospect of its symbolic value, along with the better financial return compared to what I had been earning.

Despite my underlying fears, I agreed with the management to start immediately with a training period under the resident translator, Abu Zuhair, who would gradually transfer his responsibilities to me.

And that's exactly what happened. Within a few days, the ice between me and Abu Zuhair had broken. From the moment I joined the company with the aim of replacing him in his role, I could see he was in a state of deep distress. It's not easy for someone to leave a job where they've spent the prime of their youth, a job that provided a comfortable income and filled their life with purpose, only to be asked to train their replacement. Yet, despite the catastrophic emotional toll he couldn't hide, I soon managed to win his goodwill. Bonds of friendship began to form between us, and he opened his heart to me about the real reasons driving his resignation and departure from such a lucrative position, despite the heavy losses he would incur.

He told me he had an only son who had traveled to Jordan to study at one of its universities. Though his son had graduated, he was unable to bring him back to Kuwait due to newly implemented residency laws that had come into effect during his son's absence for studies. He explained that if he were to leave, his loss wouldn't be limited to his personal income; he would also have to take his daughters with him, who were working in well-paying jobs.

When I inquired about his salary, he told me he earned a base pay of 1,400 Kuwaiti dinars, along with a set of generous incentives, including housing provided by the company, a car with maintenance and fuel covered, and annual flight tickets for him and his family to any destination of their choice. These benefits had been part of his package throughout his years at the company.

Then came the deafening shock. It became painfully clear that I had been grossly shortchanged by the company's offer. The injustice wasn't just in the meager salary compared to what the outgoing translator—whose responsibilities I was to take over—had been earning. It was also in the cancellation of numerous other incentives, which together amounted to more than his salary. But that wasn't all. My presence would save the company the wages of the secretaries the translator, Abu Zuhair, had needed to type up his translations, as he didn't know how to type. I, on the other hand, would work alone, typing my translations directly on the computer, eliminating the need for the services of four secretaries.

It became glaringly clear to me that the departure of that poor, sorrowful man wasn't solely due to his inability to secure a residency permit for his only son. The company could have easily arranged such a permit if they had wanted to—or even hired him despite the complexities of the residency system. After all, they had managed to transfer me from a government job to the private sector, something that was technically prohibited under the prevailing laws. No, the truth was far more calculated. There was more to the story than met the eye. The real, unspoken reason for his departure was the company's desire to cut costs. Here I was, about to take on his entire workload, as well as the work of his four secretaries, who had manually typed up his translations. I would do it all using modern tools that saved time and money—all for a fraction of what the company had been spending.

Despite this bitter truth, I swallowed my anger and the overwhelming sense of profound injustice. I threw myself into my work, determined to make the most of his presence during this transitional period, clinging to the hope that circumstances might change and my income from this job—which I had once considered a dream, as any ambitious translator might—would improve. To me, it represented a qualitative leap from the professional instability I had endured.

To his credit, that man served me with unexpected loyalty, despite his own wretched state of mind. He shared with me many of the techniques, tools, and secrets of translation, and provided me with previous translations to use as models. As soon as his notice period ended, he left the job—and perhaps Kuwait entirely—with a heart full of sorrow, etched visibly on his face. I never saw him again after that, but if our paths crossed, I would have stood before him with the utmost reverence.

And so, I officially began my first real job, after all those years of education, training, and working in what I had always considered insignificant roles.

Khalil Hamad

Fat Years

The first month of my employment at the company came to an end. I had greatly benefited from the guidance of the translator who left at the conclusion of his notice period. Now, I was the only human in the translation department, accompanied solely by a computer. Work in the department continued as usual, with no one noticing any real change in the quality of output—except that translations now emerged from the computer fully prepared, eliminating the need for secretarial services, proofreading, and reprinting. This saved a great deal of time and reduced expenses.

There's no doubt that those early days, even the first few months, were arduous for me. I exerted herculean efforts to produce legal translations on par with those of my predecessor—a seasoned expert who had graduated from the prestigious Frères schools in Birzeit, where the curriculum was taught in English, and who also an alumnus of Birzeit University. I managed to match his standards, perhaps even surpass them, thanks to the assistance of the computer.

I began working closely with the company's seasoned legal advisor, Mr. Ramez Samaha. He was meticulous in ensuring that legal texts were phrased with precise and appropriate wording, safeguarding the rights of the Yusuf Ahmed Al-Ghanim Group of Companies. He was adamant that no flaw should undermine the rights of subsidiary companies, expose them to harm, or entangle them in unjustified obligations. It so happened that I spent long hours—even several days—with him, debating the translation of a single clause in one of the legal agreements. Our goal was to arrive at the exact phrasing required to protect the interests of the subsidiary companies.

Most of the documents I translated were legal in nature—agreements, powers of attorney, contracts, memoranda of understanding, and related paperwork. Occasionally, however, I was tasked with translating correspondence, business plans, and other administrative documents. At times, I was even asked to handle technical translations related to the company's work in the automotive and electronics industries.

The first three months passed smoothly, then six months, and finally a full year had elapsed without any incident to disrupt my life.

By then, my translation work at the company gradually settled into a routine. Over time, I had memorized most of the legal terminology by heart and came to understand the demands of the legal department, which handled the bulk of the translation work. Meeting their requirements became second nature, requiring little effort or strain.

However, I occasionally struggled with the lack of understanding and appreciation some people had for the work of a translator. They seemed oblivious to the immense effort, time, and dedication this demanding profession required. This was especially evident when someone would, for example, hand me a technical document several pages long and return a few hours later, expecting the translation to be completed in moments. Such tasks, however, often demanded hours, if not days, of consulting dictionaries and meticulous work to ensure the accuracy and precision of the translation.

During this period, I experienced only one truly embarrassing situation, one that still haunts me to this day, despite its triviality and the years that have passed. It happened as I was walking down the hallway toward my office and ran into one of the company's vice presidents. He was engaged in conversation with another person when he suddenly asked me what the North Pole was called in English. The word—Arctic—completely slipped my mind at that moment. I stammered, unable to recall it, and he gave me a look that felt laced with disdain. I was mortified, even though such lapses are natural. Even Monir Al-Balbaki, the compiler of the renowned *Al-Mawrid* Dictionary, might struggle to recall certain meanings at times and would need to consult his own dictionary to refresh his memory.

Later, the company hired a young woman who, it was said, held a degree in political science from America. It seemed she had been appointed through connections or as a favor to someone, as she was assigned translation tasks despite having no background in the field. She knew nothing about the technicalities of the profession, yet she was placed in the translation department without any coordination or clear division of tasks with me. She was utterly clueless about a job that requires rigorous training and linguistic proficiency. To make matters worse, she was unbearably arrogant, selfish, and entirely uncooperative. She carried herself as if she were the Shakespeare of our time, but it wasn't long before she faded away like foam on the waves.

And so, life smiled upon me. I had a respectable job at one of the largest companies in an oil-rich nation, and I was earning a relatively decent salary given the circumstances. It allowed me to save a modest sum, though my paycheck was only half of what my former colleague at Burgan Bank was earning by the time I left for the United States to pursue a master's degree, hoping to improve my professional and financial standing.

As my situation improved, the idea of marriage began to tickle my mind and heart. For the first time in my life, my bank balance had surpassed a five thousand Kuwaiti dinars, if only by a small margin. Hesitation and with some trepidation, I began the process of searching and inquiring about a life partner. I had my share of adventures in this pursuit, but what ultimately settled the matter of marriage was a small living creature I found one day under my bed— a stark reminder of the harsh and bitter realities of bachelorhood.

Khalil Hamad

Enough is Enough – Emerging from the Well of Bachelorhood

During my university studies in the United States, I had dismissed the idea of marriage entirely. Even after returning to Kuwait with a master's degree, the harsh circumstances I described in detail—struggling to secure a prestigious job and living on a meager income—further pushed the thought of marriage out of reach. Despite my advancing age, now past thirty, I resigned myself to the idea of dedicating my work, efforts, and income to helping my siblings and their children. They were living in dire conditions, especially my eldest brother, Hamad, who had arrived in Kuwait before the 1967 setback.

Despite the economic boom and financial abundance of the time, continued to live in a cramped, narrow annex after his marriage. Even with multiple manual jobs, he could only afford a space that felt more like a refugee camp shelter, only smaller. The exorbitant rents forced him into this space, which consisted of a single tiny room, a kitchen barely large enough to turn around in, and a bathroom so small it seemed designed for people the size of Smurfs. Hamad, a large man, lived there with his family, as did many other Palestinian expatriates in the oil-rich Gulf, struggling on limited incomes. By the time I left for the United States in the early 1980s, he already had four children. When I returned to Kuwait four years later, nothing had changed about his living situation—except that he now had more children, making the space even more suffocating.

I was convinced—adamantly so—that sacrificing for my siblings and their children was a moral, familial, and humanitarian duty, even if it came at the expense of my own happiness. I believed it was my responsibility to help their families, bring them joy, and alleviate their financial struggles.

But then, during one of my visits to my brother's home, something shifted. I was playfully teasing—with affection, of course—one of his children, whom I had spent countless hours teaching English, his older sibling surprised me. With the blunt honesty of a child, he told me to leave his brother alone. At that moment, a sharp, icy chill swept through my body. It struck me that no matter how much I did or gave, I would always remain an outsider to my siblings' children. It dawned on me that I needed to seriously consider building my own family and having children of my own.

That moment was a deafening alarm bell, a stark reminder that if I did not have children of my own, I would be utterly alone in my old age. It was enough to reshuffle my priorities and push the idea of marriage to the forefront, especially since my financial situation and job stability—two essential prerequisites for marriage—had finally improved. But things were not easy, especially in the absence of a mother, who, in such matters, often serves as the spearhead, smoothing every difficulty to ensure her children find their partners and build their futures.

I had to rely on myself to find a bride. The opportunity arose when a former colleague—someone I had met during my time at the bank—asked me if I had any plans to marry. I seized the moment and asked him for help in finding a wife. To my surprise, he told me he had a sister and would be delighted to arrange a marriage between us. Since he was a close friend and a man of good character, I agreed to meet his family and get to know the young woman who might become my future wife.

On the appointed day, I arrived at their home, expecting to meet his sister in the presence of just him and perhaps his parents. But when I stepped inside, I found myself surrounded by what felt like an entire family reunion. All his brothers—enough to rival the number of Joseph's brothers—had gathered to welcome me, along with what seemed like the sun and the moon themselves. His father, a burly man who turned out to be a retired civil defense and firefighting officer, presided over the gathering. They all sat in a circle in the living room, and I was overcome with a sense of embarrassment unlike anything I had ever experienced. This was, after all, my first attempt at finding a bride.

Amidst the small talk—of which I remember nothing—a young girl, no older than sixteen, entered the room. She carried a tray of coffee cups, placed them down, and then darted out like a bullet fired from a gun. I did not even catch a glimpse of her face or any of her features. In the presence of that army of stern men, I doubt I even dared to look at her properly.

The encounter ended there. I never brought the matter up again with my friend, and I began avoiding him to spare us both the awkwardness. My excuse, perhaps to escape the situation entirely, was that she was far too young for me, with an age gap of over fifteen years.

Later, relatives suggested the name of a young woman who lived nearby, a university student specializing in psychology. I didn't hesitate to accept the proposal. On the day of the meeting, I prepared meticulously, dressing in my finest clothes and dousing myself in cologne. But as I drove to meet her, I saw the mangled remains of a dead dog in the middle of the road, crushed by the wheels of a passing car. The sight filled my heart with such foreboding that it solidified my decision to reject the idea of marrying her—

even before I laid eyes on her. Even if she were Cinderella herself. Still, out of politeness, I went through with the meeting.

These exploratory visits and attempts to find a life partner repeated themselves several more times. I no longer remember the exact number or the finer details, but the fishing hook never caught anything, and the souls never aligned during any of those attempts. Meanwhile, the advancing years, the harsh pangs of loneliness, the isolating solitude of bachelorhood, and, at the same time, the improvement in my financial situation and job stability all became pressing factors pushing me toward hastening the decision to marry. But the true catalyst, the reason that drove me to make that decision, was the urgent desire to escape the brutal conditions of bachelorhood in that country—conditions that felt like a slice of hell.

Despite living in a residential complex near the beach in Salmiya, one of the most beautiful and upscale areas in Kuwait—a choice inspired by the charming beachside homes of San Diego—life inside the complex was unbearable. From the outside, the residential complex might have looked picturesque, but in reality, it was a burning inferno within. As the saying goes, "all that glitters is not gold." The place was crammed with miserable bachelor tenants of various nationalities, ages, and backgrounds, united only by their need for a place to sleep at night. The living quarters were divided by wooden partitions to accommodate as many bachelors as possible, making the space filthy, noisy, and utterly unfit for human habitation. In truth, tenants were paying for a bed, not a home.

One night, I felt as though tiny creatures were crawling on my body. The next morning, I lifted the mattress to investigate the source of the mysterious nocturnal movements, only to discover an army of blood-sucking bedbugs—jumbo-sized—hiding in the cracks of the wooden partitions during the day and roaming freely in the darkness wherever they pleased.

It was a horrifying sight that left me shocked, stunned, and terrified. At that moment, I felt the dam had finally burst. The time had come to escape forward, to break free from the wretched well of bachelorhood. The only way out, it seemed, was through the golden cage of marriage.

After that, things moved at an astonishing pace. Marriage did happen, and for a while, I lived a chapter of overwhelming happiness, despite the many challenges that come with building a family. Sadly, that joyful chapter did not last long.

Our Joys on the Day of Our Return

I had just turned thirty- four when I encountered the savage, blood-sucking bedbugs that had made their home in the wooden crevices and hidden corners around me—even in my bed. These vile creatures were invisible by day, but as darkness fell, it would awaken stealthily, roaming freely while we slept, feasting on my blood and the blood of my fellow bachelors. It worked gradually, while we lay in our little death, oblivious to the silent havoc unfolding in the dead night.

To be honest, I can't say for certain whether this ordeal played a role in my decision to escape the fires of bachelorhood and hastily step into the golden cage of marriage. Several factors and circumstances had already piled up, nudging me in that direction.

As time passed after my marriage, I came to realize that such a sacred bond, with all its intricate details, is orchestrated by a higher power—a matter of pure destiny. Humans are powerless to play any real role in this affair; it is involuntary, unconscious, and tied to the meeting of souls. In a single moment, all obstacles dissolve, all barriers crumble, ignited by a spark beyond human comprehension or will.

In the heat of this battle, one might delude themselves into thinking they have finally achieved their goal by finding the person who matches their preconceived notions of a life partner—the girl of their dreams. Yet they fail to recognize or accept the truth: souls are troops collected together and those who had a mutual familiarity amongst themselves in the store of prenatal existence would have affinity amongst them, (in this world also) and those who opposed one of them, would be at variance with one another.

Yes, it is true—undoubtedly—that the soul may be influenced by the accumulation of experience, the traits, qualities, and temperaments it has grown accustomed to over the years, and the faces glimpsed through the eyes—the windows to the soul. Yet, in the end, the decision is a celestial one, written in the preserved tablet of fate. The role of humans in its realization is nothing but an elaborate illusion, a stubborn insistence on control.

This, I believe, is what happened to me the moment I met the woman who would later become my life partner and the mother of my future children. Despite my initial doubts about the wisdom of my decision and my lingering hesitation, I gradually surrendered to the will of the heavens as the days passed. At times, I consoled myself with Aristotle's words on marriage: "Take a spouse: if you find happiness, you will be content; if not, you'll gain the wisdom of a philosopher." And here I am, caught somewhere between the two.

Naturally, in the midst of the arid landscape of bachelorhood in a conservative society, burdened by the weight of my complex orphanhood, exile, the absence of a mother and sister, the flames of loneliness and isolation, the relentless march of time, and the newfound financial stability, I agreed to meet a girl—a relative of a close friend. The meeting took place at my friend's house, and it was nothing short of magical. A strange, wondrous familiarity coursed through my veins, seeped into the depths of my heart, and enveloped my soul. Fate intervened, blinding my sight as the saying goes, and with my inner vision, I saw that she was my life partner—my lost paradise and my other half.

The very next day, the families convened. We went in a grand procession of relatives and friends to meet the girl's father, a respected elder and the head of his tribe. He welcomed us warmly and was surprisingly lenient in his conditions. He didn't scrutinize my financial status too closely, adhering to the adage, "Take them poor, and God will enrich them." He asked for nothing more than a single dinar as an advance dowry for his daughter, along with the customary conditions regarding gold and the deferred dowry, as was typical in that oil-rich country at the time. Yet, he was careful to convey his responsibility with tact and clarity, saying, "A daughter is a trust placed upon her family, and once she marries, that trust transfers to her husband and his family." The meeting culminated in the recitation of Al-Fatiha, as if by magic once again.

Only a handful of days later, we went to the Sharia court to formalize the marriage contract. Just before signing, the officiant asked my bride-to-be, "Have you received the dowry, my daughter?" She stammered, unable to answer, as the question caught us both off guard. I hadn't actually given her the dowry yet. My late cousin, Taysir Salem, who was one of the witnesses, quickly pulled a dinar from his pocket and handed it to her in front of the judge. With that, the judge approved the completion of the marriage contract.

Not long after, we finalized all the necessary logistical arrangements. After preparing our marital home and furnishing it with all the essentials, and after purchasing the gold, we agreed to hold a grand, lively celebration in one of the ballrooms at the Marriott Hotel—a massive floating ship anchored on the shores of the Arabian Gulf near the Seif Palace, the residence of Kuwait's Emir.

My brother Mustafa, who managed a printing press, took charge of designing the wedding invitation. He shaped it like a map of Palestine, crowned with a phrase brimming with nostalgia for our homeland: "Our true joy will come on the day of our return." Through the invitation, we extended our heartfelt call to family, loved ones, and friends to join us in celebrating the wedding. The event was brought to life by a renowned wedding singer of the time, and the ballroom was filled with a large crowd of guests who immersed themselves in the joyous atmosphere and the singer's danceable tunes. The hall buzzed with energy late into the night, and to this day, the echoes of the song "I'll Plant You a Garden of Roses" to which I danced with my bride in pure delight, still resonate in my ears. Whenever I recall that radiant celebration, I can't help but smile.

And so, on October 14, 1987, I emerged from the inferno of bachelorhood. I now had a home of my own, a wife to return to at the end of the day, a sanctuary in her presence, delicious food, and a clean, bug-free bed-a sanctuary to retreat to as night fell and sleep took hold.

We lived in happiness and contentment during that time, though our lives during that time were tinged with the struggles of poverty and financial strain. Despite not paying an upfront dowry, the social pressures and expenses of marriage drained my bank account entirely, leaving it nearly empty after the wedding.

Yet, even amidst the disruption caused by our financial struggles, our lives were rich with the joy and delight of newlyweds—until the arrival of our firstborn son, Ahmad, the crown prince of our little kingdom. His birth marked the end of the honeymoon phase, which had stretched blissfully for a year.

We had been living in the glow of newlywed happiness, but with Ahmed's arrival, the challenges of caring for an infant began to overshadow our moments of joy. I must admit, I was partly to blame for the tension that arose—my exaggerated reactions to the newborn's needs, my overbearing concern for his well-being, and my struggles with the tools and methods of caring for him. The difference between a father and a mother in handling a newborn became glaringly obvious, especially in those early days. While my wife acted with calm and composure, guided by her maternal instincts, I found myself in a state of constant turmoil.

As days passed, the situation escalated, nearly spiraling out of control. We teetered on the edge of what is often called "the most detestable of halal things"—divorce. But I managed to step back, albeit reluctantly, and handed over the primary responsibility of caring for our child to my wife. I worked to repair the damage caused by my overthinking and excessive fear, gradually restoring peace and harmony to our home.

Meanwhile, during the 1980s, Kuwait enjoyed a life of relative luxury despite the occasional crises. Yet, just a stone's throw away—a mere few hundred kilometers on the Iraqi-Iranian border—a brutal war raged on. It was a ferocious conflict that consumed everything in its path, leaving the warring nations on the brink of collapse and famine. The repercussions of this war were far-reaching, culminating in an event on August 2, 1990, that no soothsayer could have predicted. It was like a minor apocalypse, followed by a tsunami of monumental events in every direction.

Khalil Hamad

Harden yourselves, for blessings do not last forever

How true are the words: "Blessings do not last forever." What happened in Kuwait on August 2, 1990, stands as the greatest proof of this saying. A devastating earthquake struck suddenly, without warning or preamble—an event so catastrophic that not even the greatest seers, from Nostradamus to the blind prophetess Baba Vanga, could have foreseen it. No other visionary, fortune-teller, or political or military analyst predicted it. The event marked a minor apocalypse for Kuwait and everyone who lived under its protection, benefited from its wealth, or orbited within its sphere, even from thousands of miles away.

Before that day, Kuwait had been a secure and tranquil emirate, a land where life flowed with ease and comfort. Its sustenance flowed from beneath its soil, its markets, its seas, and its lands—despite the fierce war raging just beyond its borders. Despite the treacherous bombings and hostile acts that had targeted the country, even reaching its then-ruler, Sheikh Jaber Al-Ahmad Al-Sabah. Despite the deafening collapse of the Souk Al-Manakh, the stock and business market, which sent shockwaves through its financial, psychological, and social fabric, Kuwait continued to thrive in abundance, drowning in worldly luxuries that many nations and people envied.

Kuwait floated on a sea of oil, a magnet for investment and wealth, hailed as the richest country in the world. Its dinar, worth three dollars, was the strongest currency in circulation in modern times. Both its native citizens and expatriates lived in unparalleled comfort, prosperity, and security, enjoying a level of luxury that rivaled the tales of One Thousand and One Nights. It was a life of bliss, unmatched anywhere else on earth.

Yet, amid these favorable conditions, the earth shook violently, and a cataclysm unfolded. Everything collapsed suddenly, marking the end of all glory, routine, opulent living, security, and safety. The earthly paradise that the people of Kuwait had known was shattered.

My small family and I were among the fortunate expatriates who had tasted a share of that prosperity. Despite my modest income and the exorbitant costs of marriage, which had drained my bank account at the time—leaving it, as they say, "Gone with the Wind"—the stability of a job and a salary that met our needs and even allowed for some excess enabled us to live a life of comfort and ease in every sense of the word.

We wore the finest clothes and dined on the most delicious food: shrimp, calamari, fish, quail, Iraqi kebabs, and more. Often, we indulged in meals at five-star hotel restaurants, unconcerned about the high prices, unafraid of poverty or the sudden loss of income. Our spending went beyond necessities to luxuries, as if the oil wealth were a shared inheritance between us expatriates and the native citizens— or as if we were drawing from the treasuries of Korah himself. The thought of income drying up never crossed our minds, nor did it occur to anyone else who basked in the riches of that wealthy emirate.

After emerging from the dark well of bachelorhood and embracing the blessings of marital life—its tranquility, familial stability, and professional security—I took up hobbies to enrich my days. I began fishing in the Arabian Gulf, practicing bodybuilding, and jogging regularly. I even joined the Al-Qadsiah Club to pursue these activities in a more structured way, especially after the notorious "marriage weight gain" added a solid fifteen kilograms to my frame.

One of the telltale signs of our indulgent lifestyle—a life so lavish it seemed to blind our hearts and dull our minds—was that I could fill my car's fuel tank for just one Kuwaiti dinar. On one occasion, I bought a sabat of jumbo shrimp from the fish market. The sabat, woven from dried reeds, contained twenty, perhaps twenty-five kilograms of fresh shrimp, freshly hauled from the bountiful waters of the Arabian Gulf. These delicious sea creatures packed with phosphorus and cholesterol, were sold for a pittance—just a few dinars. We cleaned and stored them, but I can't recall exactly how many shrimp I devoured that day in an unprecedented feast. By evening, I was struck with severe digestive pain, prompting my brother Mustafa to rush me to Al-Sabah Hospital for treatment. The diagnosis was a gastrointestinal disturbance, which was treated without the need for hospitalization.

The truth is, during those years, we lived a life of extravagance, akin to that of kings and princes. Our days were filled with joy, and enchanting nights reminiscent of the tales of Andalusia and *One Thousand and One Nights*.

Then, at the dawn of the summer of 1990, the stifling yellow Tooz storms swept in, blanketing the emirate's skies with fine sand in an annual ritual that occurred every summer. This phenomenon, which often obscured the sun for months on end, sent temperatures soaring to astronomical heights, sometimes exceeding fifty degrees Celsius. As was customary every year, many people packed their bags and fled the scorching heat, escaping Kuwait to spend their summer vacations away from the infernal, suffocating atmosphere.

Among those who left that summer was my father in law, who traveled to Jordan with his entire family. They rented a spacious villa in the upscale Al Rashid district, near the University of Jordan. I decided to send my wife and our firstborn son, Ahmed, to join them for a while, hoping they could escape the blazing, oppressive climate of the Gulf, especially during the blistering months of July and August. Arrangements were made, and they left Kuwait for Jordan by plane in late July. I stayed behind, immersed in my work at Al-Ghanim Company. Little did I know that the farewell moments of that trip would mark their last days in Kuwait.

Just two or three days after my wife and son departed, the great calamity struck. The world turned upside down, and Kuwaiti time came to a standstill.

Khalil Hamad

The Kuwaiti Time Stands Still

I had bid farewell to my wife and my son Ahmed, who was barely two years old at the time, at Kuwait International Airport. They were heading to Jordan to join my wife's family, where they had already traveled there for the summer vacation of 1990. Little did I know that those moments would mark their final departure from Kuwait—a departure with no return.

Back in my apartment, I returned to the life of a bachelor, living alone and commuting to work at Yusuf Ahmed Al-Ghanim's company as usual. Though I felt a strange sense of calm and quiet for the first time since marriage, the absence of my wife and the disruption of our marital routine left a bitter taste. In such moments, a man transforms from a bachelor into akin to a young widower.

On the fateful morning of August 2, 1990, just four, five, or at most six days after my wife and son had left, I woke up as usual. I went through my typical morning rituals, got into my car, and drove from my home in Hawally toward the Shuwaikh area via the Fourth Ring Road, heading to the headquarters of Yusuf Ahmed Al-Ghanim's company.

Suddenly, I heard the loud roar of warplanes soaring low over the emirate—a strange and unfamiliar sight. For the first time since arriving in Kuwait, I witnessed such a scene. The planes flew so low that their markings were visible to the naked eye.

Though the sight of warplanes was unusual and unsettling in this small emirate, where military presence was almost nonexistent—let alone low-flying, fully alert warplanes—I didn't pay much attention to it. It didn't strike me as a serious matter, and it certainly never crossed my mind that these planes were part of a violent military campaign, a brutal Iraqi invasion, and a sweeping occupation of Kuwait.

By the time the sun rose that morning, Iraqi tanks had already reached sensitive and sovereign locations in the country, and the emirate's occupation had been completed— as we would later learn. Yet, traffic on the Fourth Ring Road toward Shuwaikh continued, albeit with difficulty. One might have attributed the congestion to a traffic jam or an accident on the road.

I kept driving and eventually reached the headquarters of Yusuf Ahmed Al-Ghanim's company. Along the way, I didn't notice any unusual military presence—no tanks, no military vehicles. Perhaps I hadn't paid attention to such unfamiliar signs in Kuwait because the idea of something so catastrophic happening in this emirate seemed impossible. After all, this was a country with a prominent place on the global stage.

When I arrived at the company's headquarters, I found that several of my colleagues had already made it to work, as usual. However, they were gathered outside the building, their faces etched with confusion and unease. Though the doors were open, it was clear that something monumental had happened the previous night and that morning. Work had come to a halt, and everything was spiraling into the unknown.

The thunderous shock was that the crowd was discussing Iraq's occupation of Kuwait—the country had indeed fallen. The proof was the Iraqi military forces presence at the radio and television building, which had ceased broadcasting. Some claimed to have seen columns of tanks and military vehicles scattered here and there, while others spoke of Iraqi troops stationed at sovereign sites, government institutions, and major intersections.

I couldn't believe what I was hearing or seeing. I tried to ask multiple people for more details, hoping to piece together what was truly happening. Slowly, it dawned on me that things were spiraling out of control. In such a chaotic situation—and following the old adage, "When the wrath of God descends, bow your head until it passes"—the best course of action was to rush home, follow the news from there, and wait for clarity. I needed to grasp the extent of this madness that was gradually paralyzing life, as if the city had been struck by a devastating earthquake. The full scale of the damage and destruction remained unclear, with conflicting accounts and rampant rumors swirling.

I retraced my steps back to the company the same way I had come. Strangely, I didn't see any military presence on my way home, which seemed the focus was on the capital and key sovereign areas. But I couldn't bear to stay alone in my apartment, not even for a moment. Doing so would have driven me mad. Instead, I headed to the home of a relative in the same neighborhood, where a group of men—relatives, friends, and neighbors—had gathered. Together, we tried to piece together the news, desperate to understand the scope of the Iraqi military operation.

As time passed, the situation began to unravel, and each new detail confirmed the enormity of the catastrophe. Fear crept into people's hearts, and shock and grief were etched on their faces. Panic set in as people rushed to markets to stock up on water and supplies. By evening, the nearby supermarket shelves stood empty, as if stripped bare by a plague of locusts.

Over time, we learned that the Kuwaiti government and all its institutions had collapsed under the Iraqi invasion, with little to no resistance. The only exception was the charismatic leader, Sheikh Fahad Al-Ahmad Al-Jaber Al-

Sabah, who reportedly took up arms and fought valiantly. A former freedom fighter who had joined the Palestinian revolution, he met his end on the doorstep of his home during the early hours of the Iraqi invasion.

Soon, we learned that the Emir of Kuwait, his entourage, and many locals who had not left the country for their summer vacations—fearing for their safety—had fled in fear of the Iraqi invasion, seeking refuge in Saudi Arabia. The Iraqi army had seized complete control of the emirate, from its southernmost to its northernmost borders.

It wasn't long before an Iraqi broadcaster appeared on Kuwaiti television, broadcast in grainy black and white. The scene was a tragicomic farce, both absurd and heartbreaking. The man, with his booming voice, was someone we all recognized from his days delivering military updates during the Iran-Iraq war. This time, however, he was dressed in a white dishdasha and a Kuwaiti ghutra, awkwardly attempting to embody a Kuwaiti persona. He began reciting military statements about the "liberation" of Kuwait, claiming the invasion had been carried out at the request of a faction of Kuwaitis. It was a narrative so blatantly fabricated to justify the invasion that it failed miserably to convince anyone.

By the next morning, the presence of military forces had become unmistakable. Soldiers were stationed everywhere, their presence looming in every direction. The air was filled with the sounds of explosions and gunfire. Military vehicles lay destroyed, their wreckage littering the streets, and ammunition was scattered across the roads. Near my home in Hawally, on the Fourth Ring Road bridge, unexploded ordnance lay on the pavement for days, untouched—a silent threat to everyone passing by or living nearby.

In the blink of an eye, Kuwaiti time stood still. Everything collapsed, and the emirate was thrown into chaos. It became a hollow shell and desolate, thrust into a dark tunnel of occupation, displacement, and death. The days that followed were even more harrowing.

THE WELL OF EXILE

The First Day of the Lesser
Kuwait Resurrection

Shock, disorientation, and bewilderment—these were the dominant emotions that gripped people in the early days of the Iraqi invasion of Kuwait. It was as if everyone had been struck on the head. Without exception, people were lost, dazed, and disoriented, moving as though in a trance, circling aimlessly around themselves. They could not comprehend what had happened, as if they were trapped in a nightmare, waiting to wake up.

Most people stayed indoors or ventured only short distances, as though an unspoken curfew had been imposed on them. Men gathered in small groups—relatives, friends, and neighbors—either inside homes or outside their doorsteps. Their conversations revolved around the explosive situation and the sudden turn of events that had engulfed their lives. The government institutions had vanished, order had collapsed, and anarchy was beginning to spread. The emirate, once a haven of security and stability, had turned into a lawless free-for-all.

Personally, during those first days of the Iraqi invasion, the farthest I ventured was within the boundaries of two residential blocks near my home. This area, part of Hawalli district, was where several of my relatives lived. It was there that I met with family and friends, particularly my close friend Hussein Ismail, who had a passion for following the news and political analysis. His company brought me a sense of comfort and relief.

Like everyone else, I was consumed by shock, disorientation, and bewilderment during those early days. I was cut off from my job, not by choice but because Yusuf Ahmed Al-Ghanim Company, like all other businesses and institutions, had shut its doors. I found myself trapped in a vicious cycle, unsure of what to do or how to act. Anxiety gripped me so tightly that I even began sleeping with my shoes on. Had it not been for those gatherings with family and friends, where I could vent and unburden myself, I might have lost my mind to the horror of what had happened and its catastrophic consequences.

My greatest worry and the source of my fear and anxiety during those days was my lack of money. I had only a few dinars in my pocket, and my last salary—450 Kuwaiti dinars—had been deposited into my bank account at the beginning of the month. But the banks were sealed by order of the Iraqi military governor.

The root of my financial crisis in those critical and urgent circumstances lay in twofold. On one hand, we lived by this philosophy "Spend what's in your pocket, and what's in the unseen will come to you." On the other, we never expected—living as we were on a sea of oil—that our income would be cut off so suddenly. To make matters worse, I was still recovering from the expenses of my recent marriage, living on what was essentially a minimum-wage income, with high costs, especially rent, which consumed at least a third of my salary.

Just days before the invasion, I had withdrawn a sum of money—the entirety of my bank balance, accumulated over time—to cover the cost of tickets and expenses for my wife and son's trip to Jordan. At the time, I hadn't considered the consequences of being left without any financial cushion. Who could have known that the country would be invaded, bringing life as we knew it to a halt and cutting off all sources of income?

Despite the horror of the event, the shock, and the overwhelming fear and confusion that gripped everyone, I managed to get through the first few days. I relied on whatever food and drink was available at home, or at my brother's or relatives' houses. Food wasn't an immediate concern; I didn't even think about buying bread during those days.

Like everyone else, I waited for the banks to reopen. The military governor had ordered them to resume operations about a week after the fall of the Kuwaiti state. But the shocking and sudden decision he made was to convert all bank balances from Kuwaiti dinars to Iraqi dinars. This meant that someone who had 1,000 Kuwaiti dinars now had 1,000 Iraqi dinars. In practical terms, the Kuwaiti dinar, which had been worth three dollars, was now worth less than five Jordanian piasters. Overnight, any savings held in Kuwaiti dinars evaporated, leaving people with mere pennies.

As soon as the banks reopened, I rushed to withdraw my balance—my last paycheck of 450 dinars. I headed to my account at the National Bank branch in Shuwaikh, just a few hundred meters from the company where I worked. My salary was automatically deposited there. But when I arrived, I discovered that the branch had been looted and destroyed during the invasion and was no longer operational. This left me unable to withdraw even that small amount, which had already lost its purchasing value.

Forced to wait several more days, I finally managed to withdraw the money from another branch, despite the rumors swirling that any official financial transaction would be seen as tacit approval of the military governor's decision. Now, my primary concern was finding a source of income. My family was in Amman and would soon need financial support, while I was left with a handful or nearly worthless dinars—insufficient even to buy bread. I found myself caught in a whirlwind of desperation, willing to take on any legitimate work that could provide me with an income.

What did I choose in the end? And what actually happened? The answers would come later...

The Tissue Seller

As the days passed, the Iraqi army solidified its presence in Kuwait. The people living within the crumbling borders of this once-stable nation now found themselves under the shadow of a harsh military regime, forced to obey its every command. It was clear that the Iraqi army had entered Kuwait with no intention of leaving. They were there to stay as it had the power to remain, and they acted with brutality and aggression, always ready to kill at a moment's notice—even over the smallest disputes.

A close Palestinian friend of mine shared a story that underscored this grim reality. He had gotten into a minor argument with an Iraqi soldier, and the soldier threatened to shoot him on the spot. My friend walked away with the chilling realization that, in this new reality, human life had become as expendable as a cigarette butt.

After the decision to reopen the banks and convert Kuwaiti dinar accounts into Iraqi dinars, the military governor issued a strategic and ominous decree aimed at further cementing Iraq's control over the emirate. He ordered the replacement of Kuwaiti car licenses and driver's permits with Iraqi ones, and the process began immediately in the relevant government offices.

Navigating the streets of Kuwait under these conditions was neither easy nor safe. The brutal invasion had plunged the country into chaos, stripping away any sense of security. Real dangers lurked everywhere, threatening anyone who dared to step outside.

The risks were manifold: not only were there the threat of being targeted by the tense, trigger-happy soldiers-whose presence was neither officially accepted nor welcomed by the people—but also the dangers of bombings and accidental military operations. We often noticed military equipment abandoned on the roadsides, left neglected for days after the invasion. It was baffling how a supposedly professional army could be so careless. I personally witnessed this on the bridge where the Fourth Ring Road intersects with the Fahaheel and Abu Halifa roads, just a few hundred meters from my apartment.

Naturally, people feared the Iraqi army's harshness. This was an army scarred by an eight-year-long, bloody war with Iran—a conflict that had undoubtedly left deep psychological scars on its soldiers. These were the manifestations of post-traumatic stress disorder (PTSD), making it all too easy for them to pull the trigger over the slightest provocation.

The army's brutality was evident from the very first days of the invasion. One soldier, for instance, was seen drinking from a garden hose under the scorching sun, where temperatures soared above 50 degrees Celsius—conditions even camels would struggle to endure.

In another instance, during the early days of the occupation, the army carried out a field execution of one of its own soldiers, accused of theft. He was tried on the spot, executed, and his lifeless body hung from a crane in a public square as a grim warning to all who passed by.

Of course, the Kuwaiti resistance posed a significant threat—a shadowy force that had emerged swiftly and grown stronger with each passing day. We heard whispers of their activities, but their members and hideouts remained shrouded in secrecy. To this clandestine movement, compliance with the military governor's decrees was tantamount to betrayal deserving punishment. The governor, now the de facto authority, ruling over the land, including its civilian sectors, even down to the replacement of licenses. In the early days following the expulsion of Iraqi forces by American troops, many individuals of various nationalities lost their lives under such accusations.

Yet the dangers did not end there. The absence of security forces, institutions, and the rule of law plunged the region into chaos and lawlessness. Looting and robbery became rampant, and the pervasive lack of safety created a greatest threat. This made life under these conditions terrifying to the extreme, and every possibility seemed to be on the table.

To make matters worse, adding insult to injury, was the depletion of supplies in the markets, the lack of any clear horizon, the future was shrouded in uncertainty, and a pervasive sense of emptiness took hold. Thugs and criminals exploited the absence of law enforcement, committing atrocities that stripped people of any sense of security. It was a time when the strong preyed on the weak.

In such an atmosphere, I had no choice but to visit the Hawalli Traffic Department to replace my expired license. There was no way around it—renewal was unavoidable. Despite my hesitation and gnawing fear that this might be interpreted as collaboration with the occupiers, I went anyway. I braved the risks, endured hours in long queues, and finally managed to replace and renew it.

As the days passed, I found myself under immense social pressure from relatives and friends who were aware of my dire financial situation. They urged me to find work, and the only option available at the time for someone in my position was selling tissues on the roadside. I resisted these pressures—partly out of fear of the unsafe conditions on the streets, and partly because I lacked enough money needed to purchase tissues for resale.

After prolonged hesitation and as my financial situation worsened, I finally gave in to the pressure one day and decided to start selling tissues on the roadside. I was pushed into this venture against my will, and since I had no capital, I went to the house of a relative who owned a grocery store. Before the Iraqi invasion, his shop had been stocked with goods, and he had made a fortune during the invasion by selling everything he had. By the time I visited him, the store stood empty, as if it had been looted and stripped bare.

That day, I found him sitting on the floor, counting a large pile of money spread out on a dining tray, his children watching silently. I asked him for a small loan of just 100 Kuwaiti dinars, explaining my intention to start selling tissues on the roadside. But he refused, and with that, my venture stumbled and died before it could even begin—thank God. I never worked as a tissue seller, not even for a moment. It wasn't out of arrogance, but rather a deep disdain for such work under those circumstances—a desperate measure many resorted to when they were left with no other options, teetering on the brink of begging or starvation.

At first, I was stunned by my relative's refusal to lend me such a trivial amount, especially when he clearly had more than enough. But as time passed, I came to understand the strange logic behind his behavior. It was, I realized, a reflection of the instinctive human response born out of the crucible of war.

THE WELL OF EXILE

Fallen into Ruin

It did not take long for the collapse to paralyze every aspect of life in Kuwait, bringing it full-blown devastation and death after the Iraqi invasion. State institutions crumbled, and the absence of law enforcement triggered a seismic shock of unimaginable force, followed by a tsunami of collapses in every direction. What stood out during this period was the rampant theft of cars, often stripped for parts, with an almost obsessive focus on stealing wheels. It was a bizarre and surreal phenomenon—scenes of cars stripped of their wheels became commonplace, scattered across the city like carcasses.

As the days passed, the societal dysfunction deepened, fueled by the immense shock, panic, and bewilderment that gripped the population. The financial sector's collapse and the turmoil that struck the Kuwaiti dinar only worsened the crisis. The currency's value plummeted when the Iraqi military governor equated it to Iraqi dinar, which itself had already collapsed, rendering it virtually worthless against the dollar or any other global currency, both within and outside Kuwait.

In addition to the panic that gripped people over their savings, the loss of the currency's purchasing power, and the interruption of income, that decision led to an increase in turmoil and chaos, a sharp rise in theft and looting, and a rapid disappearance of supplies from the markets. Eventually, the shelves of commercial stores were left empty, fallen into ruin, as the days went by.

It wasn't long before many shops closed their doors—some because supplies had disappeared, others because their owners fled with whatever savings they had, desperate to escape the harsh realities of war and its terrifying consequences. This was especially true for those who had always considered their stay in Kuwait as temporary. They had the foresight and wisdom to save and invest in their homelands, securing a foothold to return to in case of disaster.

During this period, Kuwait witnessed a mass exodus of countless expatriates from various communities and nationalities—except for the Palestinian community. In a sense, they were disguised refugees, having bet on permanent residence in Kuwait, which they had come to regard as a substitution homeland. Despite the government's restrictive residency policies, they had never considered moving elsewhere. They lived as if they were there to stay forever, had not saved or invested outside Kuwait, nor did they own a penny or a piece of property beyond its borders.

As the search for basic necessities grew increasingly difficult, people were often forced to stand in long queues, waiting for their turn to enter the few remaining markets or cooperatives. More often than not, after hours of futile waiting, they would return home empty-handed. Over time, the search for a bag of rice or any essential grocery item became like searching for a needle in a haystack.

The scarcity of goods, the disappearance of most products, and the dinar's plummeting purchasing power led to exorbitant and astronomical price hikes. For instance, the price of a carton of eggs soared from five dinars to forty Iraqi dinars.

Then there was the story of bread—that indispensable staple—was a sage of its own. At first, people lined up in long queues outside bakeries, hoping to secure a few loaves. Soon, however, bread vanished from the markets altogether, and many bakeries shut their doors. The few that remained operational altered the shape and size of their loaves, harkening back to the days of kradish—a makeshift bread made from lentils during times of famine caused by plagues and wars. These bakeries replaced wheat flour with barley flour or whatever grains were available to produce a substitute bread, even though it was a poor imitation in size, appearance, and taste.

At the peak of the crisis, a new phenomenon emerged: home-baked bread. People began making bread from barley, lentils, corn, and other flour substitutes. But as days passed, even these materials began to run out, until some resorted to baking something resembling bread from birdseed.

The situation grew so dire that it mirrored the conditions of the *Saferberlik* famine that struck Palestine during World War I, when people reportedly sifted through cow dung in search of barley grains to bake bread, as the old stories go. Indeed, the difficulty of obtaining bread, the disappearance of essential supplies, and the catastrophic state of the markets—now barren of basic goods—were among the primary reasons that pushed me to consider leaving Kuwait early on. I foresaw that it wouldn't be long before life there became utterly impossible.

On the other hand, the absence of state-run service institutions—particularly municipal services—led to a rapid deterioration in living conditions, environmental health, and public sanitation. Waste piled up in the streets, forming hills and mountains of garbage. Insects proliferated at an alarming and terrifying rate, something no one could have imagined happening in Kuwait.

I witnessed this decline in public services firsthand. One day, as I walked down a street, I passed by a wall I knew had once been painted white. But now, it appeared almost entirely black. Curiosity piqued, and astonished by the change in color, I approached the wall to inspect the source of this darkness. To my shock, the wall was entirely covered—every inch of it—by an enormous swarm of black flies. What made it even more bizarre was the size of these flies—each was as large as a small cockroach. It was a far cry from the days of Kuwait's golden era, before the Iraqi invasion, when flies and mosquitoes were a rare sight.

Alongside the collapse of public systems and living conditions, Kuwait also experienced a breakdown in behavior, values, and morals. It was as if the latent forces of evil within us had broken free from their chains, possessing people and turning them into beasts driven by those hidden, malevolent forces. Good qualities—solidarity, cooperation, love, and selflessness—vanished, replaced by discord, hatred, and repugnant selfishness.

It was as though ferocious beasts had been lurking within us, tethered only by the ropes of fear—fear of punishment. But when war struck, when disasters unfolded, when order collapsed, and when the tools of law enforcement disappeared, when the state crumbled, and when chaos reigned, the thick stick of fear was snapped. Those savage beasts within us broke free, and people became like wild animals, driven by their selfishness and primal instincts, operating on the principle of "every man for himself." The once-safe place, governed by noble morals, transformed into a jungle steeped in savagery, narcissism, and cruelty. In this jungle, the strong devoured the rights of the weak, while vice, crime, selfishness, bad manners, and grotesque behaviors spread like wildfire. Every individual acted out of selfishness, driven by animalistic instincts, far removed from the balanced human behavior governed by ethics and conscience. It was as though the mechanisms of conscience, reason, and religious restraint had ceased to function, no longer able to control behavior or rein in animalistic and devilish impulses.

One might understand the ease with which a soldier's finger moves to pull the trigger during combat, how killing becomes second nature—a grim consequence of the horrors of war and the fears that hunt them. One might even understand the burning thirst for revenge in the heart of a resistance fighter who has lost everything to an unjust war. Yes, we might comprehend his drive for retribution, how his doubts, his vulnerabilities, and the calamities that befell him and his homeland could push him to commit acts that defy all norms, acts that make the soul shudder.

But what is far harder to comprehend is the collective madness, the collapse of conscience and reason, that seizes ordinary people in times of war and disaster. It is a time when masks slip away, and the darker facets of human nature rise to the surface. People turn their backs on one another as if they were strangers, as if the bonds of kinship, love, brotherhood, and human compassion had never existed.

This is what befell people during that war—a lesson for those who would pause to reflect. If the common saying goes, "Save it for a rainy day," then let me assure you, dear reader, that the days of war are the blackest of all. In such times, people abandon one another, and you are left with no one to rely on but yourself and whatever you have managed to save for survival.

It was in such an atmosphere that I had to continue my search for work, desperate to secure some semblance of income. I applied for a job, and though it became another reason pushing me to leave Kuwait, the decision to depart meant casting myself adrift, at the mercy of uncertain winds.

Khalil Hamad

Baby Formula and the Warnings of My Wife

Only a few days after Kuwait fell to the relentless Iraqi forces, it became clear that the Iraqi market was ravenous for electronic devices in particular. The road to Basra soon teemed with unusual activity, as large numbers of Kuwaiti residents began traveling there to sell such goods. Some were drawn by the high prices they could fetch, while others sought just enough money to stave off the looming threat of hunger.

Among the bitter memories of that time, stirred by the hidden forces of greed and malice, was something that happened to me personally. Two years before the Iraqi invasion, during the preparations for my wedding and the setting up of our marital home, I had purchased a video projector from a relative for 100 hundred Kuwaiti dinars. The agreement was that I would pay him in comfortable installments, as a way to ease the financial burden of wedding expenses. By the time of the invasion, I had already paid 60 dinars. Then, in the early days of the occupation, that same relative surprised me with a visit, demanding the return of the projector. Stunned by his request, I unplugged the device, still reeling from the shock, and handed it over without reclaiming the money I had already paid. Later, I learned that he had taken it to Basra, where he sold it for 1,000 Iraqi dinars, riding the wave of the frenzied demand for electronics in the Iraqi market.

As the days passed, the movement between Kuwait and Basra grew increasingly noticeable. People traveled there not only to sell goods that the Iraqi market craved—snapped up at astronomical prices—but also to buy food supplies, blankets, and other cheaply produced Iraqi goods. These

237

items had vanished from Kuwaiti markets due to the international sanctions imposed on Iraq for years.

These journeys took place under harsh and perilous conditions, on roads crammed with large trucks and military vehicles. The sides of the roads were littered with the wreckage of destroyed civilian and military cars, some stripped of their tires, and abandoned military equipment scattered here and there. One of my townsmen, the late Bassam Al-Othman, met his tragic end in a horrific traffic accident on that road, which had become a highway of death. His Mercedes was crushed by a military vehicle traveling in the wrong direction during one of his frequent shuttle trips between Basra and Kuwait.

In another incident—no less strange, amusing, and unfortunate than the story of the reclaimed projector—something equally bizarre happened to me personally, as if orchestrated by an even more sinister demon. I had joined a savings group with relatives and friends, contributing 10 dinars a month. The purpose of the group was to provide financial assistance to any member in need. By the time the war broke out, my total contributions had reached 200 hundred Kuwaiti dinars. I requested a withdrawal, assuming I was the only member of the group who had been caught empty-handed by the war, with no savings or resources to fall back on, and in urgent need of financial support. All I asked was to be reimbursed for my contributions. To my surprise, my request was denied on the grounds that the money had already been used to cover the cost of household items given to me during my wedding as part of furnishing our marital home.

These actions were an ominous sign for me, a harbinger that I would find no one willing to lend me money in my time of need—a situation that seemed inevitable given the complete loss of income, the ongoing devastation, and prices soared to astronomical heights.

The state of the country was stagnant, if not worsening, and the same could be said for its economy and businesses. Yet, at the peak of my personal crisis and the country's crushing turmoil, word reached me that Kuwait University would reopen for the academic year (1990-91). There was a possibility they might hire new teachers to replace the staff who had fled Kuwait after the Iraqi invasion.

Though I didn't know who had ordered the university to reopen that semester, I decided to take the risk. Driven by necessity, I resolved to go to the university and apply for a teaching position, even if it was part-time, in the field of translation.

At the time, I was fully aware that such a move could spell disaster for me. If the Kuwaiti side or the resistance interpreted my application as collaboration with the Iraqi occupiers—especially if the decision to reopen the university had come from the Iraqi military governor—it would mean I had committed a third violation, one that could be seen as aiding the enemy from the Kuwaiti perspective.

This attempt to secure a teaching position at Kuwait University would now added to my previous actions: withdrawing my bank balance in Iraqi dinars instead of Kuwaiti dinars and later exchanging my Kuwaiti driver's license for an Iraqi one—both decisions made in compliance with the military governor's orders and to avoid violating traffic laws.

I went to the university and met with a committee of three individuals dressed in Kuwaiti attire. I assumed they were Kuwaiti, judging by their language and body language. But the problem was, I read in their eyes—eyes that seemed to pierce through me—what their tongues did not say. Or at least, that's how it felt to me. During the interview, I couldn't shake the feeling that they were silently asking, "What brings you here, you Palestinian?" It unsettled me deeply, but I held my composure and answered all their questions. In the end, their decision was negative, citing the university's requirement that English literature teachers, in particular, hold a PhD as a minimum qualification.

I left the interview disheartened, my hopes dashed for the one opportunity that had appeared on the horizon amidst the ruin and desolation—a chance that could have breathed life back into my existence. But it evaporated, carried away by the wind, and my financial situation plummeted to rock bottom in the days followed.

During this time, under these harsh conditions, large numbers of expatriates who had been on vacation outside Kuwait when the invasion occurred began returning to check on their properties. It turned out that a relative brought me a message from my wife, urging me to join them in Jordan—or else she would return to Kuwait.

I couldn't believe my wife was seriously considering coming back to Kuwait, a land now reduced to ruins where owls hooted in the desolation. Life there lacked even the most basic necessities, especially since she was a mother to one child and pregnant with another. If obtaining a loaf of bread or a sip of water was a struggle, how could we possibly find infant formula?

Yet, I feared that the grim reality of the situation had not fully reached her, that she still held in her mind the image of a prosperous Kuwait—or perhaps she had succumbed to denial, like thousands of others who could not believe that what was once a lush, thriving oasis had now become a desolate wasteland and barren. I worried that if she returned, on the brink of a second birth amid such financial turmoil, our fate would be collective ruin.

That letter, carrying a warning reminiscent of America's ultimatums to Iraq, finally settled my wavering indecision about whether to leave Kuwait or wait for salvation. It tipped the scales in favor of departure—a choice that felt like a gamble to me—over staying, which seemed closer to suicide. In the end, I resolved to travel to Jordan without delay, especially since there was no longer any point in staying in Kuwait under such circumstances. The faint glimmer of hope that had briefly flickered on the horizon had now vanished, and I realized that a matter of such gravity could not be resolved through third-party letters.

THE WELL OF EXILE

The First Departure from Kuwait
– Like a Swarm of Locusts

As the handful of coins I had saved ran out after the Iraqi invasion, and hope of finding an alternative source of income—even as a street vendor selling tissues on a street corner—vanished, I found myself abandoned by family and friends. Destruction was everywhere, and chaos was spreading like wildfire.

It's said that chaos only grows if left unchecked. The relentless onslaught of flies and the unbearable wait for relief, waiting for circumstances to change began to feel like a slow suicide. I became absolutely convinced that leaving Kuwait, even temporarily, to catch my breath until things settled, was no longer a choice but an inevitability. For me, however, it felt like a gamble—one that could plunge me to a situation even worse than the misery, despair, and brokenness I was already in. History has shown that there is nothing worse than the life of a refugee in times of war, even if that refuge is within the borders of one's own homeland.

The collapse had reached its peak, even affecting healthcare centers and hospitals. A friend told me he had decided to leave Kuwait for good, without regret, after obtaining a loaf of bread had become an almost impossible task—though at the beginning of the crisis, he had been able to secure plenty of bread, distributing it freely to anyone who asked.

But the final straw that broke the camel's back for him, and made him leave without hesitation or remorse—despite the pain of abandoning his thriving business, which had once brought him abundant wealth—was the death of his wife's uncle, a man I also knew well. One night, he collapsed unconscious, perhaps from the overwhelming grief and despair that had gripped everyone, or from the sheer toll of how far things had deteriorated. He was rushed to the nearby Farwaniya Hospital, where he was admitted to the intensive care unit and required a ventilator. But it turned out that all the oxygen tanks in the hospital had been stolen by those who had lost their conscience. The man died of suffocation shortly after.

In such an oppressive, suffocating dire circumstances, I made the decision to leave Kuwait—though only temporarily, for a few days—to test the waters, to reconnect with my family after our communication had been cut off, and wait for a miracle that might descend from the heavens and restore life to Kuwait. Despite Iraq's stubbornness and its continued efforts to strangle the wounded emirate, amid escalating international and regional threats and the rapid preparation of the U.S.-led coalition, I held onto a sliver of hope.

I completed the paperwork for my departure and boarded a bus to avoid the dangers of the road. Despite Iraq's harsh laws and severe penalties, rumors of robberies and highway banditry, especially in the desolate, sparsely populated desert areas, were rampant.

When the time came, I left, abandoning my household belongings and my modest car to the wind. I bid farewell to my car, the one I had agreed to sell out of financial desperation and the shame of asking for help. The buyer was a fellow townsman who had originally lived in Basra and worked there. The invasion had opened the way for him to come to Kuwait, and he had come to buy a car. I had agreed to sell him my Daihatsu for 36,000 Iraqi dinars—a sum that, in Kuwaiti currency, wouldn't even cover the cost of a single car tire. But at the last moment, I backed out of the deal, fearing it might be recorded as a fourth violation by the other party and interpreted as collaboration with the Iraqi side.

The bus departed from Kuwait, crossing the former border with Iraq, and I found myself venturing deep into the vast desert toward Baghdad. Contrary to the rumors and warnings, we encountered no attacks, no threats. The journey was, in fact, surprisingly comfortable despite its length. I remember arriving a little before midnight near the city of Amarah, where the bus stopped for a brief rest. There, I stepped off and joined a few other passengers at a nearby restaurant. The air was thick with the aroma of grilled meat, and I was reminded that Iraqi kebabs have a flavor unlike any other.

What I witnessed there, however, was shocking. Despite the darkness of the night and the blazing embers, flies swarmed and landed on the skewered meat roasting over the fire. Strangely, the cook seemed unbothered, as if he had made peace with these creatures we were taught to despise. Back home, if a fly landed on food, we would recoil in disgust, as if it had tainted the meal. But here, it was as if they had been removed from encyclopedia of insects and reclassified as birds, even called them "birds" instead of flies.

We continued our journey to Baghdad. During another stop, under the pressure of needing money, a man I knew—a Baghdad local who had welcomed me with warmth and unparalleled kindness—convinced me he could sell my personal computer, which I had brought with me for this very purpose, for a substantial sum up to 15,000 Iraqi dinars. In reality, this amount was modest, barely enough to buy a keyboard in Kuwaiti currency. Desperate, I handed over the computer, hoping for a quick sale. That was the last I saw of it, and the money never materialized. To this day, I don't know what became of it. Did my friend, who must have dreamed of owning such a device, actually sell it and enjoy the proceeds? Or did he keep it for himself, perhaps considering it his share of the spoils from Kuwait? Either way, I was left to writhe on the coals of need and regret.

At the scheduled time to resume our journey to Jordan via the Traibeel border crossing, we boarded the bus again. Along the way, I was captivated by the beauty of Baghdad's geography and its rich history, as well as the stunning infrastructure beyond the city—wide roads that resembled airport runways. We encountered no significant problems during the long stretch of the journey, though fear of the unknown remained ever-present, fueled by prior warnings. Eventually, we reached the Traibeel border crossing with Jordan. There, the scene was nothing short of chaotic, like a smaller version of the Day of Judgment or a massive pilgrimage. People swarmed like locusts, some waiting to enter Jordan, others rushing to exit, hoping to return to Kuwait and salvage what they could.

What caught my attention at that border crossing, and what I overheard, was the cold demeanor of the border staff. They meticulously confiscated any valuable goods they deemed smuggled from Kuwait—even if they were personal belongings: gold, silver, currency, electronics, and anything lightweight yet expensive. However, some shipments slipped through unchecked for various reasons, including pre-paid bribes.

From what I heard—though I did not witness it myself—the border staff confiscated large sums of money, substantial quantities of gold, and electronic devices. Among these was 25,000 Kuwaiti dinars belonging to a friend of mine. I had once asked this friend for a goodwill loan of 100 Kuwaiti dinars to start a small business selling tissues on the streets. He had entrusted the larger sum to someone to smuggle across the border, but the courier claimed the money was confiscated at the Traibeel border crossing. Only God knows what truly happened.

The movement through the border crossing was a test of endurance. The process was agonizingly slow, with long waits for travelers. But the worst part of that crossing was the state of the restrooms—overflowing, filthy to the point of disgust, and their condition remains etched in my memory. They were so appalling that some travelers preferred to relieve themselves in their clothes rather than step inside.

During that interminable wait, I tried to console myself with the proverb, "The miller's day will come," and I urged myself to endure and downplay the ordeal so I could bear the suffering of that journey. Our noble Prophet spoke the truth when he said that travel is a piece of torment, but this journey felt like torment multiplied hundredfold. Relief finally came when we crossed into the Jordanian border, which, though crowded, was nothing compared to the chaos on the other side.

When I reached Abdali station, I headed straight to the apartment of my father-in-law, which he had rented in Al Rashid suburb before the invasion for his family's summer vacation. My wife and son were staying there with him. Upon my arrival, I found that the apartment had become a refuge for a large number of my father-in-law's relatives, all of whom were stranded like us, their savings nearly evaporating in the aftermath of the catastrophe that had befallen Kuwait.

I spent a few days in Al Rashid suburb under unbearably harsh conditions—overcrowded, difficult, and filled with grief over what had happened. There, I witnessed the horrors of displacement and deprivation etched on the faces of those

I met. Eventually, I returned to Kuwait through the Traibeel crossing, embarking on yet another journey of torment, one fraught with uncertainty and open to every possible hardship.

THE WELL OF EXILE

A Warrior's Respite

My departure from the war-torn land of Kuwait—ravaged, plundered, broken, and steeped in sorrow—and my journey through Baghdad, which was intoxicated with the euphoria of what it called liberation, its markets brimming with goods after years of severe and prolonged sanctions, despite an undercurrent of unease about foreign intervention and the distant drumbeats of war. Finally, I arrived in Jordan, reuniting with my family in Al Rashid suburb—all of this represented a precious opportunity to catch my breath and find solace. It was a chance to escape the circles of death, poverty, hunger, fear, thirst, lawlessness, and the chaos that followed the invasion. The absence of long queues at bakeries, supply stores, government offices, and border crossings, and the relief of escaping the bottleneck of survival, brought me a sense of peace. Reconnecting with my wife and son filled me with immense joy, though it was tinged with incompleteness for reasons I could not yet fully articulate.

Yet, the crisis in Kuwait—with all its repercussions, shocking details, and devastating consequences—loomed large in the Hiyari Villa in Al Rashid suburb. That summer, which had turned into a catastrophe, saw the villa crowded not only with my father-in-law family, my wife, and my son, but also with several other relatives of my uncle who had either come to Jordan for a summer retreat or fled Kuwait in the wake of the crisis, shattered by the horrors they had endured.

Everyone was stranded, their savings evaporated, forced to gather in that one place to share the burden of exorbitant rent, even before the new wave of displacement and refuge. The villa's floors were packed with over thirty, perhaps forty, people. Every inch of that once-luxurious villa was now covered with bedding, each spot occupied by a victim of Kuwait's ongoing calamity.

Fear, psychological turmoil, and the scars of trauma were etched on the faces of the adults. The atmosphere was thick with uncertainty, a sense of waiting for what the future might hold, as everyone tried to make sense of the unfolding chaos. Yet, beneath the surface, there was a palpable sense of regret and disappointment, mingled with a quiet denial and fleeting daydreams. No one wanted to believe that Kuwait, once thriving and vibrant, had become a hollow shell, a shadow of its former self.

As more news trickled in, stories piled up, and the full scale of the disaster became clear, and as more residents fled, the displaced began to accept that Kuwait was gone, swept away like dust in the wind, never to return to its former glory. The greatest concern now was survival—finding money in the midst of a crushing crisis, severed incomes, and frozen assets (if any remained). Family, relatives, and friends, once pillars of support, had become strangers, and the need to spend in the face of skyrocketing prices became urgent. This was a consequence of the massive wave of refugees fleeing Kuwait.

The day after my arrival, after I had recounted the devastation and painted a vivid picture of the ruin that had befallen that small emirate, one of the first things I did was sell a piece of my wife's gold jewelry. The goal was to contribute to the villa's rent and other expenses, joining the collective effort of the families who now shared this quasi-military burden. We could not let my father-in-law be forced to vacate the rented property, especially since, throughout his long years of work in Kuwait, he had never thought to build a home or buy an apartment—a refuge he could turn to in times like these.

That sale marked the first bleed in a series of painful transactions, each one draining the only strategic reserve we could turn to—my wife's gold. Each transaction was excruciatingly cruel, their pain perhaps no less than selling one's internal organs. With each sale, I could feel my wife's heart shatter into pieces as she parted with the golden treasures she held dear. One of the most painful was the loss of her beloved gold chain set, which she had cherished deeply. Even now, after all these years, she still mourns it, reminiscing and longing for what was once hers.

The bleeding of gold continued from that day onward, each sale driven by our desperate need for money. Piece by piece, my wife's collection dwindled until nothing remained. These were not mere possessions; they were part of her dowry, a sacred trust from her family, and I had no right to dispose of them. Yet, necessity forced our hand. In the end, we even sold our wedding rings—the very symbols of our sacred marital bond, as dictated by tradition and custom. We sold them in a later phase, for by then, we had endured seven lean years with my family, years of hardship, poverty, and destitution. Our situation grew so dire that a poor family, who themselves lived largely on charity due to their own difficult circumstances, offered us fast-breaking charity out of pity for our extreme need. God willing, I will dedicate an entire volume to recounting the sorrows, sighs, and stories of that wretched period under the title: Seven Lean Years.

In the days that followed, I wandered the streets of Amman, drifting through Hashemite Square and visiting relatives, especially my aunt Aisha, Umm Rida. She had tasted the bitterness of voluntary displacement after the 1967 defeat, having migrated against my father's advice and settled in the

Khalil Hamad

Awajan district. My favorite pastime during those days was riding the bus from Hashemite Square to Awajan via Russeifa, back and forth. Those journeys became my sanctuary, a time to nurse my wounds and grapple with the aftermath of the catastrophe. In the evenings, I would return to the temporary refuge of the Hiyari villa, where I spent hours discussing our bleak reality with my uncle—my father-in-law—and a group of male relatives who shared our pain and burden, all of us united in our suffering.

Sometimes, I would stop men in the streets or markets, their faces and ragged appearances betraying the scars of the disaster that had befallen us. I would ask them if they, too, were victims of the Iraqi invasion of Kuwait. More often than not, my intuition was correct. Once I confirmed they were indeed among the victims of the Kuwaiti calamity, I would gently probe for news, asking about their choices and how they had fared.

Through these chance encounters, I learned that a number of the victims, particularly those interested in stock investments, gathered at the Housing Bank Complex, the hub of the stock market and trading companies. I visited the place once and was struck by the aftermath of the shock. The most glaring signs were the dazed expressions etched on the faces of those men, a testament to their trauma. To this day, the pitiful image of one man in particular remains etched in my memory, despite the passage of so many years.

My stay in the Rashid suburb was brief, as circumstances did not permit a long-term residence. I decided to return to Kuwait, chasing my old dream of wealth and awaiting relief, especially as preparations were underway by a broad international coalition led by the United States to expel the Iraqi forces.

251

My return coincided with that of my father-in-law, who had also chosen to take the risk and go back, despite the horrifying stories he had heard about the state of the country where he had spent the prime of his youth and lost everything in the invasion. He hoped to reclaim his former position as an accountant at the Kuwait Municipality.

The road to Kuwait, however, was not paved with roses. It required passing through Tarbil—and oh, what a place Traibeel was.

Khalil Hamad

Leaping into the Frying Pan and Clinging to the Fragile Threads of Hopes

My return to Kuwait coincided with the escalation of its crisis, the deepening of its turmoil, and the mounting threats from Iraq. The atmosphere was charged with tension, as military mobilizations accelerated. Returning felt like a fish leaping into a frying pan—a desperate act, fraught with danger. People sensed the looming threat of a fierce confrontation with the international coalition led by America, and hope for a return to normalcy dwindled. Fear of the impending conflict drove many residents to flee Kuwait. Those who had homes or livelihoods abroad left in droves, while only a handful of expatriates remained: those bound by travel restrictions, those so consumed by Kuwait's consumerist lifestyle that they had neglected to secure a home in their native country to return to in times of crisis, and a small, stubborn few who preferred death to the humiliation they imagined awaited them outside Kuwait's paradise of oil, wealth, and opportunity. It was in this climate of chaos and peril that I returned to Kuwait, feeling like a pilgrim setting out on a journey while others were turning back.

Yet, even at that time, I hadn't entirely lost hope for a miracle that would end the nightmare of the Iraqi invasion, restore life to Kuwait, and return us to the days of dignity, abundance, and luxury we had once enjoyed—before it all came crashing down. I still hadn't made up my mind about whether to leave, seeking the uncertain safety and security of the unknown, or to stay and face the open-ended risks that lay ahead.

As for Iraq, which had laid its hands on the treasures of Korah and Pharaoh, unlocked the caves of Ali Baba, and seized the crown jewel, it was unthinkable that it would relinquish its dream of controlling Kuwait without a deadly, fierce battle forcing it to withdraw. This was especially true since its rulers had framed retreating from the liberation of the "nineteenth Province" as an act of betrayal. At the same time, America—the imperial power notorious for its oil ambitions and mired in its own financial crisis—would never allow Iraq to seize the earth's treasures and revel in them. Thus, the battle was an inevitability, a foregone conclusion for anyone with foresight.

The paralysis that had gripped life in Kuwait, halting businesses and work after the invasion, remained the dominant feature. In fact, it had deepened in terrifying and visible ways, fueled by the drumbeats of war and the mass exodus and displacement. Activity in the stricken country was now limited to a few supply and service sectors, as well as emergency trades, like selling tissues on street corners and at traffic lights.

But I returned there, living the life of a vagabond, relying on the kindness of relatives and friends. I didn't take up any work after that return—not even visiting the headquarters of Al-Ghanim, the company I had worked for before the invasion, to see what had become of it. I no longer thought of selling tissues, eggs, or vegetables on the street, even though I had a small amount of capital from selling a piece of my wife's gold.

Meanwhile, my father-in-law, upon arriving in Kuwait, tried to return to his job at the municipality, despite the devastation he had witnessed with his own eyes. Indeed, he went to his workplace at the Kuwait Municipality, where he had been an accountant, just once—a solitary, unrepeated visit. There, he found the world turned upside down. Familiar faces were gone, replaced by strangers, and he noticed that the chaos had seeped into his workplace. That evening, after that ill-fated day, he decided to leave for good. In the eyes of his former colleagues—those who had once shared life's sweetness and bitterness with him, with whom he had lived in camaraderie and solidarity—he saw accusations of betrayal and collaboration with Iraq. All because he had expressed a willingness, under the pressure of necessity, to return to work and serve the country's interests, and its cleanliness. He may have heard things that convinced him that he no longer had a place in that stricken land.

While my father-in-law did not stay long—packing what he could of his household belongings and leaving the wounded Kuwait for Jordan just days after his arrival, consumed by grief and sorrow that later turned into physical ailments and blocked arteries—he passed away a few years later, heartbroken and anguished over the state of affairs. Hasan Shukhtur—that was his name—was only in his mid-fifties when he departed this world for God's mercy.

As for me, I remained in the crippled Kuwait, stubbornly defying my own convictions and what my eyes plainly saw. I procrastinated, delaying the decision to stay or leave, until one day when I was at the shop of a fellow townsman, a tire repairman in the Shuwaikh area named Sayil Al-Othman. While I was there, an Iraqi soldier came in to repair a tire for a military vehicle. Surprised, I asked him, "Are you repairing the tire for the military vehicle at your own expense?!" He replied, visibly annoyed and in a wretched state of mind, that he was doing so on the orders of his unit's officer as punishment for being late to duty.

What I heard from that soldier left me stunned. I don't know why, but I couldn't help linking that moment to the inevitability of an international coalition striking Iraq, forcing its withdrawal from Kuwait. I began to lean more and more toward the belief that war was imminent—closer than the blink of an eye—and that greater destruction loomed on the horizon.

As the tone of threats and warnings from the international coalition against Iraq grew sharper, the exodus from Kuwait surged to unprecedented levels. Many families, including relatives and friends, joined the flood of people packing their belongings and leaving. I felt, more than ever, that staying under such a grave threat was nothing short of madness—an unspoken recipe for suicide. There were no guarantees of what might happen if military clashes erupted, if war broke out over the treasures of the earth in a region afloat on a sea of oil.

Even though joining the wave of displacement felt like leaping into the unknown—a sad end to my dreams of wealth in the land of oil—I made up my mind and decided to leave. The process was arduous. I had to surrender my passport to obtain an exit permit from the Iraqi authorities and arrange for the transportation of my belongings. For several days, I lived in a state of anxious anticipation, fearing my passport might be lost in the chaos and overcrowding that was all too visible in the government office.

When the approval finally came through and I had my passport back, I searched for others to share the cost of a truck to transport our belongings. This is exactly what happened. On the morning of December 27, 1990, I climbed into my Daihatsu alongside one of the men who had agreed to share the truck's cost and two of his daughters. We followed the truck, which carried not only our belongings but also those of a third companion, a refugee from the 1948 exodus. We moved when it moved and stopped when it stopped.

While the first part of the journey went smoothly, the second part brought a harrowing incident that threatened our lives. What unfolded felt like a scene straight out of a *Mission: Impossible* script.

THE WELL OF EXILE

So God repaid you with distress upon distress
so you would not grieve for that which
had escaped you

And so, I left Kuwait, limping away, on December 27, 1990—twelve years after I had first arrived as an exile. Leaving the "Pearl of the Gulf" was no easy feat, especially when I departed empty-handed, save for the wreckage of furniture that wasn't even worth the cost of shipping to Jordan. Had it not been for necessity, I wouldn't have bothered hauling it. The only other possession I took was a small, worn-out car, once used for driving lessons.

It's true that I had left Kuwait temporarily on January 1, 1980, for the United States, to further my academic qualifications. But as soon as I completed my master's degree, I returned, preferring the Kuwaiti dinar—then the strongest currency in the world—over the dollar.

Though my share of Kuwait's wealth, its dinar, its oil, and its sea had been but a trickle; though its summers felt like hellfire, its dust storms blotted out the sun, blinded the eyes, and nearly suffocated the lungs—still, leaving it against my will was bitter and painful.

I drove my white Daihatsu, accompanied by my companion in hardship, the truck driver, and his two daughters. He had arrived in Kuwait over thirty years before me, and I imagine his departure was far more bitter and painful than mine.

We moved cautiously, trailing the truck that carried our belongings, using it as a shield against the dangers of the road. We followed its tracks closely, lest we lose our way in the vast maze of southern Iraq's desert.

Whenever the truck driver stopped to rest, we stopped with him. When he moved again, we followed diligently, like his shadow. Thankfully, the journey went smoothly, and we encountered no noteworthy incidents. My hidden fears of the car breaking down due to the long distance never materialized.

For hours and hours, we trailed that truck through Iraq until we finally reached the Traibeel border crossing, infamous at the time. It was around midnight when we arrived, and the decision was made to sleep in the car at the border checkpoint. I don't remember much after that, except that I fell into a deep sleep behind the wheel, my travel companion—my partner in exile, journey, and suffering—beside me, and his two daughters in the back seat. I doubt they were any less in need of sleep and rest than I was, after all that exhaustion that could wear down mountains.

I remained submerged in a deep slumber, undisturbed by the darkness, and perhaps I did not move an inch from my spot, despite the cramped space and the biting cold in the heart of the desert. The eastern winds howled through that harsh night, sweeping across the barren expanse of the Badiya. It was only when the sun's rays pierced through the veil of night, dispelling its gloom and bathing our eyes in their golden glow, that we were roused from our little death and brought back to life. As I opened my eyes, I was startled to find the windshield completely frosted over, as though we had been sleeping inside a freezer, its walls layered with a thick coat of pristine white snow.

We crossed the Iraqi border and continued westward in silence along that narrow desert road, occasionally passing massive trucks. The morning was bitterly cold, with the eastern winds whipping around us, forcing us to roll up the car windows tightly. Little did I know that sealing the windows so firmly would lead to the terrifying incident that nearly cost us our lives, just a few hundred meters from the Traibeel border crossing, inside Jordanian territory.

What happened was this: before we reached the civil defense checkpoint built on the right side of the road for those entering from Iraq near the Ruwaished area, we encountered a massive truck barreling toward us from the opposite direction. It roared like a beast, racing against the wind as it sped toward Iraq—perhaps carrying more furniture belonging to displaced families like ours, forced to flee Kuwait. Suddenly, just before the truck reached us, a deafening explosion rang out. In an instant, the windshield of my car shattered. We couldn't immediately determine the cause. Was it the sudden pressure difference inside and outside the vehicle, coinciding with the truck's approach? Or had a small stone, flung like a bullet from beneath the speeding truck's tires, struck the windshield directly at the level of my forehead? Had it penetrated the glass, it would have reached my skull, leaving a clear mark—a central point etched deeply into the glass, with cracks radiating outward like the threads of a spider's web.

Despite the windshield remaining intact and not shattering completely, it was now in such a wretched state that driving became nearly impossible. We were in the heart of the desert, far from any urban areas, and I doubted we'd find a place to replace the glass. I removed as much of the shattered debris as I could and drove the car with extreme caution, inching forward until we reached the nearby civil defense station. The moment we arrived, the young men at the station sprang into action. They had seen the disaster that had befallen us and immediately set to work clearing the remaining glass shards. Using tools like screwdrivers and knives, they toiled diligently, their hands soon streaked with blood as they meticulously cleaned up the mess.

Despite the fierce winds and the bitter cold, we decided to press on. The tiny glass particles swirling around made driving nearly impossible, and I feared the sharp fragments might find their way into our eyes.

After a short distance, I stopped again, fearing the sharp, flying fragments. I was at a loss, but one of the sisters had a pair of sunglasses, which saved the day. I put them on and resumed driving, shielding myself from the cold with a woolen cloak I had bought in Ramadi.

Even so, the drive was excruciatingly difficult and utterly terrifying. We managed to cover several kilometers in that miserable state, but despair, exhaustion, and worry began to weigh heavily on me. Just then, a soldier driving a blue military supply truck caught up to us. He signaled for me to stop, and I complied. Without a word, he took off his red cap and handed it to me, gesturing for me to wear it. Then, he motioned for me to follow him, staying close behind his truck as he drove slowly, acting as a shield and protector against the hazards of the road. I did as he instructed, trailing him closely as he led the way.

When we reached Safawi city, the gallant soldier signaled for us to stop. He directed us to a nearby restaurant to rest, eat, and drink some hot tea while he busied himself with installing a plastic cover over the broken windshield. I'm not sure if he bought it from a nearby shop or if a kind citizen donated it, as a crowd had gathered around him. Once he finished the task and secured the cover, he called out to us, and we resumed our journey. That brief rest and the warmth of the tea lifted our spirits, giving us the strength to continue driving.

I thanked that gallant soldier, bidding him farewell with heartfelt warmth, acknowledging my deep gratitude for his kindness. I tried to return his red keffiyeh, but he refused to take it back. As I climbed into the car to continue driving, I realized that the milky-colored plastic cover made it impossible to see through. Our friend, perhaps anticipating this, immediately cut an opening in front of me, allowing me to see the road ahead.

I said goodbye to him a second time, and we set off toward the city of Zarqa. The difficulty and danger of that journey are hard under such conditions. Yet, I drove on without hesitation or pause. As we drove, the cold eastern winds whipped and tore at the plastic cover, and by the time we reached Zarqa, it was completely shredded.

And so, I emerged from the well of exile, the horrors of that final scene—which nearly cost us our lives—overshadowing the terrors of Kuwait's day of reckoning. It eased the weight of displacement, its grief, its pain, and its sorrow, and marked the end of the dream of wealth. From that day forward—January 1, 1991—my family and I entered a tunnel of seven lean years, during which we endured immense hardship on both sides of the homeland. We faced trials no less severe or painful than those of the well of exile or Kuwait's day of reckoning. Life was relentless, and we found ourselves in dire circumstances, sometimes hitting rock bottom. Those lean years came to an end on January 1, 1997, when I secured a prestigious job that lifted me out of the tunnel of poverty, destitution, and humiliating need. God willing, I will continue to recount this chapter in a separate part of my life story, under the title "Seven Lean Years."

Epiogue

Author's Picture

About The Author

Inner Child Press

Inner Child Press is a publishing company founded and operated by writers. Our personal publishing experiences provide us an intimate understanding of the sometimes-daunting challenges writers, new and seasoned may face in the business of publishing and marketing their creative "Written Work".

For more information:

Inner Child Press

www.innerchildpress.com

intouch@innerchildpress.com

'building bridges of cultural understanding'
www.innerchildpress.com

www.ingramcontent.com/pod-product-compliance
Lightning Source LLC
Chambersburg PA
CBHW070446030726
47503CB00004B/923